Last
Puffs

Last Puffs

Harley Mazuk

NEW PULP PRESS

Published by New Pulp Press, LLC, 926 Truman Avenue, Key West, Florida 33040, USA.

For information contact:
Publisher@NewPulpPress.com

Printed in the United States of America
Visit us on the web at www.newpulppress.com

Last
Puffs

To Pilar S.

Part 1

Aragón

CHAPTER ONE
Talking Baseball

Aragón, Spain, March 1938

There'd been a dusting of fresh snow in the high ground during the night, and the captain wanted our squad, which was nine men, to relieve an outpost on the crest of a hill, just up above the tree line. Max Rabinowitz took point, and I followed, climbing steadily. It was a cold, quiet morning, and we talked between ourselves about the '38 baseball season, and whether we'd be back in the States to see any games.

"I would like to see Hank Greenberg and the Tigers play DiMaggio and the Yanks," said Max. Max was dark-haired and rangy, and I always thought he looked a bit like Cary Grant, though now after a year in the field, there was nothing suave nor dapper in his appearance.

"How about Ted Williams?" I said. "We've already seen DiMaggio play in San Francisco with the Seals."

"We saw Williams play with the Padres. Besides, he isn't in the big leagues yet," said Max.

"Yeah, but the Red Sox signed him." I walked along just off Max's shoulder. I was about the same height as Max, six feet, six-one, a little thinner, and looked at least as scruffy that morning. I wore a burgundy scarf around my head and ears, under a dirty and battered grey fedora. I scanned the virgin snow ahead of us with heavy-lidded eyes. The wind was faint, just enough to pick up a feathery wisp of snow in spots and spin it around.

"He's only about 19. I think they'll keep him down on the farm for '38."

"I would like to see Bob Feller pitch to your boy Greenberg," I told Max.

Smitty came up between us. "Feller throws 100 miles

1

an hour, and he strikes out more than one per inning."

"They say," said Max, "he walks almost one an inning,"

"Keeps 'em loose up there," said Smitty, who was from Cleveland. "Hundred mile an hour heat and nobody knows where it's going."

As the three of us stepped out of the cover of the tree line, Smitty kind of hopped up on one leg and threw his arms out. I wondered what sort of a weird little dance that was; then I heard the automatic weapons fire coming down at us off the hill. It was a mechanical chatter, rather than gunpowder explosions, and the wind had blown the sound around the hills so that the bullets cut Smitty down before it had reached us. Branches near us started to snap off and tumble earthwards. Max hit the snow on his belly and rolled downhill to his right to get to cover behind a rock. I motioned for the others to get back into the trees, and dove into a low spot in the ground.

When we could look up, we saw that the fascists had overrun the outpost we'd been climbing up to the ridge to relieve, and the firing was coming from there. We returned fire. I heard cries in Spanish from behind me, a curse in a low voice, then a high-pitched prayer.

A potato-masher grenade came flipping end-over-end down the hill toward me. It seemed like slow motion. It hit a rock and bounced up. I could say a Hail Mary in about four seconds flat in those days, and I said one then. The grenade sailed over my head; I heard it explode, and felt a shower of dirt on my back. In front of me, Max was popping up and firing one round with his Springfield, then dropping behind the rock. I popped up and fired when he dropped down. I thought we were doing pretty well taking turns, but grenades kept arcing over our heads and bullets pinged into Max's rock and raked the dirt beside me. Max tried lobbing one of his grenades towards the machine gun, but his throw was uphill, and he didn't have an arm like DiMaggio.

After a few minutes of this, I tried to aim and squeeze the trigger instead of popping off quick shots. Then I didn't hear anyone behind us firing anymore. I looked around and saw Rocco and Pete sprawled in the grass. I called to a couple of the others.

"Comrades ... anyone ... sound off." *Nada.*

"Frank, this is bad," Max yelled to me.

"I'd rather be facing Feller's fastballs," I told him. "Maybe it's time for us to dust." Then we heard an airplane motor. It grew louder, and the first plane, a Heinkel, zoomed over the ridge seconds later. Max had risen to his feet and was scrambling down the slope. He looked back over his shoulder at the plane just as a cannon shot from the aircraft hit the rock he'd been behind. The explosion flipped Max in mid-air and tossed him towards me. The ground under him ripped up and clods of dirt flew towards us.

The scene faded to black, but for how long, I don't know. When I opened my eyes, I was facing the sky but I smelled the forest floor, earth and leaves. Truffles, perhaps? Max was on top of me, limp, and it was quiet. No planes, no shooting. "Max," I said, "we gotta get up. Get off me." I felt my voice in my head, but couldn't hear it in my ears. Max didn't get up. I rolled him over next to me, and saw that his hat was gone. The top of his head and the right side of his face were a collage of blood and dirt. I shook him, and he gasped for breath, earth falling out of his nostrils. He was still alive.

"Frank, Frank. I can't see. I can't see." It didn't sound like Max, but there was no one else there.

"Easy, Max." I tried to rinse some of the dirt, debris and blood off Max's head with my canteen, then I ripped open a compress from my pack and put it over his forehead and eyes. I wrapped more dressing around his head to keep the bandage in place "Hold this on your face, man. Don't try to open your eyes." I was afraid his right eyeball was going to fall out. "Hold it tight." Using the slope, I maneuvered him across my shoulder, head down in front of me, and struggled to my feet. I took off at a trot along the tree line.

Our lines were behind us to the east but it looked like the whole damned fascist army was charging down from the outpost, headed that way, so I ran south. It was downhill and my momentum carried us. The going was easy, but I felt panic building in my gut so I tried to slow down. I slid on the snow, fell on my butt, and slammed into a tree and dropped Max.

"Frank, where are you? Am I dyin'?"

"I got you, Max. You caught some shrapnel in the head from that plane. Say an act of contrition or something."

"I'm a Jew, you idiot."

"Say it anyway." I lifted the gauze off his forehead and looked under it. His wound didn't appear to be deep, but the right eye was very bad, all blood and pulp, and the bone around it may have been shattered. "Press on this, Max." I pressed the bandage back against his face and put his hand on it.

I hoisted him over my shoulder again, and stepped off, forcing myself to keep my pace steady and not too fast. We went on till the sun was high in the sky. I didn't fall again, but my ankles were burning, and my toes were pinched in my boots from going downhill. I stopped twice, and opened our *bota*. I washed my mouth out with the wine, a rustic red from Calatayud, then I cradled Max's head and opened his mouth. I squirted the wine in, squeezing the leather skin, the way I'd squeezed the trigger of my rifle. Max coughed. He seemed only half-conscious.

I carried Max down the hill and to the south, parallel to our lines, until we were deep in some woods. I was scared and it wasn't easy, but I would have done anything for Max. We had been roommates and run around together at Berkeley. We fell out of touch when he went to law school, and I started drinking, trying to forget Cicilia. When Max re-connected with me in '36, he tried to help me sober up and get back on my feet. I'd come around for a while, but always, I'd slip back into the abyss.

Max was a red, even back in our student days. I hadn't been serious about my politics then. One evening to keep me from drowning my demons, Max took me to a meeting about the Spanish Civil War and the Abraham Lincoln Brigade. Before the night was over, we'd signed up to fight in Spain. Max didn't have to. I think he did it to save me. Now I was going to save him.

When the sun dropped behind the hills, the woods quickly grew dark. There was a smell of pines, and the footing was better – no snow or ice on the ground, which was hard and covered with dry pine needles. Under the background din of war, the roar of artillery and airplanes, I heard water down to my left. I turned towards it and a few minutes later, came to a stream, probably flowing south to the Ebro. It wasn't night yet, but it was so dark under the tall trees, I would have walked into the stream without seeing it if not for the sound of the water rushing over the rocks. I put Max down on his back, head and shoulders downhill toward the stream. The blood had dried; the gauze was stuck to his head. I scooped up water with my hat and poured it on his face. The icy cold shocked him into consciousness – and panic and pain.

"Morphine, Frank," he moaned. "Gimme the morphine." But I had used our morphine one night weeks ago on guard duty on a cold hillside. We did have a flask of Cardenal Mendoza Spanish Brandy, and I gave him some, then I drank. I rinsed his wound good and put a new bandage on it using Max's kit this time. My legs felt weak and started to shake with cold or exhaustion. I don't know if I could have stood up then if the *Generalissimo* had come down the hill waving his *pistoles.* We were down low, and there were some bare shrubs and young trees sheltering us on the uphill slope. I fought my exhaustion and tried to keep watch as long as I could. I had another swallow of brandy and pulled close to Max. My eyes closed, and I fell asleep.

Chapter Two
The Zingaros

First thing I noticed in the morning, was the quiet. No more sound of gunfire, no engine noise. But when I opened my eyes, I saw gray fascist troops spread out through the woods, crouching, advancing from tree to tree towards us on our side of the river. The sun rose in their faces, on the far side of river. We were down low, and there were some shrubs above us on the slope. We had an even chance or better of not being seen in the half-light and shadows, unless Max woke up and made a noise. I clamped a hand over his mouth and moved my head to his ear. I could feel he was feverish in the frosty morning.

"Max," I whispered. "Keep still. We're surrounded but they haven't seen us."

"Frmph?"

"Yeah, it's Frank. I pushed the wrapped dressing up on his forehead. "Can you see?" He opened his left eye and blinked twice, then panicked and shook his head left and right, no. "OK. Just hold on," I said. I was hungry and I had to piss, but I couldn't get up at this moment.

Now the sun was slanting through the pines and some steam started to rise off the cold water. Dust floated in the light, and I could see spider webs in the low branches along the creek bed. I saw that there was a ford about 25 yards upstream from us. I rolled over and looked downstream, and there was a fallen log 35 or 40 yards in that direction. As they came downhill, the enemy divided just above us and crept toward either the ford or the log.

"Shhh," I said, and took my hand off Max's mouth. Our luck held. The *Nacionales* came downhill through the woods and split around us as if our clump of shrubs were the prow of a ship running through a gray sea. They advanced in silence, crossed the rushing water, some stopping to fill canteens, and started up the slope through the woods on the other side. I assumed it was some kind of flanking action, in support of yesterday's main attack to the north.

When the last of the fascist troops were out of sight on the other side, I got up to pee. My legs were shaky and unsure. Afterwards, I went back to Max and rinsed his head and face with some clean cold water.

"What are you doing, Frank?" He sounded weak.

"Cleaning you up," I said. I drizzled some cold water on his forehead. "You know, in extreme circumstances, a lay Catholic can baptize a non-Christian into the faith–"

"Cut it out."

I stopped. "I'm gonna get you out of here now, Max. Ready?"

~ ~ ~

I carried Max south and we came out of the trees onto a road that ran along pastureland on the far side. Max tried to take some of the load off me, draping an arm on my shoulder and trailing his feet along. Staying on the wooded side, we followed the road west by southwest until a little after noon, when I heard the wheels of a cart from up ahead of us around a bend. I dragged Max off the road, back into the trees, and as I saw the cart come into sight, we dropped into a shallow gully. Then Max groaned a couple times before I could cover his mouth. The cart stopped, and I heard the cocking of a weapon.

"*Hola!*" a voice called, "*Quien esta ahi?*"

I said nothing. I didn't think the voice knew where we were. "Keep quiet, Max," I whispered. He was drifting in and out of consciousness.

I heard a branch crack behind me and turned with my rifle. The cold barrel of an Astra pistol was a few feet away, pointed at my head. I blinked and looked again. Long dark hair hung out from the beret of my adversary, lush, cascading dark chestnut hair. The youngster had neither beard nor mustache, just smooth, pure cheeks, ruddy from the cold, with dark eyes and long lashes, lips a dull color, but thick and full, jaws narrow, and chin pointed. A bulky drab military jacket above wool olive pants, and low, buckled, thick leather shoes – it was an outfit that hid but didn't conceal the swell of young breasts and the feminine spread of the hips. The lad was a lass.

I put down my gun, and stood, raising my arms. "*Estamos a favor de la republica,*" I said. We are for the republic. "*Puedes ayudar a mi amigo?*" Can you help my friend?

"Papa, bring the cart," she called in Spanish. I heard a slap and then the sound of the cartwheels turning on the rutted road again. Soon Papa came up. He was of indeterminate age, with a thin grizzled face and short white hair. A rope belt holding up his trousers was cinched so that they looked too big for him. A fedora-style dress hat shaded his face and eyes. He poked Max with the barrel of his rifle.

"Please," I said in Spanish, "he's hurt bad." Max moaned and rolled his head from side to side.

"How are you called?" asked the man.

"I am called Francisco," I told him, "and this is Maximilian. We are with the International Brigades, fighting for the republic."

"It goes badly for your side," the man said. "Franco began an offensive yesterday. He drives east, with many airplanes."

"We were in it yesterday morning. My friend was wounded from the air."

The old man picked up my rifle and put it in the back of his cart. They were hauling firewood. I started to put my hands down, and the girl poked me in the side with her pistol. I raised them back up and turned to look at her. She was a striking beauty. I smiled. She averted her eyes from mine and watched her father, who slung his rifle over his shoulder.

"Come on," he said to me, "help me move some of the wood to make a spot for your friend." I did, and then we lifted Max onto the pile of logs, next to my gun. The girl kept her pistol on me while we worked.

When we had Max in the back of the cart, the girl looked at his wound. "It does not look too bad for your friend, but he may lose the eye," she said.

"That's bad enough." I told them. "He can't see."

The old man put a dark gray blanket on Max and then after a coughing spell covered him with a single layer of the lightest weight, thinnest sticks. You could walk up to the cart and not see Max lying there.

"I am called Alejandro Zingaro," said the old man. "Your Spanish passes. Take the insignia off your coat; walk in front with Fuego and Amanda." He climbed aboard, and turned the cart back in the direction they had been coming from.

Chapter Three
The Highway Is Fraught

We had had uniforms when we arrived in Spain in February 1937, but by now, most of the men wore a harlequin's mismatch of what clothing kept them warm or dry. I unpinned the small metal pin of the Abe Lincoln brigade, and my little black flag anarchist badge from my shoulder and chest, and marched along with them.

Without the pins, you might not be able to tell on which side I fought. I had an officer's topcoat, grey, but what sort of officer one couldn't really say, except that he had been about six feet tall and fit in a 42 coat. I walked along the road near the front shoulders of Fuego, who turned out to be Alejandro's mule. Amanda stood on the other side of the mule, a pace or two back from me, where she could see me. Alejandro sat in the cart, rolled a cigarette, and drove.

After we had walked for a few minutes, Amanda came up alongside me with a cheese and a knife. She cut off a block of the straw-yellow, dry cheese, pressing the knife towards her thumb, and handed it to me. "For your stomach," she said. "Perhaps this will stop its grumbling." She smiled and looked down.

I took the cheese realizing that my gut was making as much noise as the creaking cartwheels. "Thank you," I said, and began to chew the cheese, in small bites. "Sheep's milk?"

She nodded.

"Is it much further?" I asked.

"No. Perhaps three kilometers. Half an hour's walk for Fuego."

That ruddiness in her cheeks – now I saw it was faint freckles, barely darker than her flesh. "Alejandro," I said to the girl, "he is your father?"

"*Si*," she said.

I unslung my wine skin, but found it empty. Amanda turned and slowed her pace until the cart caught up with her. She spoke to Alejandro, tossing a glance and her thick hair in my direction. The old man grumbled a little but drove the mule on without changing expression or speed. Amanda reached behind him and picked up a wine bottle, then quickened her pace to come back up to me. She held out the bottle to me, and I took the cork out and rinsed my mouth with wine. The liquid was cool and soft; the wine was warming and dry, so I had another longer drink. I found myself thinking of Cicilia.

The war had kept my mind off Cici, but now the nearness of this other dark-haired beauty turned my thoughts. I dropped back a half a pace, to steal glances of Amanda walking. Cici's form drifted into and out of my vision. Cici was petite and always wore heels. Her walk was more precise and more pronounced in its sway than the long, loose strides of this country girl in her flat-soled moccasins. But watching either walk could hypnotize me.

We had gone twenty minutes or so and coming over a rise, I saw a small farmhouse at the bottom of a downhill grade. "Our house," said Amanda.

When we were half way down the slope to the farmhouse, I heard the sound of a car motor approaching from the opposite side of the farm. In a few seconds a muddy Fiat sputtered into view. We were in the open on the downhill slope, and it was clear they'd see us before we could disappear if they hadn't seen us already.

Alejandro said, "If they are *Nacionales*, we will try to bluff them. Francisco–"

"*Si?*"

"Say as little as possible. You are my nephew. Your language is Catalan, and you came west to Aragón to escape the communists. You stay with us on the farm."

He kept the mule going downhill at a steady pace, as if to announce, your car means nothing to us.

As the Fiat closed on us, the driver swung it out across the road. Only then did Amanda and I stop walking, and Alejandro called to the mule. *"Parada, Fuego, parada, hombre."*

A young soldier in a blue jacket and chocolate brown trousers got out first from the passenger side, and pointed his rifle towards us. He had fear in his eyes. An officer climbed out of the back. He was dressed all in blue, and drew a broom-handled Mauser from under his coat and held it across his chest. The driver, wearing a goatskin jerkin over a blue shirt, climbed out last. He turned to get his rifle from the back seat of the Fiat.

"Buenas," said the officer. The sun was overhead, but low in the southern sky. We were facing it.

"Buenos dias, Capitan," said Alejandro, and touched two fingers to his forehead. Amanda shuffled back, between me and the mule, and she kept her face down.

"Where are you going?" the captain said to Alejandro.

Alejandro raised an arm and pointed down to the farmhouse. "There, to our home," he said.

The officer swaggered up to me. "Your papers, *señor."*

"No tinc papers," I said. I knew a little Catalan, but I didn't have much of an accent or feel for the tongue. If this fascist officer knew Catalan, I couldn't pull it off. *"Jo sóc de Barcelona."* He looked at me as I'd often seen Spaniards look at Catalonians. I felt like he'd told me to sit in the back of the bus.

"How are you called?" He glanced at Amanda while he waited for me to answer.

"Em dic Francisco Salu. Jo visc en aquesta granja amb el meu oncle." I live on that farm with my uncle, I told him.

"You are an anarchist?" he asked me. He did a double take at Amanda.

"*No, Capita.*" I gave him a dumb grin; with no papers, I couldn't disprove that accusation. He looked at my boots, shabby, but military looking, with my khaki uniform pants tucked in.

"But you are for the Republic?" he said. He spoke to me, but now he could not seem to take his eyes from Amanda.

"*No, Capita.*"

"You have no papers from the Nationalist side, and you are from Barcelona," he said. Before I could reply, he slammed the flat of the Mauser against the side of my head. My legs buckled and I sank to the road. I remember seeing Amanda's Astra come out from under her coat, and I thought I might have heard a shot or two after I closed my eyes, but before I passed out.

When I came to, Alejandro's arms were tied around the yoke of the wagon. The young soldier with his rifle stood over him. The Astra lay in the dirt near me. I heard voices from the side of the road by the rear of the wagon – a man's grim laugh, a dull thump, a woman's cry of pain. "Hold her, hold her," a man shouted. "Pin her down." Another cry. She sounded so young. Taking the Astra, I crawled on my elbows, keeping the wagon between the youth and myself. Bleeding from the forehead, Alejandro was between the horses, looking down into the dirt. He caught my movement and raised his head a little. He was helpless, but when he saw me, he gave me an encouraging look.

At the back of the wagon, I saw the other two fascists with Amanda. Her pants were in the dirt by the road side. I saw only one of her shoes. The driver sat on her chest and pinned her arms with his knees, while the officer opened his coat, and dropped his trousers. Amanda's bare legs pumped and kicked. "Hold her, fool, and you can be next," the officer said, and forced her legs apart. Amanda threw dirt at the driver's face, and he lashed out and struck her. His blow thudded against her face, and he sank down on the girl with all his weight.

Alejandro and his daughter had helped us. They might have made it home without trouble, if it hadn't been for us. I couldn't let them down. I stood up and made sure I felt steady. Then I stepped forward two rapid paces and shot the driver in the head, twice. The fascist officer didn't know whether to pull up his pants or go for his gat. But the soldier guarding Alejandro did have his rifle in his hands, so I hurried two more steps toward the front of the wagon, and shot the young lad in the chest, twice.

I turned to finish off the officer, but now the damn pistol just clicked. Empty or jammed, I didn't know and I didn't have time to think about it. I threw the bean-shooter at the captain's head, and dived under the wagon and rolled. I saw the officer on his feet, pulling up his pants, and that gave me an idea. I slipped my belt off and watching his legs to see which way he'd come for me, I rolled the opposite way, to the other side of the wagon. He headed for the front and Alejandro; I scrambled out from under the cart at the back and took the long way around. Just as he bent over Alejandro to look for me, I looped the belt around his neck like a garrotte. It was an old belt, and I prayed to St. Crispin the leather worker that it would hold together. I pulled on the ends of it with all my strength and leaning against the wagon for balance, I bent a knee into his back.

The moments crept by as slow as a condemned man chews his last meal. It took too long for him to die, but when my wrists burned and I didn't think I could hold him any longer, he ran out of air on that dirt road in Aragón and went limp in my arms. He was the last man I ever killed.

Chapter Four
One-Eyed Jack

I let the limp body go, and ran to Amanda before it even hit the ground. The rapists beat her to take the fight out of her. Her mouth was bleeding and I saw now she'd broken a tooth. I knelt beside her and put an arm around her to try to comfort her. But she got up and pulled on her pants and rinsed out her mouth with wine. About all I could do was steady her and brush leaves out of her hair and off her shoulders.

Alejandro and his daughter had had a rough time of it but they knew they had to pick themselves up and we had to get off the road. Alejandro had a coughing spell, but he wiped his face and was soon ready and in the driver's seat. Amanda nodded that she was ready too.

We were close to the farmhouse and soon we carried Max in and put him on a straw bed. Amanda washed and dressed his wound while Alejandro and I hurried back out to clean up the scene. We loaded the bodies into the car. Alejandro couldn't drive. "I'll take the wheel," I said, "If you direct me." We drove to the river and dumped the bodies there. Then we covered the car with old brush as best we could. By the time we'd finished and returned to the farm, the sun was behind the nearby hills and dusk was settling into the valley.

The farmhouse was small. We met in the room with Max. "The eye is beyond repair," said Amanda. "I should take it out."

"No," I said

"He has the other one," said Alejandro.

"He can't see at all," I said.

"He has two eyes. The left eye appears only scratched. The sight in that one will return," said

Amanda, "but the right eye is useless. It will infect."

And that is how my oldest friend, Maximilian Rabinowitz came to resemble the one-eyed jack of hearts.

I would not put my belt back on. It ended up in the fire. We ate some weak stew, and there was fresh bread, and good wine. I drank plenty. "You will sleep with me," Alejandro told me. "*El tuerto* can sleep in Amanda's room." *El tuerto* – one-eye. "He is too weak to think of love."

~ ~ ~

Spring came to the valley in Aragón while Max recovered. Alejandro played the roles of gruff peasant and watchful father. He made a show of his authority and was protective of Amanda. He talked about how feeding us would ruin him before the next harvest. But my bowl always had more in it than his, and he poured me wine before serving himself. His heart was big, and I think he would have done anything for me since I'd saved Amanda.

He told me I had to do work to earn our keep, and I said that was fine. "But I don't want you on the farm where you can be seen from the road in the daylight."

"Understood," I said. I chopped wood in back of the barn after dark. I milked cows before dawn.

In the daytime, Alejandro went out. I stayed in the house. The rooms were small – not just the floor space, but the place hadn't been built for a six-footer like me. The ceiling and the beams were low. I went around hunched over, unable to straighten up, to put my shoulders back, to breathe deeply. Even the bed I had to share with Alejandro was short. I couldn't stretch out anywhere. Curtains were drawn across the small farmhouse windows, and I felt enclosed.

Amanda tried to make me comfortable. She made coffee, and gave me a little bowl of it. She held hers up to her lips with both hands cupped around it and blew across the surface, then drank, her dark eyes looking into the dark coffee.

"How old are you, Amanda?" I asked.

"I will be 17 in May," she said. "How old are you, Francisco?"

"I will be 26 in September." Cici had been 17 when we'd started dating.

"Do you have a wife?" she asked me. She wore a sweater of coarse wool, dark like her long flowing hair, dark like the java, dark as her eyes. She was not in pants today, but an ankle length, blood-red skirt.

"No," I said. Cici had married someone else.

"I see. Come, we will give Max something hot to drink. I have made chocolate." We went into Amanda's bedroom where Max lay on the straw mattress. Amanda sat at his side. I stooped through the doorway and stood over them.

"Amanda?" said Max.

"Yes, it is I. I have brought you hot chocolate."

I took off my coat, folded it and put it behind him, helping him sit up a little. "How you doing, Max?"

"The pain's better," he said. "But I'm scared. I can't see."

"You have a bandage around your eyes," I said. "When we take it off, you'll see again. Don't worry."

Amanda put her wrist on his forehead, over the bandage. "He has no fever today. No infection. He will get better." She started to take her wrist away, and Max latched on to her forearm. The sudden movement almost upset the hot chocolate, but Amanda held it steady, and Max relaxed his grip.

"Sorry," he said. "Your touch..."

"I know," she said. She stroked Max's hair. It was dry and dirty from being out of doors all winter, but still thick and curly.

"You have hair like the gypsies," said Amanda. I went

to the window and moved the curtain an inch or so while she spooned hot chocolate down his gullet. The sun was shining in the yard around the farmhouse, and on the road and beyond. It looked much warmer than yesterday. I watched a yellow finch search for food in the trees. Soon another yellow finch joined the first one, and I watched them together.

When I turned back, the chocolate was gone. Amanda had one thigh up along the bed and her slim ankle showed pale and luminous in the dim light, below the blood-red wool of the skirt. She was rolling a cigarette using Max's pouch of Bull Durham, and Max had a hand on her hip. "It's cold in the house," I said. "Let me take my coat, Max. You lie back under the blanket and rest."

~ ~ ~

I learned a little about making cheese, and about curing mountain ham. Alejandro had a cellar the length and breadth of the house where he made more wine than just the two of them needed. He grew the *mazuelo* or *cariñena* grape, from which he made a robust, earthy red. It was not elegant, but a good drinking red nonetheless.

There was always work to do downstairs, racking barrels, filling bottles. One day, Alejandro knocked on the end of one of his two huge oak casks, which were as tall as me, filling the cellar from floor to ceiling. Then he bent over and knocked on it near the bottom. It sounded different at the bottom.

"You see, Francisco? Empty." He pressed a spot on the rim of the giant vat and the boards across the bottom sprung open. Inside was a crescent of hiding space about two feet tall and six feet wide. "If someone comes to the house while I am out, you bring your friend down here and get in. It is safe. The floor of the wine barrel is lined with concrete. And you cannot be locked in from outside. Look, here is the release." He showed me the latch inside the door. The boards on the end of the barrel ran horizontally and the door blended in, invisible when closed.

"What about Amanda?" I asked.

He shrugged. "She will use her judgment. If it's someone she knows or trusts, she'll stay upstairs. Strangers or *nacionales*, she must hide, too."

It was not too many days later that we used the barrel for the first time. A man on horseback approached the house. I asked Amanda if she needed to join us. She said no. "It's a boy I know," she said, "but you must take Max and hurry." I draped Max's arm over my shoulder and walked him down to the cellar. We spent the next hour or so in the false bottom of a wine cask, side-by-side in total darkness.

"Frank," he whispered.

"Right here, man."

"I won't forget what you've done for me. You saved my life."

"You would have done the same for me," I said.

"Maybe so, but it didn't go down that way. You saved me. I owe you. What's mine is yours." He laughed. "Of course, I can never begin to repay you, but if there's ever anything I can do, if there's ever anything you need–"

"Forget it, man." I felt awkward.

"You'll see, buddy," he said. "I'll be loyal to you, forever."

Later, when we were back upstairs, I asked Amanda, "Who was here today?"

"Manuel Lopez."

"Who is Manuel Lopez?"

"Manuel Lopez-Ramirez, son of Carlos Lopez," she said. "The father is a landowner and a merchant, the richest man in our village. They used to call him Don Carlos. Then in the Republic, he was only 'Comrade Lopez.'" She gave me a long dash of a smile; the broken tooth made her look like a wild woman. Anything goes.

I straddled a wooden chair in the kitchen. Amanda brought me wine. I thought of Cici, waiting tables in John's Grill, bringing me a nickel beer the first time I saw her.

"So he is all right?" I asked.

"No, Manuel is not 'all right,' as you say. Carlos Lopez is a Falangist. He and his family fled the village in late 1936, just as the trouble began. But now Franco has swept away the republic and the law, and the Lopezes return to claim what was theirs."

"What did Manuel Lopez want?" I said.

"Two things. He is a blueshirt, an officer of the Falange militia. He was looking for a party of three, an officer and two men who disappeared last week."

"That is trouble, then."

"Maybe not," she said. "He is easily fooled."

"What is the other thing?"

She blushed. "He wants me. Before the war, he came to call many times."

"You were only 15," I said.

"That did not matter to him. This second thing may be trouble, because he will return." She put a plate down for me, with a piece of bread, and a small slice of ham to go with the wine. Bending her head down near me, Amanda pulled her hair back from her ear, and said, "Look."

I saw she wore a gold earring. "Very nice." I remembered how Cici used to bend over me, looking at me with her emerald eyes.

"Manuel gave them to me. He says they are from Madrid. How could he have been in Madrid? Should I wear them?"

"You are beautiful with them or without them," I told her. A blush of color began to flow into her skin, as water flows into a tide pool. I put a hand on her neck, and I brushed my lips in a light kiss across the faint freckles on her cheek. Amanda turned and smiling, drifted out of the kitchen.

Chapter Five
The Cave Scene

One evening, later that same week in March, Alejandro put his rifle under his arm, picked up a sack that clinked with bottles, and said, "Bring your gun, Francisco, and come with me." I had stashed our rifles in the secret compartment in the wine cask. After I went down to fetch mine, I joined Alejandro out in front of the house.

The sun had fallen behind the surrounding hills, and it was dark in the valley, but there was still light in the western sky behind the hills. We walked along the road half a mile or so, then Alejandro turned onto a path that I wouldn't have seen if he hadn't been leading me.

"We go to see a group of like-minded men," he said.

"Guerillas?"

"*Si*, for the Republic. Carry this would you? My arms are tired." He handed me the sack. The bottles knocked together and he swore, in the manner he used with me. "Quietly, fool. You will wake the whole neighborhood." I hadn't seen any neighbors since Max was wounded. Then Alejandro started to cough. When he stopped, he spat on the ground. It could have been blood.

"Are you all right?" I asked him.

"*Si, bueno.* Hey, *cabron*, why didn't you tell me you spoke Catalan? You almost got us killed." He slapped me on the back.

"You didn't ask. By the way, you should hear my Basque."

"Basque? Don't even joke!" He coughed some more.

The path climbed and in another 15 minutes or so, Alejandro led the way around a bush and walked right into the black side of a hill. It was the entrance to a cave, and when I came to it, a short thin fellow stepped out of the shadows and held a bayonet to my neck. But Alejandro vouched for me, then introduced me around.

"*Muchachos,* meet Francisco, the one I told you of." Jorge, the one with the bayonet, put away his blade, and shook my hand.

We sat on empty wooden crates and stones around a small fire. The smoke drew well back toward some outlet I hadn't seen. Alejandro told me to pass out the wine and I gave each man one of the bottles we had brought. Other men passed around a quarter wheel of cheese and slabs of ham in a rough string net. The food was to take home, but the wine was for now. Corks came out and the men began to drink. Some rolled smokes with loose cigarette tobacco – Picadura. Alejandro gave me one, then rolled a second for himself, and we smoked.

Santana, a white-haired, bearded man, sat opposite Alejandro, and had some news of the offensive. It went well for Franco. "He will be at the sea by the end of the month," Santana said. "Nothing can stop him now."

Jorge, to my left said, "*Mierda!* He cuts the Republic in two, driving a wedge between Barcelona and Valencia."

"Franco can go to hell," said Alejandro who was to my right. "What is important for us is that we are no longer in the Republic. Now we are behind the lines. Do we fight on?"

"What can we do?" said Santana. "We are cut off."

"We can kill fascists," said one called Diego. I looked into the fire.

"I will die for the republic," said Alejandro, "but I will not throw my life away, sniping from the hills. Better to pull our heads in like the tortoise, and wait. If there is a counterattack, then we join it. We crush the fascists between our army and ourselves."

"I am with Alejandro," said Igon. "Let us work our farms. We will be ready in a minute to serve the

Republic."

"What say you, Francisco?" Alejandro asked.

"I say pass the wine, *por favor*." They laughed with me, and we drank. In the fire in front of me I saw the surprised look on the young soldier's face when I shot him twice in the chest on the road. I made it a long drink.

Three of them favored going into the hills to fight on regardless, to die like men on a hillside, than to live under the Generalissimo's boot heel. "And besides," Diego finally spoke, "whose family had not suffered from the war? Killing, rape? Where is your daughter, Santana? Your wife, Alejandro? The killing will not end just because Franco has marched across the land."

Santana, Igon the Basque, and Alejandro favored a wait-and-be-ready approach. "We will look for opportunities to help our army," said Alejandro, "but we must not throw our lives away. What say *you*, Francisco?"

Everyone looked at me. I was squeezing the neck of the wine bottle too tight. I passed it on to Alejandro and flexed my wrist. I felt the burn in my radial muscles as when I'd pulled my belt tight around the Falangist captain's neck. "*Compañeros,*" I said, "I will kill no more."

~ ~ ~

Alejandro and I were the first to leave. We walked quietly for a while. "What did he mean about your wife?" I asked.

"Diego? He talks too much." Then there was a low rustling off to the left. I went down to one knee; Alejandro raised his rifle and fired. Something tumbled through the underbrush and then was quiet.

Alejandro went into the bushes and came back holding a large, pale grey hare by the ears. "We will eat well, thanks to you," I said. I patted him on the back and he began to cough again. This time it was clear that he spit blood at the end. "What is it, *hombre*?"

"*La tuberculosis,*" he gasped out. "Amanda does not know."

"I won't tell her. What can we do for you?"

He shook his head. "I'm dying. When the time comes, I will fight and die here with the others. But you, if you do not want to fight, take care of Amanda for me. When your friend is better, take her with you, away from here. Take her to Valencia. I will make my stand then."

"You're not dying, Alejandro."

"Carry the hare, you fool."

Chapter Six
Down by the River

One day, in April, I came up from working in the cellar. It had rained most of the week, but this day was sunny.

Amanda was in with Max. His shirt was off; his hair was cut, washed, and still wet. Amanda had put a coarse sack around his shoulders and another on the bed, and was shaving him.

"Hey, Max," I said.

"Frank," he said, and grinned, "how about this, hunh? I'm teaching Amanda English, see, and I got my hair washed and cut, now a shave. The works."

"Hold still," she said. "This razor is sharp."

"She treats you good," I said.

"I must take care of him, you know," Amanda said. She held the razor hand up and steady. "He is helpless."

"Is he?" I said. I smiled. I crossed to the window, bending to look behind the curtain. I wondered if the yellow finches would be there.

"Yes, of course," she said. "He still wears the bandage over his eyes." Amanda went back to shaving Max.

I thought it was time for the bandage to come off, and for Max and me to dust. We had been there about six weeks. I wanted to get out, stretch, and let the sun warm my bones. I saw a rider in blue on the road with a riding crop tucked under his arm. Then a second rider, then two more came into sight. "Falange," I whispered. "C'mon, Max. We have to get to the basement. Are you coming with us, Amanda?"

"Wipe your face," said Amanda, giving Max her towel, and joining me at the window. She was barefoot, and stood on her toes to look, the top of her head and her hair – carrying a whiff of wood fire smoke in it – up against my jaw. "It's Manuel again, with a patrol. I will meet him outside the house. It will be all right." She folded the razor, and slipped it up her sleeve.

"There are four," I said. "Don't do anything foolish."

"Get downstairs. Hurry," she said.

Max and I went down in the cellar, and we were in the false bottom of the barrel before you could say malolactic fermentation. "Frank," he whispered after a few moments.

"Yeah?"

"Tell me about Amanda."

"What about her?" I said.

"Is she beautiful?"

I was feeling claustrophobic. "She's all right," I said.

"C'mon, man..."

"OK, yeah. She's easy on the eyes."

"How tall?" he asked.

"Max, I haven't weighed and measured her." He was quiet for a few moments.

"I can't see, you know," he whispered. "But I sense ... something special about her, and I just wonder if she's everything I imagine."

I gave in. "I'd say she's about five-six or five-seven, kind of rangy. She seems thin, but I'm not sure. She's been dressed in warm clothes. Dark brown eyes. Long hair – chestnut you might call it."

"How's her figure?"

"For God's sake," I said. "You're the one sleeping in there with her."

"Head to toe. I haven't touched her, Frank. But I think I'm falling in love."

I'd been thinking the same thing, but I couldn't say it to Max. "Let's not talk about it, OK? I want to listen, see if I can hear anything upstairs." We were quiet.

Then we heard someone come in the door, but no boots crossed the floor above. In a few moments there were three taps on the cask. I pulled the release, and we climbed out. "All is well," Amanda said. "They are still looking for the missing patrol. Today they go south of here."

"South? That's where your father and I dumped the car and hid the bodies," I said.

"Then I must go tell Papa," she said. "He works the vineyard northeast of the house today. I want him to know where they search." She put her Astra pistol on a lanyard around her neck, and pulled on a coat.

After she left I went back to working in the cellar, but I bumped my head on a beam. I went up to Max's room. "Max, I can't stand it in here anymore. I haven't stood up straight for a month and I stink. The patrol is searching to the south. You're safe. The stream is northwest of the house. I'm going to go have a wash."

"The water will be freezing. It's April."

"Doesn't matter," I said. "The sun is warm today, and I'll build a fire when I get back."

~ ~ ~

It was a swell day for a bath, even if some inconsiderate bastard before me had already used all the hot water in the river. I took my rifle, the soap that Amanda had used on Max, and my only change of rags, and walked to the stream. I braced my rifle stock between tree roots in a grove of poplar and ash. Then I stripped to the waist, and hung my tunic and undershirt over a low limb. I tossed my last pack of Gitanes on the grass next to the rifle butt, and after taking off my boots and socks, walked into the stream in my khaki pants. There were smooth river stones on the bottom, so it was easy on my feet. The water came up to my waist when I reached the center, and it was colder than the currents around Alcatraz. I hopped a little and slipped my pants off, then washed them as best I could in the flowing waters. My undershorts hardly seemed worth saving, but I didn't know when I'd get another pair, so I rubbed them side to side, and wrung them out.

That didn't take three minutes but I really felt the icy chill so I climbed out and hung up the pants and shorts. I squatted on the bank and soaped up before going back in. I let the cold water rush over my body until I was nearly numb. When the cold became painful, I waded up onto shore, and stepped out into the full sun. What a beating my body had taken over the last 15 months or so. I was marked with bruises and scars like a drunken mapmaker's rough sketch of the coast around Half Moon Bay, with wine glass rings and coffee mug stains. I was thinking I'd drop a peseta in the scale when we went to Valencia. I doubted I weighed more than 70 kilos. Then I looked up and a blanket hovered out from behind the tree where my clothes were and glided towards me.

Before I could react, the blanket was on me, and Amanda, who'd been carrying it from behind, wrapped it around us. It was the sign I'd been waiting for, all that I needed.

"*Hola*, Francisco," she said.

"*Hola, guapa*," I replied. I brought my cold lips to her warm mouth. She parted her full lips for me, and kissing, we waltzed back to the trunk of the tree. When her back was leaning into the trunk I lifted one of her legs, and slipped down inside the blanket to one knee. Reaching under her skirt – thanking St. Lucy, patron of dressmakers, that she hadn't worn pants that day – I ran my paws along her lean thighs, against the grain of her short soft hair. The aromas were like a mature red wine from a fine vintage – rich, smoky, meaty, leathery, earthy scrubland. Love is so urgent.

When I came back up for air, Amanda's face was flushed. I felt her heart beating next to mine as our bodies pressed together. The blanket around us slid down, and I pushed her sweater up to her shoulders. She was very thin, thinner than I had expected. Her breasts were full above her slim waist, the skin on them taut, stretched over rosy points. I thought of Max, blind since we'd come to the farm. He loved Amanda, yet he'd never even seen her beauty.

~ ~ ~

We lay on the blanket in the sun for a while, warming our bodies. "*Gracias*," I said to her.

"For what, Francisco?"

"Uh, for the blanket, *quapa*. I was cold."

She rolled onto her side, put an arm across my chest, and raised a knee across my legs. We lay a little while longer. "*Gracias a ti tambien*, Francisco," she said.

"For what?"

"You know what, *guapo*." She smiled, "You know."

I retrieved my packet of smokes and fished out the last two stale Gitanes for us. We smoked. "Amanda, where is your mother?"

She rolled onto her back. Now the sun in the western sky slanted across her body, highlighting pink peaks and casting dark garnet shadows below them. "My mother is gone," she said. "She disappeared late in 1936. Papa and I were out hunting. He had shot a deer, a fine stag. We were late coming home. When we arrived, Mama was gone."

"You mean she just left?" I asked.

She shook her head. "We found no trace of her, but there had been a struggle in the kitchen. That was the night Don Carlos and his family fled the village."

"You think Carlos Lopez took your mother?"

"It was no secret that he coveted her. I think he came with his sons. It was the night of the full moon, a beautiful long night, and they would have expected Papa to be out hunting. If I had been home, I think Manuel would have taken me."

I said nothing.

33

"You see, Francisco," she went on, "that is why we need the Republic. Without it, the powerful, like Don Carlos, take what they want. There is no law for them. Is it like that in your country?"

I thought about the question. "No, we have the rule of law. No man is above the law." I smoked my stale cigarette, and then asked, "Do you think your mother is still alive?"

"If she is, it has been so bad for her that she does not want to return to us. She may be dead. She may be living on the street in Madrid. Broken. Ashamed." She smoked and I drifted into thought about what had happened. Amanda was still a teenage girl. But what a life she and her father had had in the war. Did she even know what it was like to have a new dress?

Then Amanda said, "When you leave here, where will you go?"

"I could lie here beside you forever."

"But I know you will leave."

"I'll take Max to Valencia," I answered. I flicked the stub of the cigarette away. "We'll find a ship. Max isn't fit to stay on with one eye, and I'm going to get him out. Besides, I have no stomach for the war now." Max thought he was falling in love. I wondered if I was too. I thought about what Alejandro had asked me about Amanda. "When we leave, will you come with us?"

"Papa needs me here." Amanda took a last puff on her Gitane, blew the smoke out and twisted the stub in the dirt by her side.

"To work the farm?"

"Yes," she said, "there's that. But he needs my pistol too. Carlos Lopez is back. Alone, Papa does not have a chance. They will come for him."

"They'll come for you," I said.

"Let them try." I rolled over and stretched out along the top of her. I moved slowly, and her eyes began to shine. The sun was warm on my back and Amanda's flesh heated me from below, relieving the aches and loosening the knots in my muscles as we rubbed together. She lifted her gams into the air and cried out, "Move, man, move."

Chapter Seven
Max Sees an Angel

When Amanda and I returned to the farmhouse, Alejandro and Max were sitting in the kitchen with Santana, the grey-haired man I'd met at the cave. "The news is bad," said Alejandro. "Manuel Lopez and his blueshirts found the Fiat and one body. Santana saw them an hour ago, towing the car along the road toward the village with a team of oxen."

"What will they do?" I asked.

"There will be reprisals," said Santana. "Carlos Lopez knows who is loyal to the Republic. None of us is safe. They will arrest us. Or kill us."

"You should go to the cave," I said to Alejandro.

"No," said Alejandro. "This is my home. If I must die, it will be here. And Carlos Lopez dies before me. But you must go."

"Maximiliano has a bandage around his eyes," said Amanda. "He can't travel now." She reached a caress to the side of Max's face. Her hand lingered on his cheek. "I never finished shaving you."

Max smiled and touching her hand, said in a soft voice, "The shave does not matter now. Roll me a cigarette, Amanda." He withdrew a pouch of bull Durham from his shirt pocket and handed it to the girl.

"The bandages can come off," I said. I was antsy this afternoon, but now that the local militia had found the bodies, it seemed all the more urgent to me–" It's time for us to go."

Alejandro said, "It is six weeks now. He will be healed underneath."

We decided to cut off the bandage at dusk, so that Max wouldn't be subjected to the sunlight until the next

37

day. Then we'd have a meal, sleep a few hours, and leave before dawn.

If the Falange militia came for Alejandro, it would be after first light. I packed our kits, and puttered around the house, helping in the kitchen, savoring every glance of Amanda that I could. Did I look at her with new eyes? No. She'd aroused me from the first moment. I'd seen Amanda and desired her. Again, I thought of Max, and what he felt, never having laid eyes on Amanda. Blessed are they who have not seen and yet desire.

As it grew dark, Amanda lit a lamp and turned it low. She sat on the bed next to Max in the room they'd been sharing with a bowl of water and a knife. Alejandro stood in the short doorframe, and I went over to my window, curling my shoulders and peeking behind the curtain, out the window. It was a clear night.

When I turned back, Amanda cut the bandage and unwound it – once, twice around Max's head, and then it was off. He reached his right hand out toward her, and put it on the side of her face. His eyes blinked. Neither of them spoke.

Finally, Alejandro called, "Hey, *hombre*, do you see?"

"I see an angel," said Max in breathless English.

"He sees, Papa," said Amanda in Spanish. "He sees." She took a piece of walnut-stained leather, a smooth hide like her shoes, but thinner, and fit it over his right eye. Reaching around Max's head, the wool of her sweater brushing his face, Amanda tied it tight with a thong. "I have made you a patch for your eye, Maximiliano, from a piece of sheepskin."

Max sat up and hugged her. "Thank you. *Gracias*, Amanda," he said. I told myself it was a brother's hug, a patient's affection for his nurse.

Finally, Amanda pushed away. "I must see to the stew," she said. She wiped tears away as she stood and brushed through the door past her father.

Max looked around the room. "Frank, is that you, buddy?"

"I'm here, Max." Why was it so hard to give him a smile?

"I can see you. It's dark, and you're a little blurry ... but you're a sight for sore eyes, man. A sight for sore eyes, hunh? What a thing to say!" He was excited. He stood and walked to the little man in the doorway. "You must be Alejandro." Max wrapped his arms around him and lifted him off his feet. Alejandro began to laugh, then he coughed and Max put him down.

We ate by the light of the fireplace. I didn't speak much. Max was quiet too, gazing across the table at Amanda. We had a stew of pork cheeks with carrots, and drank Alejandro's *cariñena* wine.

Old man Rabinowitz had made good dough in the lighting business back in Santa Rosa, and Max was the wealthiest bourgeoisie in our brigade. Now, he took off his belt and extracted five gold double eagles. Alejandro's eyes grew wide. "Go ahead," said Max. "They're yours."

"No, *compañero*. It's not right," he said.

"Yes, comrade. For your kindness. For Amanda," said Max.

When we'd wiped up the last of the sauce with our bread, Alejandro reminded us he'd be waking us before dawn. "Go to bed and sleep," he said. "Be ready."

"I don't know if I'll be able to sleep," said Max. "I'm too excited."

"Have another cup of wine," Alejandro said, and poured for him. Amanda held out her cup, too.

Chapter Eight
Noises in the Night

I woke twice before dawn. Or maybe I never fell asleep. The first time I heard a rhythmic panting, the creaking of wood, and soft cries, ghosts moaning somewhere. I climbed out of bed and rushed to the door of Amanda's room. The sounds had stopped. I put my ear to the door. *Nada*. It must have been a dream.

Before we had turned in, Alejandro reminded me, "Francisco, in the morning when you go, I want you to take Amanda. Take her to America if you will. I will give you the five gold coins to pay for her passage."

"Alejandro, maybe it's not such a good idea to let Max sleep in there tonight," I said.

"Ha! You want me to put you in there instead?" He wagged an index finger under my nose. "You must think I'm an old fool."

"It's not that. It's Max. He's recovered. He has his sight, he has his strength. He..."

"I have spoken with my daughter about these things, but she said she must be close to her patient. He may need her during the night."

He may indeed, I worried. "But..."

"And Amanda is a good girl. I trust her. Besides, she'll be 17 in a couple weeks, eh?"

Now I turned my back to Amanda's door, and returned to Alejandro's bedroom. The old man snored a bass line. There were a few drops of fresh red blood on his nightshirt. He was right. He was dying. I climbed into bed and put my back towards him. Did I drift off and dream again, or stay awake? I couldn't tell, but towards dawn, there was a banging on the wall, and I heard a cry. It sounded like, "Move, man, move."

I sprang out of bed and rushed to Amanda's room. I knocked on the door, paused, and then I pushed it open. Amanda lay curled like a lazy "S." Max was on his back, but sat up when I burst in. He wore the eye patch. "Frank, is that you? It's still dark."

"It's time to get up," I said. "We should go."

"OK." He tossed the blanket aside and swung his legs out of bed. Amanda and Max had not been head to toe, but at least his pants were on. "Lemme go out to the latrine, then I'll be ready."

When he'd gone I gave Amanda a smack on her rump. She was warm and soft there, and I was surprised by the loud crack my slap made. "*Guapa! Buenos dias.* Time to get up."

She pulled the hair back from her face, rubbed her eyes, and smiled at me. I grew hard.

"Amanda, we're leaving," I said, and brushed a hand across the front of my trousers. "You should come with us. It's not safe for you here."

"I will stay with Papa." She sat up and stretched her arms over her head and back.

"It is the end for him," I said.

"He needs me with him."

"He told me to take you. He gave me the gold to take care of you." I showed her the coins.

"Here," she said, and held out her hand, "give them to me." I put the five coins in her palm. "I will leave with you. That will put his mind at ease. You are going to the cave first? I will go only that far, then double back to the farm."

"That makes no sense, *guapa*. You want to die too?"

"No, but I must help Papa, Carlos Lopez and the others will come for him." She kissed a finger and put it to my lips. "Say nothing now. Go, so I can dress." I turned her shoulders to face me and kissed her. The kiss could have gone on and gone further, but she pulled away.

"Max returns. He should not see us embrace."

Why not, I wondered, but I said nothing and went out to the kitchen. She thought she was only going as far as the cave? Fine, let her think that. But I would hold onto her – for Alejandro's sake. I would take her with me ... for love's sake.

Max came back. "My vision's a little better this morning, I think," he said. "But I'm not used to seeing with only one eye."

"We'll go to the cave I told you about, Max. We're going to take Amanda out of here, OK?"

"We're taking her? That's swell." He leaned close to me and lowered his voice. "Does Alejandro know?"

"It's his idea. He's dyin', Max. That cough? He's got TB."

Alejandro and Amanda both joined us from their separate rooms. He told her of his wishes. She acted surprised. "It's for the best," he said. "I will be fine. Santana and I will gather the other men today, and we will make our plans to welcome Don Carlos when he comes."

"I will stay with you," she said to her father. She put the lanyard for the Astra around her neck. "You will kill Don Carlos, and I will shoot Manuel."

"No," he said. "I will shoot Manuel for you. To shoot Manuel is nothing." Amanda protested that she'd stay, but Alejandro was firm. They spoke like actors in a play, making speeches about killing. Finally, Amanda acquiesced, and the two of them packed a travel kit for her.

We met on the porch and said our good-byes. The western sky was still indigo above the hills. You know you can see yellow finches in the morning half-light in the country? It was a nice last memory of the place as I hugged Alejandro, and promised him I'd take care of his daughter. "If any of the men are at the cave, I will send them to your farm this morning," I told him. Then we set out along the road, which was still dark under its canopy of trees.

I took point, knowing where to look for the path to the cave. Max and Amanda walked side-by-side behind me. Amanda had nursed him back to health, while I'd rested after a tough year in the field, drank Cariñena, and climbed up my thumbs. Now I was responsible for both of them. But my mind was racing – thinking of last night, fixating on the noises I'd heard in the house.

After seven or eight minutes, we came to a little rise in the road, the last spot from which we'd see the farmhouse before the path to the cave. I stopped and turned back for a final look. Only Max was there.

"Where's the girl?" I said.

He glanced around. "She was right here. We were holding hands for a while." Amanda had been walking on Max's right side, his blind side. How long ago had she slipped away?

Now the rising sun was shining in the garden and on the front of the farmhouse. We had come maybe 200 or 250 yards. I saw a great fat man in a blue uniform sitting on a grey stallion in front of the house. He pointed and gestured, directing other men. Two blueshirts had Alejandro's arms behind him and were dragging him across the front yard. Then in the meadow that stretched out along the road, I saw Amanda, running towards the house. She had already covered more than half the distance back, her skirt swirling and trailing through the tall grasses. She pulled her Astra from under her coat and fired one shot as she ran. "Get down, Max," I said. I pulled him to the dirt at my side as I dropped down into the prone firing position and brought my rifle to bear.

"What's happening?" he said.

"They've got Alejandro; Amanda is headed into it."

Max tried to get up, and I yanked him down by his

belt. He unslung his rifle and tried to aim it, then choked out a sob. "I can't see well enough yet to shoot at this distance."

"Try the field glasses," I handed him my binoculars. One Falangist had turned toward Amanda. She fired again, and may have hit him, but maybe only a shoulder. Or maybe she missed. He didn't go down.

I heard Amanda cry out on the run, "NO! Don't shoot him."

"Shoot, Frank, shoot," said Max. There was a noise in my head like I had stopped on the tracks and a train was bearing down on me.

I said, "She's in the way," or some excuse like that. The blueshirt nearest Amanda – was it Manuel? – fired twice. Amanda fell. Her beret came off and rolled on its edge like a red wheel. She didn't bounce or move again; she just went down. I saw blood on her head.

The fat man fired his pistol from horseback. Alejandro fell back in the spring mud in the yard. The one who'd shot Amanda turned away and walked back toward the house. He holstered his pistol and put a hand on his shoulder. I could have shot him in the back then. I could hear the fat man laugh. I heard the plea in Max's voice, "Shoot, she's not in the way now. Shoot!" But I couldn't. The train roared on by.

"It's no use, Max. They're dead. Let's get to the cave. We'll save ourselves."

Who said, "Love conquers all?" Shakespeare? No, it was Latin. *Amor vincit omnia.* Must have been Virgil. The sap. I understood why my love for Amanda had been so urgent. Love passes away; only death endures.

Part Two
The Girls from Nanking

Chapter Nine
A Body in St. Francis Wood

San Francisco, Dec. 1948

Whenever Maximilian Rabinowitz wanted a little Asian nookie, he would go to the Lotus House in Chinatown. I didn't see any harm in it, so I went along one Tuesday night. Max thought of himself as a connoisseur of exotic women. I paired up with a Burmese girl named Bimla, who had taut brown thighs and turned out to be a lot of fun. Max wouldn't go with a girl until a 5' 9" bombshell named Cuifen was free. "She was a princess in Shanghai before the war," he confided in me. "She does things in bed you've never dreamed of." He had to wait in line for half the crew of a Taiwanese freighter that was in port that night, but he didn't mind. If Max didn't care, why should I worry?

Ten years had passed since we lay in that meadow in Aragón. Max had a profitable criminal law practice now, with offices on my floor of the Rose Building over on Post Street. We'd stayed close over the years, and with Amanda Zingaro having died before our eyes, I never felt the need to tell him I'd been intimate with the woman he loved so romantically. Max was still a member of the communist party, and though I'd styled myself as an anarchist is Spain, I really wasn't so deeply into politics. I was a run-of-the-mill American socialist, who believed in justice for the working man and leaned far enough towards Max's politics that we stayed compatible.

After the Lotus House, Max drove me home in his pre-war Alfa Romeo Touring Spider. It was a lot of car for a man with no depth perception, but he reveled in speed and powerful cars. I lived in Cicilia's house on Lafayette Square. Cici and I had reunited for a spectacular week in

'48, after she poisoned her husband, Rusty O'Callaghan, the gent for whom she'd dumped me in '34. Cici died, too. There would have been no future for me with her, but Cici's death really brought me to my knees. I took it hard, like I'd taken the loss of Amanda in '38, and the first loss of Cici in '34 when she'd married Rusty. I would have slipped even further into the abyss, except on our last night, Cici told me I was father of her first daughter, Brigid. She left the house to Brigid and Meaghan, her daughter with O'Callaghan, but I was executor of the estate and I moved in to take care of the girls while they were still minors.

As we approached my house, I saw one of the brand new '49 Ford police cars parked outside. Max pulled over to the curb behind it, and I climbed out. A plain-clothes dick sauntered over. He was short and a little stocky, like a beer barrel. His rumpled overcoat and suit jacket hung open, and his narrow dark tie curved over his belly.

We stood near the street end of the drive. The house was partly sheltered from view by a tall hedge, above which you could see the ornate but crumbling white limestone on the second story. Someone must have thought he was making a hell of a deal on the limestone forty years ago when they built the place. It was all over the house. But he didn't know limestone doesn't hold up well in the San Francisco climate. "Hello, Swiver," said the dick.

"Hello, Snootsie," I said, "I'd invite you in but I haven't inventoried the silver yet this month. What brings you around?"

"The Lieutenant thought maybe you could use some work," he said.

"Overby?" I asked. Sergeant Snoots usually paired up with Lieutenant Overby. They worked the homicide detail for the San Francisco Bureau of Inspectors. Snoots nodded. "Well, sure," I said. "What's the lay?"

"We got a body over in St. Francis Wood. Looks like a suicide, but the lady of the house is screaming murder. She wants to see a private license on the case. They're important people. Lieutenant Overby told me to come and get you."

"I'm your man. Just give me five minutes and I'll follow you in my crate." I said good night to Max who put the Alfa into gear and roared off. Then I went in through the house, opened the garage, and flashed the lights of my Pontiac at Snoots when I was ready to follow.

~ ~ ~

Snoots turned on his red light and took off. I tucked in close so I wouldn't be clobbered tailing him through an intersection. He headed south on Webster, past Alamo Square, and into the Castro. Soon we picked up Portola Drive, and Snoots led the way into St. Francis Wood, a neighborhood of spacious homes with large yards. On Santa Paula Avenue, he pulled his cruiser into the driveway of a three-story hacienda, and I found a spot on the street.

I belted my trench coat against the December chill and walked back to where the squat detective sergeant was waiting for me in the drive. We climbed some stairs to the front entrance. Snoots showed his star to an officer at the door and led me into a foyer with white plaster walls and mission wood framing. A wooden staircase with an iron banister started in front of us and wound up in a spiral past tall windows. Snoots bounded up the stairs and I followed.

One flight up, we headed down the hall to the first door on the left. It opened onto a bedroom with two picture windows and a beam ceiling. There was a woman's body on the bed, with the top of her head and face covered in blood. She was naked, with her knees up and her legs spread. Coarse, straight black hair carpeted her pubic mound.

Snoots put his hands in his overcoat pockets and said, "Chinese girl. She worked here as a maid. Note the gun, in her right hand lying there by her head, and there's black marks and burns right along here," he took his right hand out of his pocket and pointed at the woman's right temple. "Looks like suicide." The gun was a medium-sized revolver, like a cop might carry, and the dead girl's hand clung to the butt, her finger through the trigger guard.

I didn't have a taste for this sort of scene, but I had to lean in and get a slant, whether I liked it or not. "Is this the note?" I asked, as I bent over the body. There was a half-sheet of lightweight paper next to her chest, with Chinese writing on it.

"What the hell is he doing here?" boomed a voice from the doorway behind us.

"It's Swiver, Lieutenant," said Snoots. "You told me to go get him."

"Yeah, but I don't want him in my crime scene," Lieutenant Overby said, stepping into the room. "Mrs. Spring wanted him. Take him to see her."

"Hello, Overby. I didn't know it was a crime scene," I said.

Lieutenant Overby was as tall as me, about six foot, and sported a mustache. He had taken his overcoat off, if he'd worn one, and his charcoal suit was neat and pressed. Snoots looked disheveled next to him. For that matter, so did I. "Got a body here with half her face blown off and you don't know it's a crime scene," he said.

"Well, Sergeant Snoots told me it was a suicide."

Overby took a breath as if to calm himself. "I'm doing you a favor here, Swiver. You can probably pick up some easy dough. It sure as hell looks like a suicide to me, but when I said what I thought, Mrs. Spring wanted a private dick called in. You played ball with us before, and I thought of you. So don't give me any shit, OK? Go talk to her."

"Sure, Lieutenant. Thanks for thinking of me." I headed towards the door. "Oh, is this a suicide note next to her?"

"We'll know when we show it to somebody who reads Chinese."

Snoots braced me by the elbow. "C'mon, Swiver. I'll take you to see Mrs. Spring."

~ ~ ~

We walked along the second floor hall to the opposite end, and Snoots opened a large oak door. A dark-haired frail sat in a tall-backed, tufted leather chair studded with nail heads. Her legs were crossed at the knees and a bit of vanilla thigh showed on one side. She was facing a low fire in the grate and a Chinese landscape hung over the mantle, which had a set of miniature jade animals – a monkey, a horse, a tiger, and so on – arranged on it.

"Mrs. Spring," said Snoots. "This is Frank Swiver. He's a licensed private investigator here in the city." She turned and looked up at me. I was surprised to see that Mrs. Spring was Asian.

"Good evening, ma'am," I said.

"I'm Joan Spring," she said. "Sit down, Mr. Swiver. Good night, Sergeant, please pull the door shut." I sat down across from her, in a burgundy leather chair that matched the one she was in. Her eyes focused on me while she waited for Snootsie to leave. They were violet eyes, so I thought perhaps she was only part Asian. The firelight illuminated her pale skin, sensuous red lips, and lush black hair. She wore a red blouse that matched the lipstick and a skirt as black as the hair. Her figure was lithe, her looks exotic, and her eyelids were semi-closed as if in an opiate haze. I sat there giving her the up-and-down. She hooked me with those violet eyes. I felt the pull of the line as she reeled me in, and I didn't fight it.

Joan Spring looked to be past 20, but beyond that I

couldn't have said if she was closer to 25 or 45. It's easier to guess the weight of a farmer's wife at the county fair than it is to reckon a Chinese woman's age when she's dressed and made up.

When Snoots had shut the door behind him, she began, "Mr. Swiver, I would like to engage your services to find the murderer of Wu Fang."

"Miss Fang is the dead girl in the bedroom down there?" I asked.

"Miss Wu, detective."

I blinked. "Whose bedroom is she in, Mrs. Spring?"

"It's my husband's. Mr. Cornelius Wells Spring, Junior." I'd heard of Cornelius W. Spring, Jr., but we didn't run in the same society. Connie Spring was probably one of the ten wealthiest men in San Francisco. He owned the WellSpring Bank. His father had owned the WellSpring Bank before him, and his grandfather, Lionel Wells, had founded it, back when Custer was alive and well in South Dakota.

"Do you know why Wu Fang would have been in there?"

"I should think from the position of the body, it might be apparent to a detective what she was doing in the bedroom." If that was difficult for her to say, her face didn't show it. She kept her violet gaze steady and locked on me, as if to say, I still have you hooked on my line.

"The police say it looks like suicide, Mrs. Spring."

"It was murder," she said. She hunted about for her cigarettes, found one in a leather box on the table, and lit up. Her hand was dead steady.

"Who do you think would want to kill Miss Fan ... er ... Miss Wu."

"My husband, Cornelius Spring." Now she let out some line and let me run with it.

"Does your husband keep any guns in the house?" I asked. "Revolvers?"

"Several." She blew out a long stream of smoke.

"Why would Mr. Spring want to kill Miss Wu?" Just then there was a crash against the outside of the thick wooden door. A log settled and the fire crackled and popped. I got to my feet. Mrs. Spring remained seated, her posture erect. She crossed her legs at the ankles. A lock clicked, the doorknob turned and there was another crash as the door swung open and hit the wall inside the room. A man took up most of the doorway, and he looked as solid as the door he'd pushed open. Tense, taut cords of muscle stood out on his thick neck, as if it were a piece of split oak. His legs were tree stumps, firmly planted in the rug. He wore a brown cardigan, the color of bark, over a white shirt and golden tie. His sandy hair was cut short and brushed straight up.

"What are you doing in my house?" he asked.

"Oh, you must be Mr. Spring. Just talking about you, sir," I said, and put out my hand. I didn't think he'd take it. I hoped he wouldn't. He probably had a grip like a baler. I gave him a smile, one I used with only the wealthiest of clients. "Frank Swiver, sir. I'm a private detective."

"Get out of here, or I'll throw you out."

"I asked to see him, Cornelius," said Mrs. Spring.

"I don't need a shamus."

"I want him," said Mrs. Spring.

"Mrs. Spring," I said, "perhaps now isn't the best time to talk. Here's my card. Why don't you give me a call tomorrow? I'm more than happy to try to help you on this." For a man whose physical characteristics reminded me so much of a rooted tree, Cornelius Spring proved agile. He moved between us and snatched the card out of my hand before Mrs. Spring could take it and tore it in half, then into quarters. While he concentrated on tearing the quarters up, I took out another card, winked at Mrs. Spring while Connie's back was turned, and tucked it face down under the jade dragon on the mantle.

"I'll be going," I said. "Thank you for your time."

I gave Connie Spring a wide berth, and left the room. I didn't see Overby, and went down the stairs. I wandered around the main floor until I came upon Snoots who was studying the liquor cabinet in the dining room, probably looking for clues. I said goodnight and thanked him for calling me in.

Outside the air was cool and damp. I stopped in the courtyard beneath the house off the driveway, and tipped back the brim of my fedora. I stood with my hands on my hips and looked up. A dark window on the second floor slid open, and a hand came out. I was quick enough to catch what the hand tossed down. Undoing a rubber band I found my card around the jade monkey. On the back of my card it said, "Talk to Wu Cuifen." It was signed with a Chinese character that looked something like this: 牛.

Chapter Ten
Dead Women

At 9:00 the next morning, I stopped in Max's office, but his girl said he was in court. I walked down the black and white tiled hall to my door, stenciled "Old Vine Detective Agency," and called Overby. "Anything new on the case in St. Francis Wood?" I said.

"The suicide? No, nothing really new, Swiver. Mr. Spring wants the investigation to be quiet. He also wants it to be closed quickly, with little bother to him."

"You don't take orders from Spring."

"No, but he called the captain," said Overby. "Seems WellSpring Bank holds the mortgage on the captain's house in Richmond. Spring told the captain it was a suicide. He also told the captain to come down to the bank today. He's eligible for a half a percent reduction in his interest rate."

"He's offering a police captain a bribe?"

"Mr. Spring says the bank's having a new promotion on home loans starting today."

"How about the note?" I said. "Did you get it translated?"

It sounded like Overby moved some papers around. "Seems like pretty standard stuff. 'I have betrayed my sister. I am so ashamed. I cannot go on.' Signed, 'Fang.'"

"Is it her handwriting, Overby?"

"Hell, I don't know," he said.

"Chinese writing is different from person to person. Like ours."

"My boys are being thorough. We always are. If we find a sample of the girl's writing, we'll compare them. Listen, you won't mess us up on this if you know what's good for you."

"Who holds your mortgage, Lieutenant?" I asked.

"Bank of America, but I'm thinking of refinancing." He hung up.

I walked to my window and looked down on Post Street. The Rose Building was a survivor, an old ten story pile with a cast iron façade. I looked down on a row of retail survivors across the street – a jewelry store, a lunch counter, a seedy hotel. Max's practice was lucrative. He could have moved out but he liked the proximity to Union Square. I was lucky to keep up on the rent.

Attorney Rabinowitz's girl called me at 10:30 to let me know he'd come in. I went back down the hall. Max was all smiles.

"I just saved Louie Cyrgryzs from the electric chair," he said.

"Cyrgryzs? The consonant murderer?"

"Hunh? Oh, you're puttin' me on, right? Dr. Cyrgryzs, the physicist from Stanford accused of espionage. Government didn't have a case. Hey, I feel like celebrating. Want to go back to the Lotus House tonight?"

"Maybe," I glanced around his office. The morning sun was shining in through his blinds. "Who's Wu Cuifen?"

"Wu Cuifen? I don't know."

"Could it be that Princess Cuifen girl you were with last night?"

"Maybe. I don't know her first name. Or is 'Wu' the family name? Why, Frank?"

"I'd like to talk to her. You want to ride over there with me?"

"OK, but the girls won't be up yet. How about we go after lunch?"

I felt anxious, and I went back to my office hoping Joan Spring might call. She didn't. We made it an early lunch. Max and I loaded into his Alfa Romeo and drove to lunch, south of the slot at the Black Lizard Lounge. I had the blue-ribbon chili and Max ordered a Hangtown Fry. We split a bottle of Zinfandel. It was just a few minutes before noon and not yet too busy at the Black Lizard when our food arrived.

"Tell me about your case," said Max.

"Not much to tell so far. My client is Joan Spring, the wife of a wealthy banker." Max had been concentrating on his fry, but when I mentioned the name he looked up.

"Banker? You don't mean Cornelius Wells Spring?"

"The same." I said. "Know him?"

"Not really." He drank his Zin. "I know the WellSpring Bank, though. Very solid."

"So is Cornelius Spring. Anyhow, the wife, Joan, she told me to see Wu Cuifen."

~ ~ ~

The Lotus House was on an alley off Washington Street. There was a dark alcove at street level, where a red lantern hung, and we walked up one flight on an outdoor wooden staircase. The door was shut, but Max knocked and a peephole slid open. He smiled; the peephole shut and we heard the bolts slide back.

It was quiet inside, compared to the hawking and bustle of the streets of Chinatown. Jade Mama greeted us. "Roosters rise early, that for sure," she said. A half dozen chippies, including Bimla, were draped around the lounge in shorts, slips, or robes. Cuifen was not among them. Joss sticks burned, but something more than smoke, something dark hung in the air.

"We'd like to talk to Wu Cuifen," I said.

"Princess Cuifen not up yet. She sleeping. She have busy night. Many sailors in town."

"What room?" I said.

"She's usually in number four, left rear," said Max. I rushed for the steps.

"You want to see Princess, you give me three dollar,"

said Jade Mama.

"Pay the woman, Max," I yelled back, taking the stairs two at a time. Max peeled off some bills for Jade Mama and followed me.

One flight up, the hall smelled sour with last night's lust. A lazy fly buzzed around my head when I found number four. The door creaked open at my knock. Max reached the landing and headed down the hall toward me, as I eased into the room. The window was open halfway, and thin curtains backed away from me as if in trepidation. Cuifen lay on the bed, her long gams draped at the ankles over the iron foot of it. At first I thought she was wearing a silk scarf, but then I saw someone had knotted a sandy beige stocking around her white, long, elegant neck. I didn't touch it. Her tongue protruded between her lips. Her eyes were open but they weren't seeing anything. I turned, thinking to keep Max away from the scene, but he was practically on top of me.

"She's dead, Max. Someone strangled her." Max was an emotional guy. I could only see his eye patch side, but he pulled a handkerchief out of his suit coat pocket and dabbed at his mug on the other side.

I called it in to Snoots. He and Overby showed up in less than ten minutes, but they were grumpy. "Chinatown's not my beat, Swiver," said Overby.

"It's a homicide, Lieutenant," I said.

"I'm gonna call the local precinct. They could handle this better than us. Snootsie and me don't know no Chinese." Overby had changed into a navy blue suit and looked fresh. Snoots looked like he'd slept in his clothes.

"It's related to your homicide from last night," I said.

The lieutenant stood eye-to-eye with me. "I don't see how, Swiver."

"The girls are both named Wu." I had confirmed Cuifen's name with Jade Mama.

"That don't mean nothing. It's probably like Smith,"

Overby said. "What are you doing here, anyhow? Dipping your wicks early?"

"Lieutenant, my client told me to talk to Wu Cuifen. When I got here, she's dead. These two murders are connected–"

"Now stop right there, Swiver, and listen to me. There's only one murder."

"But Wu Fang–" I started, but he cut me off.

"Wu Fang's a suicide," he said. "As a matter of fact, I'm expecting the coroner to return that verdict this afternoon."

"What the hell, Lieutenant?"

"Dammit, Swiver, don't you understand?" he said. "Spring has clout. Now, listen, you're in a cathouse. These women don't want me and Snoots here. If they knew any English, they forgot it when we came in. I don't like anybody killing women any better than you, but I can't help these girls. Maybe the local boys can. C'mon, Sergeant."

"Overby, wait." He turned to face me and put his hands on his hips. "I looked around the girl's room," I said. "She didn't have much, but the stockings in her drawer – they were seamless."

"So?" he said.

"So, the one around her neck, it had a seam," I told him.

"So it wasn't hers. Swiver, that don't mean nothing."

"Yes it does, lieutenant. It means the killer brought the stocking with him."

They left. Max had been sitting on one of the sofas in the lounge sobbing and holding a couple of the girls. They were rolling him smokes with his Bull Durham. He rubbed his good eye with a knuckle and standing up, lifted his eye patch and dabbed under it with his handkerchief. "Let's drift, Frank." He collected his tobacco.

We drove back toward Union Square. Max told me the other girls had said Wu Cuifen had taken in a late customer. Nobody had a good look at him, but they agreed from seeing his back and clothes he was well dressed and not a sailor.

"I'll wait and see if Joan Spring calls me. Otherwise, I'm at a dead end," I told him.

"You're sure these two girls are connected?" he asked.

"I know it, Max."

"I'll go over to the coroner's office," he said. "I'll explain to him that he'll have to appear in court and show cause if he hands down a suicide ruling today without a proper inquest." He dropped me in front of the Rose Building and drove off.

Chapter Eleven
The Redwood Room

I had just poured a glass of red from the office bottle when the phone rang. "It's Joan Spring, Mr. Swiver. I'm at the Clift Hotel. Can you meet me now?"

The Clift was just around the block. "I'll be there in ten minutes, Mrs. Spring."

"My driver is in front of your building," she said. "A dark blue Chrysler."

"See you in five." I downed the Louis Martini and headed out.

I found the Chrysler, a big New Yorker four-door, by a hydrant out in front of the Rose Building. A heavy-set Chinaman with a low center of gravity stood by the side of it. He wore a snap-brim cap on a bald head, a navy-blue suit, and chestnut-brown leather driving gloves. His suit was an old one, but showed evidence of care. The Chinaman ushered me into the back of the car. We glided over to the Clift, and in five minutes I was stepping into the Redwood Room. Joan Spring was in a booth alone. Her hair was pinned up under a pillbox hat. Dim light from sconces and from dark shaded lamps on the tables, reflected off polished redwood walls. Joan kept her dark green wire-rim sunglasses on. I slid in opposite her.

"I ordered Champagne, Mr. Swiver," she said. "Bollinger. I hope you'll join me."

"What are we celebrating, Mrs. Spring?" I picked up a slight fragrance from her, bergamot or vanilla.

"Let's drink to Wu Fang. May she have a sweet life in a celestial place. Her life on earth was more bitter than one would have wished." The wine was on the table and uncorked. She waited for me to pour for us both.

"To Wu Fang," I said.

"To my sister." We drank.

"Do you mean that literally, Mrs. Spring?"

"Yes, Wu Fang was my half-sister," she said. "We were born in Nanking. My mother was a French woman, not married to my father. He was a wealthy and powerful man, a Chinese man."

"Nanking?" I said. "I hear things were very bad in Nanking."

"Yes. Things did not fare well for my father's family. The Japanese murdered him, and his wife, Wu Fang's mother, after they raped her. Her daughters were also raped. Wu Fang was 14. They did not kill her afterward, as they did with so many girls, but kept her and her sister as slaves for their army." She took a package of Chesterfields out of her purse and fit one into a cigarette holder. I held out a light for her, and she touched my hand as she took it. Her fingers were chilly, but steady.

"The Japs didn't bother you?"

"No, I lived in a European household, with my mother. That and good fortune saved me." She blew out a long cloud of smoke. "I am in more danger now. I need your help."

"What brought you to San Francisco?" I asked.

"I met Cornelius Spring in Nanking in 1946. The WellSpring Bank had considerable investments in the Republic of China, and in Chiang's government. Connie had come to pick up the pieces after the war."

"You fell in love?"

"I wanted to get out of China. There was civil war; there were shortages of food, fuel, medicine. In three months we were married in Nanking. I was a foolish girl, I admit it. But after we married, it was easy for Connie to bring me to the U.S. And he was able to help Mother leave China, too."

"And your sister?" I asked. I'd finished my first glass of Bollinger and I poured another, and topped off Joan

Spring's glass. Thousands of tiny bubbles sparkled in the Champagne glasses, and their reflection danced in the dark lenses of her shades.

"Yes, Connie got her out too. That was more difficult; it took a year. She's been living with us. There are three rooms with a private terrace on the lower level of our house. I tried to give her a good life."

"The police said she worked as your maid." A waitress came by and asked how we were doing. I told her we were doing all right.

"She was very grateful," said Joan. "She wanted to help out. But she was my sister first," She finished her cigarette and took a long drink of Champagne. Rosy-fingered dawn began to peek through her pale makeup, putting color in Mrs. Spring's cheeks.

"Why would Mr. Spring want to kill Fang?"

"Because he could. He feels entitled, powerful." She was hard to read. If she felt sorrow for her sister or hatred for her husband when she said this, I couldn't detect it.

"That's not a motive," I said. "Did he have a motive?"

She took a deep pull on her Bollinger. "Fang came to me and said my husband forced himself on her. It had happened while I was away last month to visit my mother, who lives in Vancouver now. Connie kept Fang in his bedroom that week. Since I returned, he has been breaking into her rooms at night and taking his pleasure with her. She wanted it to stop. Yesterday, I had it out with Connie. I told him he must stop. He laughed at me, Mr. Swiver. We argued." She stopped and finished her wine. I poured her some more.

"Oh, it's all my fault. I pushed him too hard. I should have let him do as he wanted with Fang. God knows, I didn't love Connie anymore. But I was jealous nonetheless. I felt humiliated. How would you feel if your wife cheated on you?" I thought of telling her I was not married, but decided it was a rhetorical question.

"He grew angry," she continued. "He slapped me. He screamed, 'Fine. You want it to end; I'll put an end to it.' He locked me in my room."

"So you think he killed her? That was how he '...put an end to it?'"

"Yes, while I was locked in. I heard Connie and Fang together. I heard him yelling. I heard Fang scream. And I heard the gunshot. It was terrible."

"Who called the police?" I asked.

"I did," said Mrs. Spring. "I have an extension phone in my room. After I called, Connie unlocked my door. 'Come and see,' he said. 'This is what you wanted.' He was in a frenzy. If I hadn't already called the police, I think he would have killed me too last night. He seemed hysterical. I'm so afraid, Mr. Swiver."

"Can your husband read or write Chinese?"

"No." She took off her sunglasses. I could see her violet eyes again.

"There was a suicide note..." I said.

"It must be a fake, or a forgery."

"Who else in your household could write Chinese?"

"Only Fang and I," she said. "My driver reads traffic signs but cannot write."

"Do you have a sample of Fang's writing?"

"That will prove nothing. He may have forced her to write it, before he killed her."

I asked for a sample anyhow, and she agreed to look. It was a bad time, but I had to tell her about Wu Cuifen. I put the jade monkey and my business card on the table by her hand. "Mrs. Spring, I'm sorry to tell you, but I didn't get to Wu Cuifen in time."

She put the shades back on, then, "What do you mean?"

"She's dead too. I take it she was another half-sister?"

She picked up the monkey and turned it in her fingers. "Cuifen, yes, but how–?"

"Strangled. A late customer, perhaps."

Her expression didn't change but her face grew more flushed. "Mr. Swiver, I can't go home now. Would you get me a room here please?" She opened her purse and dug through it for her wallet.

"Sure," I said. I stood up. She tossed some bills down for the Bollinger and a generous tip. Getting up, she took a few steps, and then started to wobble. I caught her. "Lean on me if you have to."

"Better get another bottle of Champagne," she slurred. "For Wu Cuifen."

Chapter Twelve
Head Full of Bubbles

I checked Mrs. Spring into a standard double. I went out onto Taylor Street, which was noisy with traffic, and told her driver to take a few hours and come back around dinnertime. He touched his cap and drove off. Stopping in the bar, I picked up a couple Champagne saucers and another bottle of Bollinger in an ice bucket, and charged it to the room.

Joan Spring had hung up her dress and was climbing into the bed in her skivvies when I stepped in. Her skivvies consisted of a black silk camisole, and a black lace garter belt to hold up her fully-fashioned stockings. There wasn't much standing between her and a good time.

I draped my sport coat over a chair, opened the Champagne, and sat down on the bed next to Joan. Now the vanilla scent was more powerful, along with jasmine and rose aromas. She was on her back with her head and shoulders propped up on her pillows. I lifted that damn silly hat off her head, but left her cheaters resting on her nose.

"Wu Cuifen was in the Lotus House. Do you know that place, Mrs. Spring?"

"Call me Joan," she said. She fixed another Chesterfield into the holder. I lit her up, then shook one out for myself. Chesterfields had been my grandmother's smokes, and she'd died of heart trouble. I'd always wondered if there could have been a connection. I'd never trusted them.

"Do you know what your half-sister was doing in the Lotus House, Joan?"

She giggled. "Do you want me to show you, Mr. Detective?"

"I'm trying to find out why you had one sister working for you as a maid and another in a whore house," I said. "And I'd like to know who would kill Wu Cuifen."

"My husband. He must have gone out after you left. Zhao, my driver – Connie drives himself, but Zhao cleans and maintains both our cars – he thought Connie had used his car last night. I'm terrified of my husband, Frank. I think I'll stay here."

"But why would your husband kill Cuifen?" I said.

"To protect himself. Connie killed Fang. Cuifen could have testified against him." She drew one knee up.

"What could she say? She wasn't at your house when Fang was murdered."

"Not what she could say, but what she *knew*," Joan said. "Yesterday, Fang visited Cuifen and told her about her relations with my husband. My sisters were close. Cuifen would have known Fang did not kill herself. She would have known it was murder." Joan drank. "How did she die, detective?"

"Strangled, with a woman's stocking." She gasped a little and gave up her poker face. "Why, what is it?"

"Zhao. He found a nylon in Connie's car. On the floor behind the driver's seat."

"What kind?" I said.

"I don't know. Zhao has it."

"Why was Cuifen working in a can house?"

Joan shrugged. "She wanted to. Connie and I brought many refugee women over from China after the war. They were victims of the Nanking massacre, living victims. Connie and the bank did it as charity work. I arranged marriages for these women here in San Francisco. They were ruined in China, but here there are many men who came to America alone. Now they have work; they want brides. They want to start Chinese families. These men know many bad things happened during the war with Japan, but they don't ask questions.

They are happy to have beautiful brides, hard-working grateful brides.

"Sometimes, though," she went on with a sigh, "things do not work out as planned. I had a fine man for Cuifen. He went to college and has a job as an engineer in San Jose. But the man's mother was an old-fashioned witch, and she asked many questions. Cuifen was not good enough for her son. She made him call off the wedding. Now I had Cuifen here, but without marriage, her visa expired. She would not be allowed to stay in America. And so she had to disappear into Chinatown. She chose to disappear in the Lotus House." Joan shrugged again, and as she did the silk camisole drew up and slid down over her nipples. I could hear its rough caress. "Fill my glass, Frank. Will you stay with me? I'm so frightened." A tear rolled down from behind her sunglasses.

"I'm not going anywhere, Joan." This was a lot to think about. We were halfway through the second bottle of Bollinger, and my head was full of bubbles. Joan Spring untied my tie, and starting at the collar, unbuttoned my shirt. She circled a long red nail in my chest hair. She kissed me on the lips. Her tongue was cool from the wine. She made me forget I had a couple murders on my mind.

~ ~ ~

I forgot about the murders the rest of the afternoon, and into the gloaming. "I have a headache," said Joan.

"That'll happen if you drink too much Champagne early and then stop. Have another glass, kitten." We both had another, then I stood up and began to dress. Joan took off her sunglasses and looked hard at me with her violet eyes. I didn't know if she was looking at the dark hair on my chest or trying to read my mind.

"We haven't talked business," I said. "I'll take your case. I get $25 a day, plus expenses. We know Cuifen was murdered. If Fang was murdered, I'll look for proof, and I'll find out who did it. Maybe it's the same killer."

"Thank you, Frank," she said. "It will give me peace. It will bring peace to my sisters, too."

"I may find that Cornelius Wells Spring was not the murderer." The room had a window on Geary. I looked down. The blue Chrysler was waiting.

"That is not a likely outcome," Joan said. "That is what he wants you to think." Then I saw worry in her eyes. I wished she'd put the cheaters back on. "What if he offers you more than $25 a day?"

"I'm for hire, but I'm not for sale. Your car is outside. Good night, Mrs. Spring."

Chapter Thirteen
The Rat

I walked north eight blocks and let the cool air clear my head. I stopped for dinner at a Chinese joint on Jackson. My food sizzled and smelled of sesame oil when they brought it out. I ate it while it was still hot and drank tea. I had a paper place mat with the signs of the Chinese zodiac printed on it. I was born in 1912, so I was a rat.

I hopped on a cable car headed back to Union Square. I'd decided to drive out to the Spring house, and poke my little rat nose around. The evening was growing foggy and damp. I walked over to the Rose Building, and went down to the garage. Max Rabinowitz was in there, just leaving for the night. "I'm going out to the Spring place," I told him.

"Great," he said, "I'm not doing anything. I'll drive."

"Max, this might involve a little breaking and entering. I don't want you to risk it."

"Risk stimulates me. Besides you may need an attorney, Frank. Come on, hop in." He fired up his Alfa. It snarled like an angry tiger in the underground garage, and Max chirped the tires as he headed up the ramp.

"Max, it's starting to rain. Let's take my heap."

"Nonsense. I'll get some speed up, and the raindrops will miss us."

Max took Twin Peaks Boulevard. As we climbed above the houses below, we were ahead of the fog, but I could see most of the city behind us was blanketed. Soon we were out on Santa Paula, and I told Max stealth was now more important than speed. He let the engine drop to lower revs and we cruised past the Spring house. The Chrysler was in the driveway by the main entrance. So, Joan had decided to come home? Max pulled around the corner onto a side street and cut his lights.

"Wu Fang, the dead girl, had some rooms on the ground floor. I'm going to have a look around," I said.

"I'll come with you," said Max.

"No, you stay here and erect the top. Looks like we're going to need it."

Instead of going up the drive, I pulled my fedora down to protect my face and dove through some bushes, then made my way across the grounds to the rear of the house. The rain was growing steady now and I hoped it would cover any noise I made. I reached a low wall and crouched down. On the other side of the wall was a small terrace with a lounge chair, a round table, and an umbrella for shade. French doors opened off the patio. Looking up I saw a light in the back room where I'd met Joan, and where the jade monkey had come out the window. I thought I could make out the top of Cornelius's head in the room, moving and bobbing.

I hopped over the low patio wall, and my shoes slapped the porphyry paving of the patio. I crossed to the French doors, and flattened against the house. The window that had opened last night opened again and Connie Spring, Jr. leaned out and looked down. I didn't move until he pulled his head in and shut the window; then I slipped my knife blade up between the French doors and in no time, I was inside, dripping on the tile floor.

I stood in silence for a while, but I didn't hear anything from upstairs. Taking out my pocket flashlight, I scanned the room. Like the exterior, the room was a Spanish design. The walls were plain, whitewashed plaster; the windows were high and set deep into the walls, and the lines were clean and austere. The furniture, though, had a touch of Chinese playfulness. There were two wooden interior doors. The first one opened onto a bedroom and bath. The bed was made.

There were few possessions in the rooms. Slippers, sandals, a chest of drawers with simple clothes folded and organized. I went back to the main room. A little jade boar sat on the desk, next to an old cloisonné fountain pen. There was a sheet of paper under the jade boar, and I stopped by the desk to have a look. Just then the other door swung open and the light from the hallway of the house spilled into Fang's room, around the hulking silhouette of Connie Wells Spring. I lifted the paper from the desk put it in my jacket pocket.

"I could plug you now," said Connie Spring. He had a revolver in his hand, a big dangerous-looking frontier Colt.

"Would you tell the cops it was suicide?"

"Why? I can shoot a man who breaks into my house. You might be interested to know, however, that I changed the suicide story today. I called the police. I confessed that I had been unfaithful to my wife, and that I no longer believed Wu Fang had killed herself."

"You confessed?" I was surprised.

"To adultery, yes. It makes quite a powerful motive for murder, as a man in your business should know." There was a pounding from the front of the house, above. "Ah, that would be the police," he said. "I don't think I'll plug you. But unless you want me to press charges for breaking and entering, I'll thank you to come upstairs with me and exit through the front door. Now." When I walked by him into the hall, Connie Spring put a thick thumb on the hammer of the single-action gun, and eased it down.

Upstairs, Spring admitted Overby, who carried an umbrella, and a very wet Snoots. Max followed them in. Joan Spring stood at the foot of the curved stairs, facing the foyer.

"Mrs. Spring," said Lieutenant Overby, "you're under arrest for the murder of Wu Fang. Sergeant, take her in."

"Are you kidding, Overby?" I said.

"Keep out of this, Swiver," Overby said.

"It's not Joan, it's Cornelius Spring you want," I said.

"Shut up." The lieutenant stood his ground in the foyer. He motioned Snoots towards the stairs. "Mrs. Spring found out her husband was screwing ... uh ... having an affair with the maid. She was jealous. She shot her."

"That's crazy," I said. "Anyhow, what about Wu Cuifen? You think Mrs. Spring went to Chinatown and zotzed her other sister?" Snoots squished across the stone floor in his wet shoes.

"I told you they're not connected," said Overby. "We have two Chinese sailors in custody for the Lotus House murder."

"Frank, help me," said Joan. The sergeant reached her and yanked her arms behind her back. Then he snapped the bracelets on.

"Don't worry, kitten. I'll get you out."

"Kitten?" said Connie Spring.

"Let's take a powder, Frank," said Max, stepping between Spring and me. "There's nothing we can do here."

Chapter Fourteen
Joan Makes Bail

Max had dropped me at home Wednesday night, and I'd invited him to come in. We drank a bottle of Inglenook red, and he left around one a.m. I fell asleep in my damp clothes.

At 9:30 the next morning, Max stopped by my office. "I'm going to go over to the arraignment and see what it'll take to spring the Spring doll," he said. "I'll represent her."

"She doesn't have any money of her own," I warned him.

"That hasn't stopped you, has it?" There were still some good lawyers in this city, more interested in justice than in money, and Max was one of them.

Max left and then I remembered that note from Fang's desk that I'd picked up last night. I spread it out flat on the desk blotter now. It was in Chinese. I decided to take it over to the Lotus House to see if Jade Mama would read it for me.

But that was a bust. Jade Mama wasn't there. The other chippies either couldn't read or write, or they clammed up. Bimla was sympathetic, but said, "I Burmese girl. Don't read China writing."

A friend of hers could read Chinese, but couldn't speak English. She read the note to Bimla, whose Chinese was rudimentary, and when Bimla translated it for me, it didn't make sense. It might have been a poetic love note. It was about love, fear, and abandonment, and the characters were a boar, an ox, a monkey, and a dog. Maybe it was a children's story.

"Who wrote it?" I asked.

"It's from 'Dog,'" said Bimla.

"Could Cuifen write Chinese?"

Bimla asked the Chinese girl something. "She says maybe Cuifen. Cuifen could write good *hanzi*."

"You know what this is about, don't you, Bimla?" I said.

"I can't tell you."

"Who are you afraid of?"

"I not afraid," she said. "I don't know."

"Come out for coffee with me."

"I can't leave."

"You can't or you won't?" I said.

"Jade Mama put me in charge."

"All right," I said. I thanked them, gave them the usual line about, if you think of anything else, call me, and I gave Bimla my card. Now I was handing out business cards in a Chinese cathouse to girls who didn't read English. What next?

~ ~ ~

When I got back to the office, Max was in the outer waiting room with Jade Mama. "How'd the arraignment go?" I asked him, as I unlocked the inner door to my office.

"I'd say it went well," said Max. "They charged Joan Spring with second degree murder, but bail was reasonable." He guided Jade Mama in behind me, and I noticed he kept a firm grip on her elbow.

"Reasonable?" I said. "Even reasonable might be too much. Joan says everything's in her husband's name, and I don't think he's going to put up the bond."

"Mrs. Spring is already sprung," said Max. "Guess who was there with cash."

"Turn me loose, One-Eye." Jade Mama squealed, pulled her arm away, and whacked Max on the blind side of his head with her purse. She headed for the door, but I lunged over and put my back to it. She swung her purse at me, but I could see it coming and blocked it. "Let me go!"

"Let's talk first, Jade Mama," I said. "Why would you post bail for Joan? What's your connection with the Springs?"

"I have nothing to say," she yelled at me, but she sat down. "You'd better let me go. This is kidnapping."

"Read me this," I said, and put the note in front of her. Her eyes got wide.

"Where you get this?" she said.

"Who wrote it, Jade Mama?" I asked. "Wu Cuifen? Is that her writing?"

"I not tell you. I want police."

I sat down behind my desk and picked up the phone. "OK, Mama. We'll have some law. But I don't think you'll like it. Those girls in the Lotus House are afraid of something. And if you won't help me, you'll take the rap for it."

"Rap? What rap?" she said. "You're bluffing,"

"How about white slavery to start?" I said. "They're afraid to leave the house. They know what's going on but they're afraid to tell me. Who scared them, Jade Mama? You?"

"No!"

I dialed the phone. "Last chance," I told her. She kept clammed and gave me a hard look. "Hello, police?" I said. "Give me Lieutenant Overby..."

"All right," she said. She lowered her eyes, and said in a soft voice, "Joan Spring."

"Why did you post bail for her? Where did you get the money?"

"$20,000, Frank. She brought cash," said Max.

"It's her money," said Jade Mama. "Joan Spring is the boss of Lotus House. She owns the place. She keeps the girls there."

Chapter Fifteen
At the Black Lizard

Muscovy duck was the blue-plate special at the Black Lizard Lounge and Max bought us a bottle of Burgundy to wash it down. It was a Faiveley Gevrey-Chambertin and one of the first wines of the 1945 vintage we'd seen here. It was an extraordinary young wine, rich and elegant even in its youth.

"The killing of Fang seems plain enough to me," said Max, "knowing what we know about what was going on between Cornelius Spring and Fang. Joan Spring confronted Connie with the facts. He shot Fang. Then he arranged the body to make it look like a suicide. A good lawyer might make a case for temporary insanity."

"If that's how it went down," I said, "then the rub-out of Cuifen makes sense. Connie locked Joan in her room, and drove to the Lotus House to kill the sister, who could have given evidence that Fang's death wasn't suicide. But where does the suicide note fit in?"

"Spring could have forced Fang to write it before he bopped her," said Max.

"Then the handwriting should be the same as the note I found in Fang's room." Jade Mama told us the Chinese note was from Fang to Cuifen, and said something along the lines of *"Sister Boar, I love you. Tell the monkey. I am afraid of the master. I must get out of this house or I will die. Do not abandon me to the ox. Help your sister."* There was potential for ambiguity there, and beyond that, I didn't even know if the translator was giving us a straight line.

"But I can't take Fang's note to Overby and ask him to compare them. If he found out I took evidence out of the Spring house and concealed it, he'd run me in." I took a mouthful of Burgundy and swished it around my palate. I hadn't made a nickel on this case yet, but I couldn't kick. People were buying me choice quality wine.

The owner of the Black Lizard kept a new Wurlitzer filled with old Southern blues records, what they used to call "race" music, before the war. Just then a tenor voice that sounded aged in corn whiskey sang,

"She's a kind-hearted woman,
She studies evil all the time."

I ran with my thoughts. "Could have been the other way around," I said. "Joan could have been jealous and chilled her sister. She could have written the suicide note to remove suspicion from herself. Then when she saw her husband played along with the suicide story, she brought me in to keep the case open."

"If Joan killed Fang, why would she want to keep the case open?" said Max. "She'd want a tidy verdict of suicide even more than Connie. Besides, after you left there, Spring locked his wife in. She couldn't have gone out and committed another murder. But Connie could have."

I shook my head. "I don't know how she did it but it must have been Joan. Cuifen was a prisoner in the Lotus House and was loyal to Fang. Joan was running the Lotus House operation."

"We have no confirmation on that. Jade Mama might say anything to save her own neck," said Max. Jade Mama translated the note, but wouldn't tell us anything else, and I'd turned her loose.

"Jade Mama wants to save her skin," I agreed. "What does Connie want?"

"Connie's a conservative businessman, a banker. He wanted to have a little fun with the Wu sisters. But things got out of hand, and now he wants it all to blow over. He wants to get away with whatever crimes he committed, and hang on to his property and position."

"What does Joan want?"

"She wants justice for her sisters," said Max. "Maybe she wants revenge on her husband."

"If Joan wants justice for her sisters, why would she keep one as a servant, and put the other to work in a whore house?" I said.

"Don't you trust anyone, Frank?" Max rubbed a piece of sourdough bread around his plate, and then divided the last of the Faiveley equally between our two glasses. "Joan called you in and told you the whole story of her own free will. Why would she take a chance on implicating herself?"

"Let's go stir things up, and maybe we'll find out," I told him.

Chapter Sixteen
Connie, in the Conservatory, with a Revolver

We were in Max's car again, speeding out to St. Francis Wood. I'd called Overby from the phone booth at the Black Lizard and asked him to meet us. This time Max pulled into the driveway. I was out of the car before the gravel stopped flying, and up through the front door. There was a long sun room on the first floor, with glass walls, stone tiled floors, palms and ferns, and a skylight overhead running the length of the room. Joan Spring and her husband were in there, sitting in wicker chairs at the near end. Cornelius had his long cavalry Colt on a low table in front of them. Zhao stood with his arms crossed part way down the hall.

"Frank, what are you doing here?" said Joan

"What are **you** doing here, kitten ... Joan?" I said. "I thought you were terrified of Connie, but you keep coming back."

"It's my home. I have nowhere else to go. Zhao is here. He will not let Connie harm me."

"It's **my** home," said Cornelius Spring. It had the air of a threat to it.

"Joan, read me this note," I said. I took Fang's note out of my pocket and smoothed it on the table, next to the gun. Joan Spring looked at it, and blinked.

"Where did you get this?" she said.

"Just translate it for me, kitten." I said.

"Oh, it's nothing," she said. "Just 'Dear Sister, You have been very good to me since I come here from China. I love you. I am afraid of the master. He hurt me. I must get out of this house or I will die. I know you love your sister and will not abandon me. Your loving sister, Dog.'"

That was close to the reading Jade Mama gave us. "Do

you recognize the writing?" I asked.

"It looks like Fang's," she said.

A low moan came up from Connie's center. "That's not how it reads," he said.

The front door opened again. I glanced over and saw Lieutenant Overby and Sergeant Snoots come in. When I turned back I had the impression something had moved.

"What's that you say, Mr. Spring?" I said.

"I know a little Chinese. That's not what the note says."

"He's gone crazy," said Joan. Connie Spring had a desperate look in his eyes. He knew nothing about losing. He was a man who'd always won.

"What's the note say, Mr. Spring?" I asked.

"I don't make it all, but the gist of it is, *'Sister Boar.'* She uses the zodiac character. *'I love you. I am afraid of the mistress.'* Not master, *mistress. 'If ox will divorce the monkey, and marry you ... you ... find love ... monkey gone ... we will be free. You will not abandon me, sister. I must get out of this house or I will die.'* Signed with the zodiac character for Dog."

"He can't read *hanzi*," said Joan. "I told you the truth, Frank. Connie's a killer." Joan looked dangerous. She looked very dangerous.

I thought before saying anything. I didn't have any proof – just a couple jade figurines and a placemat from a Chinese restaurant, that and my intuition. "I don't believe he's a killer," I said. "He was dizzy with your half-sister. He wouldn't kill the dame he loved."

"He loves *me*," she hissed.

"Maybe he did once. Maybe before you enslaved the girls he was bringing out of China in his refugee work. You told him you'd find them homes and husbands. But you put them to work turning tricks in the Lotus House."

"No!"

"Yes, Joan. Jade Mama told us that much. You kept

them there without papers. They couldn't go out into the world because they didn't have legal status in this country. If they left you could have them picked up and sent back to China. Or worse."

"I never knew, I swear," said Connie. "Not until Joan went to Vancouver last month. Then Fang had the courage to tell me. I'd brought all these girls out of China, fifteen of them the last three years. They had been sex workers for the Jap army; I thought I was helping them start new lives. Instead I'd consigned them to a brothel – a whore house where this bitch kept her own sister a prisoner."

"Dog was Cuifen," I said. I unfolded my paper placemat from the Chinese restaurant. "She was born in the year of the dog, 1922, wasn't she? Raped by the Japs at age 15, and you showed your compassion for her by putting her in a whorehouse. She wrote the note. The boar of course was Fang. You already told me she was 14 when the Japs took Nanking. 1923 was the year of the boar. And I imagine the ox is your husband, who looks to be in his late 40s and was likely born in the year of the ox, 1901. If the ox divorced you, the monkey, and married the boar, you'd have a comfortable settlement, but you'd be losing a chance at millions, maybe tens of millions."

"Between $20 and $35 million is about right," said Max.

I'm slow sometimes, but I had finally realized what was out of place. Zhao had moved closer, and now he pulled a nylon stocking out of his coat pocket, stretched it between his hands, and moving fast towards Connie, looped it around his neck. There was a revolver shot from behind me and a flat crack of a bone splintering in Zhao's knee. I turned and saw Snoots had drawn and fired. I turned back and the Chinaman sank down, the nylon slipping to the ground.

But while I'd turned my head Joan had grabbed the

cavalry revolver off the table and was trying to thumb back the hammer while holding the heavy gun up. "Stop," yelled Overby.

I dived for Joan, got her elbows, and pulled her to the floor. It was a good thing I got in there. Snoots had the drop on her, and he's an old-fashioned police sergeant who pumps lead first, and sorts it out later.

Chapter Seventeen
Sign of the Ox

Connie Spring admitted he'd withheld evidence of a murder – for about half a day. He said that on the evening of Fang's death, he'd finished taking his pleasure with her, and had gone downstairs to his wine cellar, leaving her in his bed, two flights up. He wasn't even sure he'd heard a shot, but when he went back upstairs, Fang was dead and posed as a suicide with a Chinese note next to her. He didn't understand, but said he'd taken it at face value.

Connie was still a wrong number in my book. Wu Fang was his employee, somebody under his roof he should have been protecting, not sleeping with. But Connie claimed that living with the gentle Fang, he'd fallen in love. He said he hadn't known his refugees were ending up in white slavery until a few days ago. Overby let him off the hook. The chief of police was refinancing, and even the mayor was in the real estate market then.

To his credit, the following Monday, Spring had an attorney and an employment manager from the bank over at the Lotus House, seeing about getting the girls permanent immigrant status, English lessons, and trainee jobs in the main office.

Joan Spring had caught her husband in the act with Fang, and kept out of sight until he left. Then she had shot her sister, scribbled a quick note, arranged the body to look like a suicide, and called the police. That much seemed certain and Overby pinched her for the murder, but she wasn't talking.

My personal attorney gave me his legal opinion that clamming up might be Joan's best defense. Max was in good spirits when he came by my office the following

Monday. He was going to take her case.

"Don't do it, Max," I said. "She's a killer. You saw how she grabbed Connie's revolver. She was going to shoot Connie then."

"Or maybe she was going to shoot you, Frank." He pointed an index finger like a gun at me. "Why do you think Cornelius Spring gave you the right translation of the note? Joan's and Jade Mama's translations agreed."

"I found it in Fang's room, so I think it went from Cuifen to Fang. Both Jade Mama and Connie had it as 'to: Boar.' And Joan told me a little about her sisters when we were drinking in the Redwood Room. Fang was 14 when the Japanese took Nanking. That means she was born in 1923, which makes Fang the Boar."

'What about Dog?"

"Well, Joan and Connie said 'from: Dog.' If it was to Fang, the Boar, then it must have been from Cuifen, and she must be the Dog character. I think Connie was reading it straight."

Max shook his head. "But why?"

"When Joan Spring found out about the affair, she wanted to kill Connie. But then, she still would have had to deal with her sisters, because they understood. If Connie had died in suspicious circumstances, Fang and Cuifen would have suspected murder. So instead, Joan popped Fang, and she hired me to pin it on her husband. That would get him out of the way just as well as murder, and the way she figured it, at less risk."

"But if she bumped Fang off," said Max, "she would have known you wouldn't find any evidence against Connie."

"And at that point, she sent Zhao on his mission of murder to the Lotus House," I said. "He took a pair of Joan's stockings – they had seams, and were too short for Cuifen. Zhao left the murder weapon around Cuifen's neck, and then Joan told me he'd found its mate in the back seat of Connie's car. That was the evidence she wanted me to turn up, and it would have been natural to tie both killings to Connie. And if I hadn't noticed the stocking, Joan probably could have coerced one of the chippies or Jade Mama to testify Connie had been to see Cuifen."

"She's not the killer," said Max. "If my client ordered Cuifen's death, why would she have tossed the jade monkey, and the note – 'Talk to Wu Cuifen' – out the window?"

"Joan didn't toss me the jade monkey. She hadn't even known it was out of the house. When I showed her the jade monkey at the Redwood Room, she was surprised. She didn't know how I'd come by it. So she distracted me – with her body."

"Then who tossed the monkey out the window?" said Max.

"Connie," I said. "He caught on quick after he'd run me off. When he realized what was going on, he wrote the note to try to save Cuifen and threw it out the window."

Max shook his head. "I don't believe that."

"The girls from Nanking called Cornelius 'Ox.' *Niu* in Chinese. He signs notes with his Chinese Zodiac sign of the ox, 牛." I still had my paper placemat from the Chinese restaurant, and I showed Max the character.

Max sighed. "You're getting me depressed, Frank. Look, let's go to dinner. How about a steak at John's Grill? I've had enough Chinese for a while. And afterward, I hear there's a place on Trenton Street. They got a girl working there looks like Hedy Lamarr at 19. What do you say we get to know her?"

"I don't think so Max. I wouldn't feel right."

"Come on, Frank. These girls are pros. They're from the City, like you or me. They're in business for themselves."

"You don't know that, Max. Not when there's dough

involved. Besides, I've got a date with a bank teller."

"Oh, yeah? A bank teller? Hot stuff, eh? OK, well, I'll see you tomorrow. I'll tell you about Hedy Lamarr, and you can tell me about your bank roll."

What did I care? He'd probably have to wait in line for Hedy, and I was taking Bimla out to dinner, and then to see Bogart and Bacall in *Key Largo*.

Chapter Eighteen
Max Takes a Powder

Bimla moved in with us at the old O'Callaghan place on Lafayette Park, "us" being the girls, Brigid and Meghan, and me. Although I'd done my best all year; being a dad was something new for me. Brigid and Meaghan hadn't warmed up to me much. I was Brigid's father, but we had no history together. Hell, she was already thirteen when I met her. But the girls really took to Bimla; she was 20, much closer to their ages, and as much a big sister to them as a new mom.

I drove Bimla downtown to her job at the bank when I went to work in the mornings. Sometimes we'd see one another for lunch. Bimla had been in San Francisco three years, but hadn't been out of Chinatown much. I had fun taking her for Italian food or coffee in North Beach, riding a cable car, strolling through Golden Gate Park, or climbing Coit Tower. The four of us drove out to Muir Woods one Saturday to see the giant sequoias and have a picnic.

Then I had a surprise in April of '49 when Max and I met for one of our regular dinners at *Chez Cici*. Cicilia's restaurant had been the best joint in town when Cici had been cooking there. I hadn't driven it into the ground yet, but was barely keeping it afloat. *Chez Cici* had 19 employees – hat check girls, bus boys, waitresses, valet parkers and a kitchen staff – and I didn't want anybody to be out of a job just because I didn't know squat about the restaurant business. I hired an assistant manager and started training a new chef, which cut into the profits, but I kept the restaurant going. My sleuthing wasn't lucrative either, but it kept the girls in shoes, gas in the cars, the lights on in the house, and paid for an occasional pack of butts.

Max usually paid the freight when we went out, whether it was lunch at the Black Lizard or a night on the town. That worked for both of us – Max made good money, and could afford it. But after Cicilia had died, I never disabused the staff at *Chez Cici* of their notion that I was the new owner, so we ate and drank there for free. It gave me a sweet way to repay Max's kindness.

Cici's was a two-story restaurant in a townhouse just off Fillmore. Max and I sat at a quiet table in a dark, wood-paneled room downstairs. The room was lit by red or white candles in straw-covered Chianti bottles on tables covered by long red and white cloths.

"I'm closing my practice here and moving to Fresno," Max said as we gnawed on Cici's famous fried chicken

"Fresno? Are you kidding me? I thought you were successful here."

"I am. But I'm taking a job as public defender there."

We drank California sparkling wine. Max insists on bubbly with fried chicken, says it cuts the grease. This one was Korbel, and a good dry one from the Russian River Valley. I topped off our glasses.

"But why Fresno?" I repeated. "It's supposed to be awfully hot there."

He shrugged. "It's a dry heat. And it's nice, sunny weather. Look, Frank, I'm not going there for the climate. I've made money here and I'm a good lawyer. But who benefits from that?"

"You."

"True," he said. "But who do I represent? The wealthy, the white-collar criminals, the upper class and the bourgeoisie." I winced at "bourgeoisie." I hoped he wouldn't launch into a Marxist lecture. I'd heard all that before. But I needn't have worried. "Now it's time to give something back. Serve the people. You know what the average farm worker in the Central Valley makes in a year?"

"$2,000?" I guessed. I had just filed my taxes, and 1948 had been my best year ever. I'd admitted to $3,400.

"Lucky if they make half that," he said. He picked up a thigh and crunched down on it. He chewed for a couple moments, elbow on the table, holding the chicken part aloft. "Now suppose a worker gets in trouble and needs a lawyer?"

"I guess he could pay his attorney in raisins," I said, "over a period of years." I selected a breast.

"Frank, I want to help people get justice, the people who are least likely to be able to buy it. And there are plenty of them around Fresno."

I couldn't argue with that. I hoped I had as strong a commitment to justice in my gum-shoe business as Max had in his legal work. "Are you going to be happy on a public defender's salary, Max?"

He shrugged, and pushed a lock of his dark hair up and across his forehead. "All right, we both know my tastes are expensive. But I think a man can live cheap in Fresno. I have some dough in the bank, and some income from my investments. We'll see. Besides, being a public defender is not a life sentence. If I'm really not cut out for the life, I can come back in two or three years, and set up shop again."

"What about Joan Spring?" I asked.

"Right now, things are moving slowly. She's in the cooler, and the trial date's not set yet. I can come up when she needs me. It's only a few hours' drive."

"Is she going to plead guilty?"

"Why should we? As long as Joan keeps buttoned, all the D.A. has is circumstantial evidence." We stayed for chocolate cake, walnuts, and port.

~ ~ ~

Things may have been moving slowly for Joan

Spring's trial, but Max moved fast on his plans. By May 1, he had left San Francisco.

I missed having Max around. Oh, I still saw a few of my other drinking buddies, like Charles Krug, Louis Martini, and Paul Masson, but I missed Max. It was fortunate that I had Bimla and the girls, or I might have slipped back into my darkness.

Chinese communist troops took Nanking that spring, but if Bimla and I stayed up late we weren't discussing world affairs. Our relationship was physical, but I had a genuine affection for Bimla. I thought it might be the youthful vitality she brought into my life. I'd never expected to be with anyone like her. Could she replace Cici? I don't know but Bimla brought delight into the big house on the park for all of us.

Chapter Ninteen
Another Death in St. Francis Wood

At the end of June, I was in my office, confessing my sins to the Christian Brothers, when the phone rang. It had been a foggy morning, but now it was just muggy up on the seventh floor with the windows open. "Old Vine Detective Agency," I answered.

"Swiver? It's Connie Spring." I wouldn't have been more surprised if it had been Joe Stalin on the horn from the Kremlin. "I need to see you, Swiver."

"Certainly, Mr. Spring," I said. "Shall I come over to the bank?"

"I'd rather not see you here," he said. "It's a personal matter. You remember where I live? I wonder if you could come out this evening, say at seven?"

"I'll see you then," I told him.

~ ~ ~

After work, I picked Bimla up at the bank. I fixed us an early dinner of ham steaks, home fries, and opened a can of peas. I told the girls I'd be out a couple hours but should be back early. "You two hit the sack by 9:30 if I'm not back, OK?" I said to Brigid and Meaghan.

"I want to hear Lux Radio theater tonight," said Meaghan.

"All right, but get in your pajamas, and rest on the couch. Stay in the house. Keep the doors locked. Go up to bed at ten when the show's over."

"We will, Dad," said Brigid.

I kissed the girls on their foreheads and gave Bimla a long one on the lips. I took my Pontiac, and chose the route across Twin Peaks. It was a dry clear night behind me, and still light in the sky, but as I wound down to the southwest, I drove into some fog, and had to slow down so that I wouldn't outrun my headlamps.

I found Santa Paula Avenue all right, but I was late pulling into the driveway at the Spring house. Joan's dark blue Chrysler was nowhere to be seen. Connie's Lincoln Continental was in the drive. I climbed out, and felt the hood of the Lincoln on my way past. The engine was cool.

I used the big knocker on the Spanish oak doors and waited. It was 7:12 by my watch. No answer. I knocked again. I could almost feel the raps from the brass, amplified through the thick oak, echo around a vast empty house. When no one came, I tried the door and found it unlocked.

"Mr. Spring," I called. In contrast to the damp fog outside, the air in the house felt dry and acrid. No lights were on in the foyer, but an open archway led to the sitting room, where a low fire burned, so I walked that way.

Spring's house was on a grand scale, even compared to our place on Lafayette Park. I'd hiked only half the distance to the living room, when I saw a pair of feet, in men's shoes coming out of chocolate-brown trousers on the floor next to the couch.

The room was dark except for the fire, and the corners were far away in shadows. I felt along the wall inside the arch for a light switch, and flicked it up with my forearm. The man lay on his face, the right arm thrown up, the left arm down at his side in a pool of blood. An automatic pistol that looked like an old Browning lay in the blood. The firelight danced on the side of the pistol and I saw a five-pointed star on the grip. It was not quite a Browning, but maybe a foreign copy of one.

I knew it was Connie; I bent over him. Touching only his yellow cardigan, I rolled him up on his side. I could tell he was dead so I tried not to look in his eyes. I tried, but they were half-open and looked at me. There was a blackened hole in his chest, and his shirt and the front of his sweater were soaked from the blood.

It could have been a Dutch act. But Connie favored American revolvers. Why shoot himself with an automatic? Not that I cared for the suicide angle anyhow. There was no note in the sitting room.

I let him drop back down, then felt his right wrist with the back of my hand. He was warmer than the hood of the Lincoln. A chill went through me when I realized the killer might still be in the house.

I should get out.

I didn't owe Connie Spring. He'd called me, but I wasn't working for him. I didn't want to explore the other rooms. There were too many. The house was too quiet.

I could call it in, but from a safer place.

I reached down again and checked the pockets of his trousers, shirt and sweater. I found a wallet; there was a license, but no cash in the wallet. Connie also had keys and change, a linen handkerchief, and a black, ruled notebook with a paper cover.

The first third of the notebook was used. The last used page had an entry that read, "*Frank Swiver,*" and my office phone number, then "*7:00 p.m., home.*" The next line read "*Cyrgryzs – 7:30.*" I decided to take the notebook. I took the run out, too.

I wiped down the knocker and the door handles. My heart was still pumping fast when I reached my car. I had to drive all the way up Portola to Woodside before I found a gas station with a phone booth. I called in a shooting and gave the cops the Santa Paula address. Then I hung up.

Chapter Twenty
Cold Coffee

I bought a cup of coffee in a cardboard cup at the Cliff House the next day, but the wind coming in on Ocean Beach was so strong, I couldn't tell if the microscopic needles it drove into my face were sea spray or sand. I couldn't drink the coffee at the beach, so I got in the car and drove up around Lincoln Park. When I arrived at Fort Point, my coffee was cold. I popped the hood, and set the cup on the hot radiator while I watched white fingers of fog reach in under the Golden Gate Bridge, and stretch out to Alcatraz to caress the rock. It's no use, Swiver, I said to myself. Every cup of coffee ends up cold.

I hadn't opened yesterday's mail until this morning. I found a letter from Max, the first I'd heard from him since he'd moved two months ago. Now I'd driven out here for an early breakfast and to think, and I took the letter out of the pocket of my Harris Tweed jacket to reread it.

I couldn't seem to hold the letter flat in the wind, so I closed the hood of the Pontiac, climbed back in the driver's seat, and spread the paper out against the steering wheel.

"Dear Frank," Max wrote. "I need your help on a case. The pay's not going to be much – I'm a humble civil servant now – but maybe we'll have some fun."

Hah! Max Rabinowitz might have been working for the state, but he'd never be a "humble" civil servant.

"This boy I'm defending is innocent, I'm sure of that, but I've nothing to go on, and he's not helping me with an alibi or even an explanation. He seems resigned to taking the fall in a murder rap. Maybe you read about it. I've enclosed an article from the Fresno Bee, in case it *didn't make the papers up there."*

Even the Fresno clipping hadn't said much, and at Ocean Beach, it had blown away. But I'd read it – couple of Mexicans, one accused of stabbing the other. Now one was a corpse; the cops pinched the other, Max's client. Good old Max. He was probably trying to direct some business my way. I could use the dough, but what about the girls? And Fresno in the middle of summer?

"Down here they say Mexicans kill over three things," I read on, *"gold, land, and women. There doesn't seem to be any gold or land in this case. But a señorita's name came up. I went to see her, and that's when I knew I'd better call you in. Frank, it's been more than 11 years, and I've only got one eye. But the woman is Amanda Zingaro, I'm sure of it."*

Amanda Zingaro in Fresno. I wished it were true but it was as likely as the Dodgers leaving Brooklyn.

But I would have to go see for myself, and Max knew that I would. I started up the car, and as I drove away, the fan belt shredded my coffee cup.

~ ~ ~

I thought about taking Brigid and Meaghan along to Fresno, but I didn't know what sort of place Max had, or if he could accommodate them. I asked the girls if they'd like to stay with Bimla. It was a hard sell, but I convinced them.

"You'll be fine," I said.

"We know," they said.

"You'll like spending time with Bimla," I said.

"Bimla's great," said Brigid.

"Don't worry. As soon as I solve this case for Uncle Max, I'll be back."

"Take your time," said Meaghan.

On Sunday, we went to early mass at St. Agnes', my old parish on Masonic. After mass, we had breakfast together at the Eagle Café.

Rusty O'Callaghan, the bootlegger, had operated on a cash basis, and the house and Cici's car, a '41 Cadillac Coupe Deluxe were paid for. I changed the oil in Cici's old Caddy and packed.

Chapter Twenty-One
Snoots and Overby

Dusk came with delicious slowness Sunday night, and there was still a rosy glow in the west after dinner. We'd had a roast, and a good bottle of Zinfandel. I walked around Lafayette Park with Bimla, and had a smoke. From the hill we saw the city lights sparkling around us.

She leaned close to me, her buffalo-hide sandals slapping as we walked. I ain't saying Bimla was in love with me, but she seemed happy with her new status.

I was thinking about her. I felt content for once. All right, I know contentment ain't love, but from where I stood content was pretty good. All of a sudden, I didn't want to risk losing her. I thought about calling Max and canceling the trip, but I couldn't. It was a one in a million chance that Amanda would be there. After all, I'd seen her shot down. But she was worth a one in a million chance. I would go to Fresno, and then Bimla and I would talk about things when I returned.

~ ~ ~

There was a prowl car waiting at the curb as we crossed the street from the park. Sergeant Snoots was sitting on the fender smoking. Then the passenger door opened and Lieutenant Overby unfolded his long body and climbed out. The lot the house was built on sloped downhill from the park to the north, and Snoots and Overby ambled down the drive with us. Overby tipped his hat to Bimla, and Snoots gave her a friendly leer.

"It's Sunday night, boys. What are you doing working?" I said.

"Crime don't take weekends off, Swiver," said Overby.

"Well, come in and I'll buy you a drink," I said, and

turned towards the door.

When we were all inside, I took out a raisiny late harvest Zinfandel from Amador County for myself. Bimla fixed a cup of tea and went upstairs. I asked the boys what they'd have.

"Rye," said Snoots.

"Rye and ginger ale," said Overby. I poured their drinks and we all sat down in the living room. O'Callaghan hadn't been an interior decorator, but he'd done the room to suit his tastes, which meant overstuffed chairs and a plush davenport, all of which were no doubt out of fashion, but comfy.

"You remember Cornelius Spring?" said Overby.

"I do," I said.

"I wonder why we might have found him in a pool of blood in his house," said Snoots.

"I don't know. What happened?"

"I wonder," said Overby, "who might have called in a shooting anonymously?" He leaned his armchair back on two legs.

I shrugged. "Beats me. What happened to Connie Spring?"

"He's dead," said Snoots. He took out a pencil and a notebook, flipped some pages back, and licked the tip of his pencil.

"Where were you Friday night, Frank?" said Overby.

"I came home after work. I made dinner for myself and the girls. We listened to Lux Radio Theater."

"*Hound of the Baskervilles*?" said Snoots, arching an eyebrow.

"Uh, no," I said. "*Treasure of the Sierra Madre.*"

"Bull! They ain't done that one yet," said Snoots.

"Sure they did. I just heard it. 'Badges? We have no badges. Who needs badges, señor? I don' got to – '"

"Can it," said Overby. "Will the girls say you were here all night?"

"Sure," I said.

"Where are they?" he said.

"What is this, Overby, an interrogation?" I took a breath. "They're upstairs."

"If we asked 'em, would they remember what was on radio?" said Snoots.

"Sure." I kept my gaze on Overby.

"What about your Chinese whore?" said Overby.

"Burmese, and she's a bank teller. You're out of line, Overby."

"Will she vouch for you?" he said.

"Her English isn't very good, but she listens to the programs with us." I sipped my wine, and glanced over to the stairs Bimla had just climbed.

"When did you see Spring last?" said Overby.

I squeezed the bridge of my nose between thumb and forefinger, and thought hard. "Must have been December, when the case ended."

"Talk to him since then?" Overby asked.

"No, we're not pals. And I'm not refinancing my mortgage." I winked at him.

"He never called you?"

"No," I said. "Why are you asking me about him?"

"I told you," said Overby, "he's dead."

"Yeah, but why are you asking *me* about him?" I said.

"We like your whiskey," said Snoots.

I got up and poured Snoots another, while I thought. I waved the bottle at Overby and said, "Lieutenant?" but he shook his head. They couldn't have anything on me.

"We went by Spring's office," said Overby. "Your phone number was on his blotter. Why would he have that? Your office phone."

"I don't know. Because I was on his wife's case? Thanks to you," I added.

"We got a phone call about 7:45 Friday night," said Overby. "Caller said there'd been a shooting at Spring's address. I think someone popped in on him after he was shot, found the body, and got out in a hurry. But it was someone careful not to leave any traces. Maybe too careful. The place was wiped clean."

"Maybe it was the shooter," I said. "Maybe he wanted the body to be discovered right away."

"If that was the case, he could have used Spring's phone," said Overby. "It was working. But he didn't. We checked with the phone company. The call came in from a pay phone."

That didn't sound like a question, so I kept clammed.

"Where's your shyster friend?" said Snoots.

"Max Rabinowitz?" I said. "He left San Francisco."

"Vacation?"

"No, long term," I said. "Better finish your drinks and go; I'm tired." Tired of this questioning.

Overby picked up his drink and finished it. "Sure. We're done, for now. You know, Swiver, I don't get you. You're livin' here on the park, trying to raise your daughters, and you bring a hooker into your house."

"Bank teller," I said.

"No, see, that's what I don't get about you," said Overby, getting to his feet. "Are you living in a dream world? You know what that Chinese bim was as well as I do, but you're pretending she's something else. And what about the O'Callaghan dame?"

"Don't go too far Overby," I said. Overby walked over to the liquor cabinet, took out my rye, poured about two fingers, and dipped his bill. I turned to Snoots. "You can take the bottle, sergeant," I said. Overby replaced the cap and passed the bottle to his sergeant, who slid it into the side pocket of his suit coat.

"I took the call when Rusty O'Callaghan died," said Overby. "I met the wife that day, right here in this house. I was standing with her in the kitchen over her husband's body. Then I saw her again with you the night she died. I know what she was. Are you kiddin' yourself about her too?"

I stood up. "Get out, Overby."

"It was no accidental poisoning," he said.

"Cicilia is dead," I told him. "Drop it."

"I'm getting a lot of heat about Connie Spring's death, Swiver. The captain, the police commissioner, even the mayor. Cornelius Spring was an important man–"

"And that strangled China doll over at the Lotus house? Wasn't she important, too? Don't get righteous with me, Overby."

"I come out here to see if you can help, and I feel like you're playing me," he said. "Playing me for a fool. Why? I've always been square with you."

He was right. Overby didn't have much charm, even for a homicide dick. But he'd given me every break. That didn't give him the right to make cracks about my women. "Is there a law against lying to the cops."

"No. We expect it," said Overby. "Glad we got that straight. So long, Swiver. Don't leave town."

Part Three

We'll Always Have Fresno

Chapter Twenty-Two
Lunch at the Basque

It was 55 degrees in San Francisco when I swept by Candlestick Point on highway 101 driving Cici's old Caddy. At Gilroy, I turned east and followed route 152 into the Diablo Mountains. The road started to climb, and I broke open a deck of Camels. It was warmer now, must have been over 70, and I rolled down the window and smoked.

I stopped at a Chevron station and filled up the tank when I turned south onto route 99. The thermometer at the gas station read 100 degrees. I took off my sport coat, folded it and laid it on the back seat. Not yet noon and 100? I circled back to the gas station and bought a bottle of cold beer. It seemed to me I could make it to Fresno in time for lunch with Max.

When I pulled into Fresno, I was feeling as desiccated as a Hollywood has-been. A steel frame arched over the road, and the sign on the arch read "Fresno – The Best Little City in the U.S.A. – Entrance." It was 11:30. I'd made good time coming down, about four hours to do the 180 miles.

For a city of about 90,000, Fresno was a sleepy burg. It was a low flat town, spread out across a low flat valley. Fresno wasn't exactly ugly, but it lacked charm.

Route 99 became Broadway Street, and I stopped at the Hotel Fresno, a faded block of about six or seven stories, once painted "desert rose," where I dropped a nickel in a machine to buy a cold Coca-Cola. Then I found a phone booth.

If it was hot outside, the inside of the phone booth was a steam bath. I slid the door to until a noisy fan in the ceiling started to swirl the hot air around. I dropped another nickel to call Max.

"Frank, it's good to hear your voice," said Max. "Where are you?" I told him. "Hotel Fresno? That's a dive, but it's near here. I'll come and pick you up. Have you had lunch yet?" he asked. I told him no, and he said, "Five minutes. I'll see you out front." It was 11:45 a.m.

~ ~ ~

It took him closer to ten, but I drank another Coke, then stood in the shade under the marquee. From my left I heard a sound like ripping canvas, and when I looked up the street, Maximilian Rabinowitz pulled up in a little red two-seater that looked like a small powerboat with headlights. I hopped over the door and slid down into the passenger seat. "Max, what the hell's this?"

"Ferrari," he said, and pulling the shift lever back into first he put his foot to the throttle and we roared away from the curb.

"What's a Ferrari? What happened to your Alfa Romeo?" My neck snapped back and forth as Max worked the clutch and slid the shifter up into second. No sooner had he put it in second than the engine wound up to high revs and it was time to shift again.

"Ferrari's the future, Frank. Alfa Romeo has had its day. Enzo Ferrari used to run the Alfa racing team. He left after the war, and set up his own shop. This is a 166 Barchetta, Ferrari's first passenger automobile."

"What does he make besides passenger automobiles?"

"Race cars, man. Ferrari loves racing."

You could tell from the ride. Only a minute or so later Max pulled over to the curb alongside a shabby brick building. It was two stories and took up the whole block, with two tiers of windows the length of the wall, though some were bricked over. Telephone poles provided the only shade. "This is the Basque Hotel. C'mon," said Max, shutting down the engine and climbing out. The Hotel Fresno hadn't been much, but it looked like the St.

Francis compared to this joint. "Shepherds seem to like the Basque Hotel. I wouldn't put you up here, but the food rates."

The only light inside came through the windows, but I had a feeling the lack of illumination didn't detract from the décor any. Max started us off with a bottle of cold white wine that the waiter poured from his shoulder height in a long stream into our bistro glasses.

"Txakolina," said Max. I couldn't say it as well as Max, but it was crisp, light and refreshing. We had some chilled, lemon-scented shrimp in garlic, and when the Txakolina was pretty much gone, Max ordered a bottle of red. I couldn't read the label in the dark room, but I guessed from the brutal, pungent aroma that the wine was from the Basque region, a tannic, black wine like we'd had sometimes in the countryside in Spain. The fruit was brambly and the wine was smoke-tinged and chewy. I'd never run across it in California before.

Max was right about the food being good. There was beef tongue, shepherd's stew, oxtail, and just about all of it was smothered in garlic. While we ate, Max brought me up to date on his murder case.

"My client is Sebastian Diaz. He's a lector. He's about thirty, and never been in any trouble with the law before."

"What's a lector?" I asked.

"You forget all your Latin? A lector's a reader. Sebastian reads to the workers in the cigar factory while they roll cigars. Cigar rolling is quiet work, see, and the reading is good entertainment."

I'd never had much interest in cigars. "I don't know if I can picture this, Max. What does he read?"

Max blinked as if surprised by my question. "Frank, I don't know what he was reading them. *The Fresno Bee,* maybe? The Bible?" he said. "It's what they do in all the cigar factories."

"I didn't even know they made cigars in California."

"Oh, yeah. You can make most any agricultural product here. In fact, the university did a study back in '29, and said tobacco would grow in any county in the state. But it barely got going before the war effort. There's not much acreage devoted to tobacco, and I couldn't even tell you if there are any other cigar factories still operating." Max was well dressed in a navy-blue suit despite the heat, and now he took off his suit jacket and draped it over the back of his chair, then readjusted his napkin on his lap.

"Anyhow," said Max, "this one is called the Rosas y Coronas Cigar Company. It's a family business. Well, a couple of weeks ago, Felipe Rios-Ortega, son-in-law of the owner and a vice-president of the company turns up dead in the Hotel Californian. Now *that's* a joint I would put you in. Air conditioning. But don't worry about that. You're staying with me, at Casa Rabinowitz. "

"Thanks. So what was the V.P. of Rosas y Coronas doing at the hotel?"

"Hah!" said Max. "It was a little after 1 a.m. One of the guests on the eighth floor hears a woman scream and calls downstairs. The house peeper, an ex-cop named Bullfinch, comes up. Half the floor is up and out in the hallway. Bullfinch knocks on the door. No answer; he calls Señor Rios-Ortega by name. Still no answer. So he uses his pass key and goes in and finds Felipe on his face in bed." Max paused here, and sipped his wine. "Victim was buck-naked, except for a little decoration on his back – the ornate hilt of a knife. It was a nasty long-bladed affair, and it had gone through his pump. There was blood all over the bed and on the carpet, and some on the windowsill." It was a good story, and I watched Max as he told it. The light from the window fell on the right side of Max's face, the side with the black eyepatch. In the darkness of the Basque restaurant, I remembered watching him that last night in Aragon drinking another bowl of wine with Amanda and Alejandro. It could have been the same leather patch Amanda had made for him 11 years ago.

"The whole façade of the Californian has a network of fire escapes – it's the code here. Bullfinch sees the man is dead and there's nothing he could do for him. He throws open the window and climbs out on the fire escape. Now this is eight floors up, and Bullfinch is fat and fifty, but the way he tells it, he takes off down the fire escape stairs like Batman."

I pictured an out-of-shape flatfoot on the face of an eight-story building, and grinned. "Bullfinch has a pocket flashlight," Max continued, "and says he saw a trail of blood and followed it down. The middle of the building is set back from the two wings in a U-shape, but the bottom two floors contain the lobby, and the fire escapes from the wings let out onto the lobby roof. That's where Bullfinch finds Diaz, with a twisted ankle. He also has blood all over his paws, his t-shirt, and his pants." A lock of Max's dark hair drooped down over his eyepatch.

"Well, the cops come and take Diaz into custody. They rough him up a little, but that's standard here. To the Fresno police it was just a couple greasers who ended a quarrel with a knife. They've seen it before. However, Felipe Rios-Ortega wasn't a Mexican. Pure-blooded Spaniard it turns out, as are the Rosas y Coronas owners. Felipe married into the family while they were still in Spain. They came over here in '45."

"Was it the victim's blood on Diaz?"

"According to the cops, yes."

"Was it Diaz's knife?" I asked.

"He says no. But that's about all he says." Max held out his flippers, palms up, helpless. "Sebastian Diaz says he didn't kill Felipe, but he declines to explain what he was doing on the lobby roof of the Californian, or why he was covered in Felipe's blood. There were prints on the shiv; it hadn't been wiped. But they're not Sebastian's."

"Whose?"

"No one known to the Fresno police, or they'd probably release my client," said Max.

"You been over to the scene of the crime?"

Max dabbed at his lips with his napkin before answering. "Sebastian Diaz was taken into custody at 2 a.m. I arrive at work at 8:30 the next morning, and they assign the case to me. I go and meet my client who's already in court being arraigned. I enter a plea of not guilty. Bail is set at ten times what Diaz might expect to make in his lifetime, so he's cooling his heels in the Fresno caboose. I stay about 40 minutes, but Sebastian is not talking.

"I drive to the hotel about 10 a.m. The cops had already removed the body, and were getting ready to release the room to the hotel cleaning staff. I don't see anything that's not jake with the story."

"Did you talk to the hotel dick?"

"John Bullfinch? Yeah. We didn't take a shine to each other, but his story seemed on the level."

I sat back with my glass of wine. I held it up to catch the light from the window, the only light in the restaurant, but the wine was black to the core. "Felipe Rios-Ortega – you say he married into the family?" I asked. "He must live around here if he works at the cigar factory."

Max nodded. "He and his wife live with the father-in-law out in the Van Ness Extension."

A local married man takes a room at the Hotel Californian, and turns up naked and dead. It wasn't much of a leap for me. "Did you talk to Señora Rios-Ortega?"

"She's in seclusion. Distraught. The family sent their *abogado* to give me a statement." Max had carried a leather portfolio in to the restaurant and now he extracted a few sheets of paper. "Here is the statement," he said. "It's just dust. The family wants Diaz convicted and fried." I reached across and took the papers from him.

"Any prior bad blood between your client and Felipe?" I said.

"Could have been," said Max. "Rosas y Coronas employs 75 workers, most of them Mexicans. About 55 of them roll cigars. Felipe managed operations. He was negotiating to buy a machine to automate the manufacturing process. One machine could match the daily production of 25 workers, so they could cut costs."

"Is it a union shop?" I asked. I remembered Max's letter and Amanda Zingaro, and I wondered where she would fit into this.

Max rolled his eye. "Nix, it's closer to a feudal system. Anyhow, the machine could be at the heart of the issue. You don't have to read to a machine."

"But it only replaces half the rollers, you said."

"If Felipe installed the machine, the noise would drown out the lector. They couldn't read to the remaining half. Sebastian Diaz would have lost his job."

That was an interesting angle. "But so would all those workers," I said. "Wouldn't the more likely suspects be the cigar rollers replaced by the machine, not Sebastian?"

Max leaned in over the table close to me. "The cigar rollers are mostly women, and the word around the shop is that Felipe was with one of them at the Hotel Californian the night he was killed."

"Who?" I said. Now I had a hunch where Amanda came in to the story. I poured the last of the wine in our glasses and pushed back from the table. I was stuffed. We had eaten well.

Max took out his Bull Durham pouch and proceeded to roll one. "I drove to the Rosas y Coronas factory," he said. "No one had kind words for Rios-Ortega. 'The Castilian,' they called him. They say both he and his brother-in-law, Manuel, preyed on the girls at the factory for sex."

"So, do we know which girl was with Felipe? Have you questioned her?"

Max was still leaning in to the table. Now he beckoned me closer with two fingers. Max was always discreet about his cases and he wanted to speak softly. "The other workers there liked Sebastian. They called him, 'Chico,' by the way. Did I mention that before? Everyone says Sebastian was easy-going, quiet, friendly, well-read, as you might expect befits a lector. Speaks Spanish of course, and reads and speaks English very well. He was going to school nights at Fresno State. I asked who Sebastian's best friends were. They pointed out a frail who worked there. She goes by the name of Pilar Avila." He licked his cigarette and lit up, then had a drink of wine.

"Avila's a common Mexican name."

He turned his head slightly to the right so that his left eye was looking straight at my face. "Right. Rumor is that Señorita Avila was Felipe's latest romantic interest."

"And if Pilar Avila was Sebastian Diaz's best friend, probably his girl, that points back to your client," I said. "If Sebastian's not talking, he could be covering up for his girl friend."

Max shrugged at that, stayed in close and lowered his voice. "I found Pilar Avila sitting at a table at Rosas y Coronas, rolling cigars in her lap. At first I couldn't even speak; I just stood there, staring at her."

"Why?" I asked. It barely came out. I knew what the answer was going to be.

"Because Pilar Avila *is* Amanda Zingaro. I swear, Frank, it's got to be Amanda. She looked, well, maybe eleven years older, but it was her."

My mind raced. I saw the scene play out before my eyes for the hundredth, no, the thousandth time.

"Amanda's dead, Max. We saw her shot in the head."

"No, she can't be dead. I saw her in Fresno." He grabbed my wrist across the table. Then he let go. "Sorry, man. I guess I still get too emotional about it. She was special to me, you know?"

I looked around for the gents. I wanted to get away from this, but I had to hear it. Amanda had been special to me, too. Was there any hope?

"I think I caught some hint of recognition in her eyes when she saw me. Naturally, I was excited," said Max, "but she looked away. 'Amanda! I thought you were dead!' I said. She acted like she didn't know what I was talking about. She kept her head down, wouldn't look at me again. She said her name was Pilar, not Amanda, and asked me to leave her alone. Her voice – it was similar, as well as I can remember – but it was scratchy, hoarse. Her face – well, you know, I can't be sure. All I remember from 11 years ago is she looked like an angel. So does Pilar Avila. I'd only seen her that last night, and my vision was still just coming back. But you'll know when you see her, won't you Frank?"

"Where's the men's room?"

Max ignored me, "I looked back when I was walking away, and I saw Pilar looking after me. I think her eyes were moist. And it reminded me of that night when I first saw Amanda, when she had a tear in those big brown eyes."

"I gotta go, Max. Long ride." I pushed my chair back. I still couldn't talk to Max about Amanda. He was my best friend. But Max was so in love with his romantic notion of Amanda, and I'd never told him that she and I had made love. It made me uncomfortable.

"Over there by the bar," he said, and sat back. "Turn right."

We spent close to two hours over lunch, like old times at *Chez Cici*, or the Black Lizard Lounge, only darker, hotter, more smoke hung in the room, and there was more garlic in the food. We settled our stomachs with some sort of brandy mixed with a bitter orange liqueur. Max bought one for the owner and he came out and drank with us. "It's very dark in here," I told the owner.

He pointed at the window. "No lights, only window," he said.

"What do you do at night?"

"Turn on the lights." He put his head back and knocked down his brandy. He shook hands with Max and left.

Max took a $10 bill out of his pocket and put it on the table. I took out a sawbuck and put it on his.

"What's that?" he said.

"For my half."

"Pick it up, Frank. I got this."

"With a ten?" I said.

"You can eat and drink for very little here. Life is cheap in Fresno."

The waiter came over and scooped up the bill. "Keep the change," Max said. The waiter smiled and bobbed his head in thanks, backing away.

When we stepped out of the dark restaurant, the sunlight and heat hit me with a power undiminished by any shade. Max paused on the sidewalk outside and slit the cellophane on a new deck of Pall Malls with his thumbnail. "Finished my Bull Durham," he said. He shook the Pall Malls out and offered me one.

I took it and Max lit us both up. "I'd buy you a java, Frank, but it's no good here."

"That's OK," I said. "It's too hot for coffee anyhow."

Max pulled a little pocket notebook out of his inside jacket pocket. "Here's directions to the Rosas y Coronas factory," he said, and tore out a page. "And here's directions to my place. I'm going to drop you back at your car, and then I got to go. I have to be in court this afternoon. See you this evening, at *mi casa*, all right?" He gave me the second sheet of notebook paper. The pages reminded me of the notebook I'd picked up off Cornelius Spring's body.

"That's a handy little pocket notebook," I said.

"It's French, Frank. The kind Hemingway uses."

I shrugged it off. "You ever hear from Connie Spring?" I asked.

"No," he said. "Why would I?"

"Well, you're defending his wife...."

He gave me a steady look. "I really shouldn't talk about it, Frank. I don't even think Spring cares. He's not paying me."

"I don't know why you're still defending her. She's guilty of murder, Max."

"I have to do it. If a guilty person can't get a fair trial," he said, "how's an innocent man supposed to? Too bad I haven't heard anything from Spring."

"You won't hear from him now," I said. "He's dead."

Max looked surprised. "Dead? What happened?"

"Friday, when I got your letter. Gunshot to the chest."

Max's one good eye started to blink. He brought it under control. "Suicide?" he asked.

"Could be," I said. I decided to put him wise to what I knew, including that Spring had called me and that I'd found his body, but I didn't mention the notebook.

"I don't get it," said Max, climbing into the Ferrari. "Do you know why he wanted to see you?"

"No," I said, getting in. The car seats were baking. I put my jacket behind them. "Do **you** know why he might have wanted to see me?

Max stared ahead through the windshield. From the passenger seat, all I could see was his right profile with the eye patch. I couldn't read anything in that.

"No," he said. "He didn't like you anymore than he liked me. Probably less."

"I wish I'd arrived at his place ten minutes earlier," I said. "It was foggy."

"If I'd been driving you..." said Max. We were quiet going back to the Hotel Fresno. Max dropped me by my car. The back of my shirt was soaked in sweat; I had to peel myself off the leather seat cushion.

"See you tonight," he said. "I'll be home by 5:30-six o'clock, OK?"

"All right," I said. "Thanks for lunch." I climbed out over the door.

"*De nada*, man. Find out what you can about the Rios-Ortega murder. But most important, find out if Pilar is Amanda." He smiled, waved a hand, and roared away. "And if she is," If he finished the sentence, I lost the end of it in the clamor from the Ferrari exhaust.

Chapter Twenty-Three
Rosas y Coronas

The inside of my car was nowhere near as hot as summer on Venus. Still, the chrome door handles nearly seared my flesh. Once inside, I had to use my handkerchief to hold the window cranks and roll them down. I stopped at a gas station for a city map. Then I followed Max's directions to the cigar factory. I tried to get up enough speed to blow the hot air out. More hot air blew in.

I found Rosas y Coronas southwest of route 99 along West Church Street, spread out under the sun like a woman in Palm Springs working on her tan. It was a low deep building, like a long shed, with windows that flipped up and out to allow for ventilation. I pulled into the lot, parked under a palm tree, and leaving my car windows down, walked in a side door that was propped open by a concrete block.

There were rows of tables, like picnic tables with leaf tobacco sorted by type and spread out across them. The workers had individual desks mixed in among the tables, with low benches for seating. Every fifteen feet or so along the arched ceiling in the center of the building, an overhead fan rotated, not fast enough to blow the tobacco leaves off the tables, just enough to stir some air. I don't know if you ever smelled fresh tobacco, but it has a sweet musky aroma. It's not what you'd expect if you've only smelled a smoker's dirty clothes.

The workers were in about a dozen rows. Most had lamps on their tables, and some wore eyeshades. Most of the overhead lights were off. There was a raised platform in the middle of the front three rows, and a thin man in a light grey suit with a narrow black tie sat on the platform holding a book in his hand. He was reading aloud in a clear, steady voice:

"*...but she was walking around the room, and I saw something I hadn't noticed before. Under those blue pajamas was a shape to set a man nuts, and how good I was going to sound when I started explaining the high ethics of the insurance business I didn't exactly know.*"

I guess they were done with the *Fresno Bee* and the Bible for today. While he was reading I scanned the room. About a third of the workers were men, older gents, slim, relaxed, and comfortable with tanned leathery faces and arms in sleeveless white undershirts or short-sleeved sport shirts. Maybe they were retired from a life in the melon fields, or picking grapes, and now they sat in the shade all day, and picked up a small wage rolling cigars. The men were working on their tables, where they could put the rolled cigars in little vises to trim and close the ends.

The other two-thirds of the workers were women, dark-haired, dark-eyed women, many of them not much older than school girls. Some were mothers, with infants in baskets next to them. Some of the women made their cigars the way the older men did, on the tables, but many were busy with their hands down in their laps. I walked along the rows toward the back of the shed.

"*But all of a sudden she looked at me, and I felt a chill creep straight up my back and into the roots of my hair. 'Do you handle accident insurance?'*

"*Maybe that don't mean to you what it meant to me. Well, in the first place, accident insurance is sold, not bought. You get calls for other kinds, for fire, for burglary, even for life, but never for accident. That stuff moves when agents move it, and it sounds funny to be asked about it. In the second place, when there's dirty work going on, accident is the first thing they think of.*"

I was about three rows from the back when I spotted her at the second desk in. She sat on the bench with her legs loosely apart and her eyes down, her hands working in her lap as the overhead fan turned. She wore a loose cotton dress held up by a pink halter ring around the neck; her shoulders were bare. The dress was light green with a soft pink floral print. It was a long dress with buttons down the center below the waist, and I saw enough buttons were undone that some bare thigh showed along the wooden bench.

She had loose tobacco in her lap, leaves lying along her long thigh and just as I stopped by the corner of her desk she reached for another large tan leaf. "*Hola, guapa,*" I said.

She glanced up just then and saw me. Did she bat an eye? Oh, yeah. She batted. She swung and missed, then tried to pretend she'd checked her swing and taken a bad pitch. She placed the leaf along her thigh and began to fill it with it with smaller bits of tobacco. "Amanda, it's so good to see you again," I said.

"My name is Pilar," she said, head down, not looking at me.

"No, *guapa*, you could pull that with Max, but I know you."

"Please, señor, I must do my work." She pushed her hair back behind her ear on the right side of her face with a quick motion, and got a slant up at me. I saw a thin, white scar that disappeared under the hairline, and a gold earring in her ear, the earring Manuel Lopez had given her so many years ago. But I also saw a dark remoteness in her visage that hadn't been there when I knew her.

"What are you doing here, Amanda? My God, all these years, I thought you were dead." I put a hand and a finger out to touch the scar. She drew away.

"My name is Pilar Avila. I don't know you, sir."

"No?" I said. "Look at me Amanda. It's Francisco."

"Can I help you, sir? *Puedo ayudarle, señor?*" said a voice behind me.

127

I turned around and saw another fellow had come up on us. He was a slim, bookish gent in a clean white shirt with two cigars and a fountain pen in the chest pocket. Two bigger Mexicans stood behind him, with their knuckles dragging on the wooden floor, and it was clear they were there in case I gave the bookkeeper a hard time.

"I'm Frank Swiver," I told him. I took out one of my business cards, the ones that read *Old Vine Detective Agency*, with my office phone in San Francisco. "I'm trying to get some information in the Rios-Ortega murder case."

"*Policia?*" he asked.

I pointed at the card. "Private," I said. "I'd like to talk to people who knew Sebastian Diaz."

"Chico?" He brightened at first, then he stepped close to me, away from his two thugs, and gave a half turn to shield our faces from them. Putting a hand on my arm, he lowered his voice and spoke in good English, "We would like to help Chico, but it is the position of management that he killed Don Felipe. I cannot let you speak to the employees. It would mean my job." Then he stepped back and said, "I am Jose Alonso Alvarez, the office manager. My employees have already answered questions of the police. I will have to ask you to leave."

"All right, Mr. Alonso," I said, but I plucked the card from his fingertips. I wrote Max's local phone numbers on the back. "I'll go. If you or your staff thinks of anything that might help, give me a call at one of these numbers, *por favor.*" I gave him a big grin. "By the way, I would like to pay my respects to Señor Rios-Ortega's widow, and his father-in-law. Could you please tell me where they live?"

He took out one of his cards and putting it on the edge of Amanda's bench, where no one else could see what he was doing, wrote on the back. "Try 6000 North Van Ness Boulevard, *señor.*" I noticed Amanda had been watching me. Eleven years had been kind to the girl from Aragón. She was a woman now, more beautiful than ever; there was new fire in her dark brown eyes.

Alonso left his card there. "I'm sorry your trip was for nothing," he said, and pointed at the side door where I'd come in. "You can find your way out?"

"Yes," I said. "Thank you." I palmed the card. As I turned toward the door, Amanda drew a finished cigar from her lap and held it across her table towards me. I took it from her, nodded and said, "*Gracias*," and started out.

I listened to the lector, still reading as I strolled toward the door:

"*I was going to get out of there, and drop those renewals and everything else about her like a red-hot poker. But I didn't do it. She looked at me, a little surprised, and her face was about six inches away. What I did do was put my arm around her, pull her face up against mine, and kiss her on the mouth, hard. I was trembling like a leaf. She gave it a cold stare, and then she closed her eyes, pulled me to her, and kissed back.*"[1]

Now some of the older women and the mothers hooted at those lines, "*Escucharlo*," "*...se va...*" and the old men grinned. The young girls were wide-eyed. I stepped out of the big shed and crossed to my car.

Like I said, I don't know much about cigars. But I'd seen people hold them next to their ears and shake them, so I did that with the one Amanda had given me. It sounded all right to me. Then they'd usually run them back and forth under their noses so I did that. Rich, smoky, meaty, leathery, earthy scrubland aromas.

If I ever found a wine that had that bouquet I'd buy it by the case. I'd remembered the smell all these years from our interlude by the river. It was Amanda, alive, for certain.

---

[1] Reading from *Double Indemnity*, by James M. Cain

Chapter Twenty-Four
The Ramos Place

Jose had written *6000 North Van Ness Boulevard* on the back of his card. Then he'd drawn a line, and under it, he had also jotted a note: *"El Camino, S. Hughes after 4:30."* It was only a few minutes before 3 p.m., so I set a course for North Van Ness.

After a twenty-minute cruise, I was in an area of large lots, with estate-style homes set far back on the grounds. 6000 North Van Ness was gated, and one pillar bore the name *"Ramos."* I understood that Felipe lived with his wife and in-laws, though I hadn't asked Max the name. It could be Ramos as well as anything else. There was an intercom and bell-push. I pushed it.

I looked inside at the estate while I waited for an answer. The property sloped uphill from the gate, and the lawn stretched out dry and thirsty between the wall and the house. A couple hundred yards back from the street, on the far side of the house, I saw a big man riding a large grey horse. He was cantering around a dirt oval, which took him out of sight behind the house for longer than he was in sight. I rang again.

"*Si?*" a woman's voice answered.

"Like to see Mrs. Rios-Ortega, please."

"Who is there?"

I had been in a bit of a daze from the heat and the lunch. I knew I wanted to meet the family but I hadn't thought much about what would make them want to talk to me. "I'm here about the horse." If Papa liked riding, maybe the daughter did too. There was a click and the gate popped off the latch. I walked it back to clear the drive, then climbed into the Caddy and drove through, heading up the driveway toward the house.

It was a big Spanish style house, like the Springs' place but Joan Spring's house was still an urban-sized estate, whereas this was a rancho. There were about six steps from the driveway up to the front door. I had just climbed them and rung the bell when the rider came around from the back of the house at a lope. He was a very big, heavy man; seeing him on horseback I found myself trying to recall some dim impression from the past.

The door opened and a young woman in a black dress stood there. She was a beautiful broad, with a dark, sultry Mediterranean look about her, and I took my time giving her the up and down. She looked at me with a blank expression, blank as a canvas waiting to be painted. It was a canvas I'd like to paint. If the black dress denoted mourning, she must be Felipe's widow. I took off my hat and was about to address her when the rider came right up the stairs between us. He stared down at me from atop his horse with a fierce look.

"Who are you? What do you want? What are you doing on my property?" he yelled. The horse skittered on the marble steps. He bobbed his head a little and snorted but the big man held him in check with the reins.

"*Buenas tardes,*" I said. "I'm Frank Swiver. I'm an investigator with the Fresno public defender's office, and I'm here to pay my respects to Señora Rios-Ortega."

"I am Señora Rios-Ortega," said the woman in black in the doorway. Her raven hair was long and tied behind her. It was the color of her mourning dress. The neckline was cut a little low for mourning, I thought, but then I don't know what they're wearing this season. Neckline aside, I could see that the dress was elegant. It set off Rios-Ortega's soft pure skin and the upper reaches of a healthy bosom that suggested ripe fruit below. The dress wouldn't have looked out-of-place on the dance floor, and I doubted it was off-the-rack. "This is not about the horse then? You are *guardia*?"

"No, señora, not Guardia Civil, I–"

"Veronica, go inside now," the man on the horse boomed.

"Sir," I said. "It will only take a few minutes–"

"No," he said. "Get out. Get out the way you came." Veronica Rios-Ortega stepped back into the shade of the foyer, and pushed the door shut, but left it open about twelve inches to watch. I could still see her bright red lips and white décolletage in the shadows.

"How are you called, señor?" I asked the man on horseback.

"I am Carlos Ramos," he said. He was a solid man, tending towards fat around the collar and the middle. He wore a dark felt hat with a round brim and crown, and it was tied under his chin. He moved his horse forward now; it was still breathing heavily from his run around the house. The stallion's neck and chest caused me to back down, from the fifth step to the fourth.

He had paused a tick, or half a tick between "Carlos," and "Ramos," though I had to give him credit for rolling his "r" in Ramos. "Sir," I began, "are you the owner of Rosas y Coronas?"

"You should leave now," he said. "You're not welcome here." Now he drove the horse down one step, and I had to let him waltz me back to the third step.

"I am sorry for the loss of your son-in-law, Don Carlos. I'm interested in seeing that Felipe's murderer pays for this crime. Can you help me by answering a few questions?"

"His murderer is Sebastian Diaz, the red who worked at my factory." He pulled the horse's head back and up, and its sweaty muzzle brushed my chest. I had to back down another step, and I was going to need a clean shirt.

"Don Carlos, I understand you came here from Spain. I take it you were on the Nationalist side?"

"Clear off, damn you, or I'll ride you down."

I was tired of backing down for this bastard. I reached into the slack in the reins that hung below the horse's neck, and yanked down and to my right. That surprised the horse. The shoe on his forward leg slipped on the marble steps and went down one. His shoulders dipped and the heavy rider tilted forward on the neck, unbalancing the horse for a moment. I danced around the stallion's head to my left and went up a couple steps.

It was a good strong horse and he held his position. The fat man knew how to ride and recovered himself but now I was between him and the door. He pulled the reins to come up on me, and then a woman's voice called out from the doorway . "Carlos, halt. Now." She spoke in Spanish. Carlos Ramos reacted to her command. "Take your horse down off our steps." Ramos turned the horse with the reins and gave it a boot heel in the side.

"*Buenas tardes, señora,*" I began again. This second woman stood just in front of Veronica Rios-Ortega. She was a bit shorter than the widow, and perhaps 15 or 20 years older. Her hair was chestnut brown and long, brushed back at the forehead and flowing loose on the sides. She wore a simple white blouse with long sleeves, and a long black skirt, an amber bracelet, amber earrings. Her brown eyes burned with a familiar light. She had a good figure, if you liked them trim and less dramatic than Veronica.

"*Buenas tardes,*" she said to me. It came out very icy on such a hot afternoon. "Don Carlos has asked you to leave, and I advise you to do so." She stepped out onto the threshold. Ramos had walked the horse down the stairs, and sat facing us now.

"I have some questions for your daughter," I said.

"*Señora* Rios-Ortega was recently widowed, as I'm sure you know. She is in mourning. I understood that our attorney had come to your office and provided a statement from the family."

"Begging your pardon, *señora,*" I said. "I have that statement, and I just wanted to ask–"

"This is not the time or place," said the woman. I couldn't take my eyes off her face. Maybe it was because I had just come from seeing Amanda for the first time in eleven years and I had her image in my mind. I could swear there was a resemblance. "Give me your card," she said; "we will consider your request for an interview and someone will call you tomorrow."

I thought about this as I extracted my cards. Then a young man came out of the doorway. He was dressed in a white shirt and light charcoal slacks, and wore a dark green silk robe over his shoulders. His right arm was nowhere to be seen. However, his left arm was in its sleeve, and he held a Mauser pistol in his left hand at his side. His pupils were tiny points, but I imagined everyone's were in this sunlight. *"Cual es el problema?"* What's the problem, he asked.

"Manuel," said the woman, "Get back inside." He looked at me with dull unfocused eyes and stepped back inside next to Veronica, his left arm and pistol closest to the open door. I wrote Max's office number on the back of the card and handed it up. "Now please leave, *señor.*" I looked at my watch. It was 4 o'clock, a good time to head for El Camino.

I thanked them and said goodbye, and walked back to the Cadillac; Carlos Ramos, who had not said a word since the second woman had come to the door, walked his grey stallion alongside. I didn't want my drive out here to be a trip for biscuits – I still hoped to get something out of Carlos.

"Your son, Manuel," I said. "He was *herido en la guerra?"* Wounded in the war?

"You leave my son out of this."

I had arrived at the car, opened the driver's door, and

began to roll down the window. "Yes, I believe I saw him shot in the right shoulder..."

Carlos spat in his driveway, and yelled "*Rojo cabron*," reared back on his horse, turned and took off for the back of the house at a reckless gallop. I started up the Caddy, drove out the gate and turned south, back towards downtown.

Chapter Twenty-Five
El Camino

I looked at my new map and saw South Hughes was back near the factory. At the corner of South Hughes and West California, I found it – a shady grove of palms and live oaks. It was another flat dry lot, like the one on which the cigar factory stood, but here a sign hung over the drive reading

"El Camino
Beer-Wine-Liquor
Garden Seating."

I pulled in and saw a few men at two picnic tables under the trees along the back of the lot. I parked and went into the roadhouse.

It was dark, but high-ceilinged and airy. Some farm workers sat at the bar. I peered across at a chalkboard that listed some of the popular offerings. A short dark man with the unsmiling visage of an Indian walked down to me. He wore a white apron.

"*Si, señor?*"

"Pint of Gallo Burgundy," I said.

"Gallo Burgundy? *Medio?*"

"*Si, medio.*" He took out a carafe with a chip in the lip and drew wine from a barrel, handed me the carafe and a bistro glass. I put a buck on the counter, and took the wine outside.

I recognized Joze Alonso Alvarez from the factory, and a couple of the fellows he was with looked familiar. I nodded at him and with a wave of his hand he invited me to sit with them. Jose and a couple others drank wine, and I topped off their glasses. I took my Camels out of my shirt pocket and offered them around while I made a little small talk. But most of the gents were already smoking cigars. Jose lit up one of my smokes. Another man took out a Kool.

Then I led with, "Tell me about Sebastian Diaz, Jose."

"We like Chico, *Señor* Swiver," he said. "We don't think he's a killer." A couple of the other men nodded.

"Why would Chico have been at the Hotel Californian that night?" I asked.

He held up his palms. "I don't know, *hombre*. Usually Chico was in school, or with his girl."

"Did he know about the rolling machine Felipe planned to purchase?"

"Oh, yes. He didn't worry about his job, but he didn't want to see 20 workers laid off. He said if we all stuck together ... he would talk to Felipe. I think he had a plan. Me, I'm in the office, so I wasn't affected, but these *viejos*..." The old men nodded their heads or looked from Jose to me. They probably liked the small income from the cigar factory, and didn't want to jeopardize it, so they let Jose do the talking.

We talked a bit more about Diaz. The kid must have been a saint – no one said anything negative about him. But most of it I already knew from Max. "What do you know about the owners?" I asked.

"Carlos Ramos," Jose said. "He come over from Spain after the war. He is an old-fashioned Spanish gentleman, I think. He is only 55 or so, but he prefers not to come to work. He stays at his house. Rides horses, I think. Felipe Rios-Ortega came in every day, run the business for Don Carlos."

One of the fellows made a comment under his breath in Spanish about Felipe when he heard the name, and he accompanied it with a rude gesture. Jose laughed at it.

"No one will miss Felipe. He was good with the business, but not a good man. He did not care about people."

"What about Ramos' son?"

Jose shrugged. "Manuel? He is a mystery. Maybe he's lazy. Maybe he's spoiled. He is the co-owner, but the only time he would come to the factory was with Felipe when they wanted women. Now we will see. Someone has to manage the business with Felipe gone. Not me." He laughed. "They don't pay me enough." One of the men gestured with his right arm, flopping it at his side like a busted wing. "Si," said Jose. "Manuel has a bad arm. We think that is why he prefers to keep to himself."

"I'll get some more wine," I said, and stood to go in.

Jose put a hand on my knee. "Sit. Carlota," he called with a gesture toward the back of the grove. A woman sitting in deep shade rose and sauntered over with a tray. She had dark skin and curly dark hair. "Carlota, *mas* Gallo Burgundy, eh? *Un litro completo, si?*" Jose ordered. I took out two bucks, and held it out for her. Jose took the bills, folded them twice, and tucked them into Carlota's cleavage. She turned and walked toward the road house, like an Aztec princess, swaying barefoot in the dust. Fresno was growing on me.

"How about the wife?" I asked.

"Neither Carlos nor Manuel is married. Manuel may never have been married, I don't know. Carlos had a wife, I think. I heard she died in Spain, before they came to California."

"Does Ramos have a sister?" I asked.

"Oh sure, Manuel Ramos has a sister, Veronica. She was married to Rios-Ortega." There were then general expressions of praise about Veronica's appearance, some crude. Her personality was not so widely praised, but it was clear that none of these men would pass up a chance to get to know her a little better, after a suitable period of mourning had passed of course. All were confident they could provide for her needs as well as or better than Felipe.

The wine came. Carlota refilled my glass and put the

full carafe down. I passed it around the table. Gallo Burgundy was not for swirling, sniffing, sipping and swishing around in your yap. We went direct to the swallowing part. And I went on with my questions.

"You mentioned Sebastian had a girl?"

"*Si*, he goes with Pilar Avila." One of the other men said something. "He says they were engaged."

"What can you tell me about *Señorita* Avila?" I asked. "Where is she from?" He didn't seem to know.

"*De donde es?*" he asked his amigos.

"*Quien sabe?*" There were shrugs. "*De donde?*" "*No se.*" Then one man said a few lines in Spanish I didn't hear.

"Ah," said Jose, "now she lives with Chico's parents." Good, I thought. At least I might be welcome there. I would take Max with me.

One of the men piped up, "*Felipe esta cogiendo a Pilar.*"

"Ah," said Jose again. He leaned in to me and continued with a worldly look, "the word is that she was Felipe's latest romantic interest."

"Maybe Sebastian was trailing Pilar?" I offered. "Trying to protect her from Felipe? That could be why he was at the Hotel Californian." Some of the men shrugged; some looked into their wine.

We finished that carafe and ordered another. This time Carlota dipped over me and I tucked a $2 bill into her cleavage. Jose and another fellow lit cigars and offered me one, but a slant at my watch told me it was time to go see Max.

Chapter Twenty-Six
Under the Milky Way

At about 6:45, with the sun at our backs, Max and I were in his Ferrari, zipping across the east side of Fresno and out of town. Highway 180 was a smooth, two-lane blacktop through the valley, and Max's speed ate up the miles. Then we climbed about 1,000 feet and the road grew twisty.

"I drove out to the Ramos place this afternoon," I told Max. He had taken off his jacket, but still looked sharp in a pale blue shirt and yellow silk tie, loosened at the neck. I was a wilting mess by comparison, sweating Gallo burgundy through every pore.

"Ramos? The cigar factory owners?"

"Yeah, I wanted to pay my respects to the Rios-Ortega widow. Have you ever seen her?"

"No," he said, "I haven't met any of them. They wouldn't talk to me."

"They didn't want to talk to me either. Señora Rios-Ortega was in mourning, but she reminded me of that Lucky Strike commercial. 'So round, so firm, so fully packed.'" I sighed. "I don't know how you can take this heat," I told him. "You know, it must be 40-45 degrees hotter here than what I left this morning. Does it cool off much when the sun goes down?"

"Goes down into the seventies."

"How am I going to sleep?"

"I've been sleeping in the hammock some this month," he said. I hadn't seen many mature trees in Fresno, but somehow Max had found himself a lot with a couple ash trees out back. There was a hammock under them. "Anyhow, I own a little cabin about 40 minutes out east in the Sierra foothills. That's where we're headed.

We'll drive out there and spend the night. It gets much cooler at the altitude there."

I told Max about Carlos Ramos, the horse on the steps, and the mysterious woman who backed Carlos down. "I don't know who she was. The workers told me they believe Ramos' wife died before he emigrated, and they know of no sisters."

Max took it all in while he kept his eye on the road, giving an occasional grunt or "ahh!" of acknowledgment. He said he couldn't imagine who the dame who seemed to pull the strings on Carlos Ramos was.

I also told him about my interview with Jose Alonso and some of the men over at El Camino, and their suspicion that Pilar Avila may have been with Felipe when he was killed. At 2,000 feet elevation, I started to feel a little relief from the swelter of the valley. We kept climbing to 3,000 feet at Badger. There were fewer passing zones, but there were turnouts where a slower car could pull over. Max drove hard and when he saw a turnout coming up, he'd flash his lights at anyone ahead of us. More often than not they'd pull off and let him by.

At 4,000 feet, there was a straightaway, with no solid yellow line on our side. Max downshifted and whipped out into the left lane. The power came on smooth and we shot by a farmer in a Dodge pickup. A bus came into view around the curve in front of us and Max pulled back over to the right with room to spare. "This car's made for mountain roads," I told him.

"It's made for racing, man. Fortunately, the same virtues that make a good race car are the ones you want for alpine driving. When you come to a passing zone you need quick response and power to pass while you have the chance."

A good detective, I mused, has to have a quick response to opportunity, and the power to act when he has the chance. "Well, you've got plenty of power," I said.

A big round white-on-black gauge, a tachometer, was the only instrument in front of Max. The speedometer was on my side. "It says you're going 140."

"That's kilometers per hour. Works out to about 85."

At 5,000 feet above sea level, I asked, "What is this, man? Doesn't sound like a straight-six."

"No."

"It's too small to cram a big V-8 under the hood." We went across a sudden dip in the road. Max downshifted and stood on the gas and the down force caused butterflies in my stomach like on a roller coaster. Then we crested a little rise, and I swear the short-wheelbase sports car went airborne. We touched down in a bend, and Max feathered the wheel just enough to keep us on the road.

"You need good brakes that slow you down in time for the next curve. And you want good handling through those corners," said Max. "No, not a V-8."

The case was full of curves. A good sleuth had to slow down, so as not to miss any of them, then stay on course. I was bracing myself by pressing my feet into the firewall, and looking for a grab handle. "I'm out of guesses, Max."

"It's a V-12," he said.

"You're shitting me? In this tiny thing?"

"Twelve small cylinders displacing two liters. It's smooth, and revs up faster than six big cylinders. Italian engineering is second to none." If you heard it sing, you wouldn't argue with that.

We kept climbing and by 6,000 feet, the air was fresh and much cooler than in the scorching valley. The sun sinking behind us cast stroboscopic shadows through the trees and across the road in front of us. All the time there was the sensation of wind in our hair, and the tremendous roar from the exhaust pipes, tailing us a few feet behind.

I saw a sign for the entrance to King's Canyon Park

ahead. Max slowed down, double-clutched, downshifted to second, and eased the car off the highway onto a dirt road on the right. He kept the Ferrari in second and we rumbled along uphill. In a few minutes, we came to a redwood cabin deep among some trees.

"I have to drive up to S.F. in the morning," Max said. "I might be back tomorrow night. Actually, it's about Joan Spring's case, or I wouldn't leave you alone when you just came to town." He put the transmission in reverse and pulled on the parking brake lever. "It's about 57 miles from my house in Fresno up here. We did it in 49 minutes." He shrugged. "Not bad time. I can do it in less–"

"You're a good driver, man." I didn't know how he did it with one eye. Some day, I was sure he'd kill us both.

"Anyhow, you'll have the run of both the house and the cabin while I'm gone."

~ ~ ~

The cabin was rustic. No furnace. You wouldn't think I'd notice that with all the complaining I did about the heat in Fresno, but when the sun went down, the temperature in the woods dropped fast. No electric. No phone. Max said, "There's an outhouse out back if you need to take a crap, Frank. But feel free to pee off the back steps if you want." There was a pump in the kitchen, and a well, and the water was cool and delicious. The rest of the cabin consisted of two small bedrooms and a sitting room with a fireplace. An old Springfield hung on the wall over the fireplace.

"Is that the rifle you carried in Spain?" I asked him.

"It ain't Chekov's," he said, and smiled. I didn't recall any Private Chekov in our brigade, but Max had hung out with some of the Soviet soldiers over there.

Max built a fire outside. He had an icebox in the cabin, and took out steaks that were red and still cold to the touch, and he nestled a couple spuds among the coals to bake. "Pick out a wine you like," he said. "Most of my wine's in town; I only have a couple cases up here." I found an old Simi Zinfandel from Sonoma. I'd enjoyed some of those in the past, so I selected it.

By the time the steaks were done, the stars were out overhead. I hadn't seen the Milky Way for years in San Francisco and it was a glorious sight. We sat at a wooden table outside. Max lit an oil lamp and put it on the table.

"So ... what do you think? Pilar Avila – is she Amanda?"

"Oh, yeah. She denied it, but I'm sure of it." I told him about the earring and what looked like a scar along the right side of her head. It had been her earthy scent that brought it home for me after eleven years, but I didn't mention that. "Of course, it's possible that when she was shot in the head she lost her memory and doesn't recognize us. But I think she just doesn't want to talk to us at the factory."

"Why?"

"I don't know, Max. But she's staying with your client's family. We'll go see her there tomorrow evening and find out."

"You forget," he said, "I'm going up to the City."

"Damn. That's right. I'll have to go over alone then. Where did Diaz live?" He gave me the address.

"Do you think Amanda croaked Felipe?" he asked.

"No," I answered. "I think Amanda *could* kill to protect her virtue," I went on, "but she's not so naïve as to go with Rios-Ortega to a hotel and not know what was coming. If she was out to kill him, would she put herself in such a vulnerable position?" I would clear Diaz if I could, but I wasn't about to incriminate Amanda, now that I'd found her again. "But something's going on, Max. It can't be coincidence that we run into her in California after eleven years.

Max kept his eye down on his steak, and trimmed off

some gristle. We ate and drank in silence for a while under the stars. The oil lamp had a dark metal shade. It didn't put out enough light to spoil the Milky Way. "Max, your eyes were bandaged at the time. You didn't see him, but there was a Manuel Lopez in the Zingaros' village who was sweet on Amanda."

"I remember his name though. He was in the Falangist militia, wasn't he? Isn't he the one who shot her?"

"Well, his father was Carlos Lopez, and he's the one who shot Alejandro that last day. Did you see him?"

"Not that well," said Max. "Big guy on a horse, right?"

"Right, very big, maybe 250-280 pounds. Well, Carlos Ramos is big like that. When I saw him today, he was riding a big grey stallion."

"It's not likely the same horse, eleven years later."

"No, but it could be the same Carlos. Maybe he favors big stallions," I said. "Maybe he breeds the grey ones. And Carlos Ramos has a son, Manuel Ramos."

"Very circumstantial. Carlos and Manuel are common names."

"Very coincidental, though."

"Their side won," he said. "What are they doing here? Why aren't they in Spain, enjoying the fruits of Fascism?"

"I don't know, but here's another thing. I think Amanda shot Manuel Lopez in the right arm or shoulder."

"So?" said Max with a shrug.

"So, Manuel Ramos can't use his right arm. Remember Amanda's pistol? It was an Astra—"

"Those things were devastating." He swirled his wine in his glass.

"Right,' I said. "So maybe the Ramos family used to be the Lopez family.

"You think the cigar factory is owned by the Lopezes?"

"Maybe. The same ones who cut down Amanda's father."

"And you think she's pursuing them?" Max said, chewing on a bite of steak. "What for? Revenge?"

"A blood feud. It's possible." I paused to drink my wine, a '39 Simi, ten years past the vintage date, but the fruit still held up to the char-broiled meat. I savored the finish on the Zin, and looked up at the Milky Way again. Infinite possibilities.

"So that would explain why she's keeping her identity secret at the factory. Let's open another bottle and talk this out," said Max.

We drank another bottle, but didn't find any answers in it. Nevertheless, it was good sitting under the Milky Way and dipping my beak with Max.

~ ~ ~

I slept well, under two Pendleton wool blankets. When I went out in the morning to pee, there was a light frost on the grass.

Max was in the kitchen. He had made coffee. "I'll buy you breakfast on the road, Frank. Let's get an early start." He drank a cup there; I drank a cup and took a tall mug with me in the car, only half full so that the coffee had room to slosh.

When we came to highway 180 at the end of Max's dirt road, we had to turn left or west to head back to Fresno. "Anything coming on your side?" he said, and started to roll out onto the highway.

"Yeah, hold it, Max!" A Hudson came steaming down the hill from the direction of the park. Max hit the brakes and we were fine. But I realized he did have a driving weakness – his blind side.

The drive back to town was fast, aside from a stop at a diner in Squaw Valley for breakfast. I picked up my car at Max's joint and followed him to the county building, where he introduced me to his girl, Florence, and fixed me up in his office. I told him I was low on cash. He peeled off $50, and said, "I'll stop at the bank and get a couple hundred before I see you again. Will this hold you for now?" I said $50 would do. "I'll be back late tonight, maybe tomorrow, I don't know," he said.

"Tell Joan Spring, 'Hi,'" I said. Max just smirked, and by 8:45 or so, he was on the road to San Francisco.

Chapter Twenty-Seven
Interview with the Accused

I walked up Mariposa Street to the city pen, and asked to see Sebastian Diaz. He was slim, in his late 20s, and looked a little like Valentino, with a narrow mustache. He also sported a lingering shiner, I assumed from when the cops had worked him over. He limped into the interview room, favoring his left leg. That was probably the sprained ankle; those take forever to heal.

The room was an institutional green, and the chairs were metal. Diaz had a full head of dark brown hair, which he wore slicked back and long on the neck. I offered him a Camel when he sat down. "I don't smoke," he said.

"How they treatin' you?" I asked.

"OK, since they gave me this," he pointed at his eye. "And my ankle would probably be better if they'd let me see a doctor."

I told him I was working for his lawyer, and we didn't believe he'd killed Felipe, but we were going to need his help to convince a jury.

"I didn't kill him," was all he said to that.

"Who did?" Sebastian said nothing.

"You don't know, do you?" I said.

He said nothing.

"But you're not spilling because you think Pilar Avila killed Felipe." He jerked his head a little to get a closer slant at me and his eyes blinked, but still no comment.

"Did you ever ask her?" I said.

His look made me think it hadn't occurred to him, and he hesitated. "No."

"When did you first meet Pilar?"

"Pilar has nothing to do with this," he said.

"Sebastian, believe me, I would do nothing to harm Pilar Avila. I don't know who stabbed Felipe, but if I had to choose between you and Pilar to take the fall for it, I'd hang the frame on you so fast..." His mouth opened. "I know her," I explained. "I met her years ago, and I'd do anything for her. And your attorney, Max Rabinowitz, feels the same way. He owes her his life. So you don't have to cover for her to us. We're not trying to find anything against her, we're trying to find something to help *you*."

I think he was beginning to believe I was sincere. He searched for words, but the hell of it was, he didn't know anything. I threw him a curve. "Where were you when you heard the scream?"

"In the eighth-floor stair–"

"Now we're getting somewhere," I said. "So you didn't even see the murder. You don't know who killed Felipe. What did you do after Pilar screamed?"

He was silent and looked down at his feet. "C'mon," I said. "Just tell me what you know. You didn't see the murder – you couldn't testify against Pilar even if you wanted to. What did you do after you heard a woman scream?"

"I ran to the room. She had told me, 'Whatever happens, whatever you hear, don't come in,' but I had to. She screamed. I had to go. I kicked the door a couple times at the lock and it opened. I went in."

"Good. What did you see?"

"I saw Felipe Rios-Ortega, lying on the bed with a knife in his back. There was blood, a lot of blood..."

"There was a woman..." I prompted. I kept my eyes locked on Sebastian. Now he looked up from his shoes, and met my stare. He had the brave look of a truthful man.

He began to talk a little. He was cautious, like a fellow testing his soup to see if it was too hot. He told me yes, there

150

had been a woman on the bed face down under Felipe, trapped under the dead man. I was uncomfortable with that detail, but at least the fact that Amanda was face down pretty much cleared her. She sure as hell couldn't have reached around and stabbed Felipe in the back during the sex act from that position.

"Ever see the knife before?" I asked.

"No, *señor*. It was a big knife, not a clasp knife or a kitchen knife, a weapon. The handle was highly decorated – maybe it was an antique. A collector's knife."

"Good. What did you do?"

He said he closed the door. The dame was crying, "Get him off me. Get him off," so Sebastian lifted the body by the shoulder and one side. He tipped Felipe up on his side and held him while the woman scrambled out from under.

"The blood was still coming out, wasn't it?"

He said yes, that's when he got Felipe's blood all over his hands and shirt. The woman had been naked. "She picked up her clothes and her shoes," Sebastian said. "We went to the window with the fire escape."

"Now think a second. Could there have been anyone else in the room?"

"*Dios mio*! Yes! Because no one had come out the door when I ran to the room, and the window was shut."

"Air conditioning," I said.

"Yes, the window was closed for the air conditioning, and no one had opened it to go out. I remember, it was locked when Pi – when the woman and I went out."

The rest of it fit with what we'd expected. Sebastian and the dame he was so careful not to name descended as far as the lobby roof. Sebastian dropped from the bottom rung of the fire escape, and twisted his ankle bad. The woman dropped safely and got dressed. She wanted to stay and help, but Sebastian convinced her to keep going and at least save herself.

Having told his story, he seemed encouraged. He

promised to get word to Max or me if he thought of anything else that could help us identify the killer.

"Anything at all, Sebastian," I said. "Sometimes a scent, a sound can be a clue."

"There was a smell in the room."

"Can you describe it?"

"I can tell you what it was not," he said. "It was not tobacco. I think the killer was not someone who worked in the factory." We talked another five minutes, and I asked Sebastian who might have hated Felipe enough to kill him, who knew he was at the hotel, who Sebastian suspected. But he had dust for me on those counts; he'd never even thought about it. The sad thing was, neither had the Fresno police.

~ ~ ~

I said *adios* to Sebastian Diaz, and walked back down Mariposa Street to Max's office. The day was heating up, and I had to take off my jacket. I stopped at a haberdasher and bought a summer hat, about the same style as my felt job, but made of straw.

It was nearly 11 when I returned, wiping my face and neck with my handkerchief. Florence, Max's girl, sat behind a wooden railing at her desk. She said I'd missed a call.

"Did you take a message?"

"No, Mr. Swiver. The party asked for you but wouldn't give her name. When I said you were out, she asked where the office was. Said she would call on you later. She had an accent ... like a Mexican, you know? She said, 'Sweever.'" Flo seemed to think that was pretty comical. She was a tall, busty redhead, in her late thirties, and I wondered if Max had hired her or if she'd come with the territory. I decided to go over to the Rosas y Coronas factory.

Chapter Twenty-Eight
Emma and Rodolphe

When I arrived the lector was working through a steamy scene in *Madame Bovary*, or as steamy as Flaubert gets. I stood for a while by the side door watching Amanda at her table, rolling brown tobacco in her lap, sunlight from the side windows streaming across her head and shoulders, dust motes rising under the quiet overhead fans.

"The broadcloth of her habit clung to the velvet of his coat. She leaned back her head, her white throat swelled in a sigh, and, her resistance gone, weeping, hiding her face, with a long shudder she gave herself to him."

The women seemed on the edges of their seats. The men took it in stride, or rubbed the stiffness out of their fingers and stretched. One *mamacita* got up and put her hands over the ears of the young girl in front of her. The girl blushed nearly scarlet and everyone had a good laugh.

"Here and there, all about her, among the leaves and on the ground, were shimmering patches of light, as though hummingbirds winging by had scattered their feathers. All was silent; a soft sweetness seemed to be seeping from the trees;"

It was pretty hot stuff, listening to those lines. I wondered if they were really picking up the language, listening to an English translation of a French novel. I glanced around the faces and saw bright understanding in the dark eyes. What a great country.

"...she felt her heart beating again and her blood flowing in her flesh like a river of milk."

I lit up a Camel, dangled it from my lips, and walked around the Caddy, picking pebbles out of the tire treads with my pocketknife. I could still hear the lector droning on:

"...Rodolphe, a cigar between his teeth was mending a broken bridle with his penknife."[2]

Before I knew it, it was 11:30. Amanda came out in a crowd of workers. She spotted me, and took off at a fast walk. "Amanda, wait," I called. She ignored that, head up, looking forward. Now I didn't want to shout "Pilar," so I tossed my butt in the dirt and got in the Cadillac.

By the time I threaded through the workers and pulled out into the street, she'd turned onto Hughes. I followed; walking, Amanda arrived at El Camino just ahead of me. She went inside, while I parked my car. I hurried in ahead of most of the crowd from the cigar factory, who had taken their time. Amanda was at the bar, one sandaled foot on the rail, the other on the sawdust-covered floor. She wore a lightweight black dress with a pink and white daisy print. Slip-like straps held up a modest neckline. The waist was cut slim and fell high on her torso. Amanda had the figure for it. The skirt flared from the high waist and ended just above her knees. Her calves were lean and her ankles slim. *"Hola, guapa."* She picked up her lemonade and moved away from me down the bar. The Indian bartender came along before I could follow. I ordered a bottle of Petite Sirah from Foppiano and two glasses.

"You want lunch, *señor*? Burrito? Tamale?" I hesitated. "I'll make you a cheeseburger, *hombre*."

"Cheeseburger'd be good." I waited for the wine and moved on down next to Amanda. "We should talk," I said. I gave her a glass and poured her some wine.

She looked across the bar, straight ahead. "Not yet," Amanda said, without moving her lips. The lips were very

---

[2] Reading from *Madame Bovary* by Gustave Flaubert

red, but it appeared she wore no makeup. She gave an almost imperceptible jerk of her neck, and glanced to the side. I saw the two big guys from the factory from yesterday at a table in a quiet dark corner, nursing a couple beers. "Come outside when you get your food." She was almost whispering. "Bring your wine. I could use some." Then, louder, "Don't follow me, *señor*." Amanda moved away from me again and sat at a table to wait for her food. She started to cough but quieted herself drinking the lemonade.

When the food came, she slipped outside. I waited a little longer for my cheeseburger, then took the wine and the glasses and headed out too. I spotted Amanda off by herself at the last table across the yard. A group of four women, more my age than Amanda's, sat drinking beer and eating their lunches at the table closest to her. I passed Carlota sitting in the shade, on lunch duty, and gave her a nod.

"California," Amanda said, when I sat down. "What a crazy place. I tried to get a tortilla when I first came here. You know what they gave me? Not a tortilla *Español*. It wasn't even eggs. Here a tortilla is a flat disk of corn flour."

"What is that you're eating?" In San Francisco, I could tell *moo goo* from *mu shu* at 30 paces, but I was not well versed in Mexican food.

"Beef enchilada," she said, "and black beans. I cannot eat it all."

"Your English is good."

"I learned much from Sebastian. He was the lector here, but..." She changed direction. "I also learned a lot in six weeks from Max." Then her voice became tender. "How is he?"

"He is well. He doesn't understand why you pretended not to recognize him."

"Do you?"

"No. We thought you were dead."

"You left me for dead," she said. She pushed out a lower lip. I put a gentle finger on it and pulled down. Yes, she had the chipped tooth, the souvenir of the rape attempt along the road.

"Amanda—"

"It's all right, Francisco. I thought I was dead too. Manuel Lopez thought I was dead."

"There was a lot of blood," I said.

"The shot went along the surface of my scalp." She tilted her head to the left and turned her chin down, while moving her hair on the right back with her fingers. I saw the beginnings of a livid scar that led into the hairline. "It made a long but shallow cut and the power of the bullet knocked me out. But it was only a flesh wound. When I woke up, I was in the cave. Santana – you remember, the old one? – had found me after the Falangists had left and taken me there. It was half a day later, Papa was dead, and you were gone."

"We were on our way to Valencia."

"I never knew what happened to you," she said.

"Amanda, what are you doing in Fresno?"

"There is so much to tell, Francisco." Looking across the parking lot then, she frowned. "*Matones.*" Thugs. "No, don't turn around."

I already had. It was the two muscle boys from the cigar factory, just coming out of the roadhouse door. I don't think they saw me looking; they were eyeing the women on their side of the parking lot, closer to the bar, and harassing some old men who'd been playing dominoes and now fell silent.

"I think they want to know what you're doing," Amanda said.

"I'm eating my lunch."

"They should not see us talking."

"You saw which car is mine?" I asked her.

156

"Yes."

"Get in on the far side. Keep down out of sight." Amanda got up. "Take the wine." I slapped the cork in the bottle with the flat of my hand. Looking around, I signaled to Carlota to come over. Jose Alonso was sitting with Carlota, feeling her leg, grinning, while she giggled, but she got up and came over. "*Cuatro cervezas más para las mujeres, Carlota, los fríos, y mantener el cambio.*" I ordered four more beers for the women at the nearby table, gave her $3, and told her to keep the change. She shuffled away.

Amanda was in the car now and had closed the door quietly. Keeping my back to the door and the goons, I finished my cheeseburger. I wiped my mouth and stood up. I started to walk to the car.

"Hey, *hombre.*"

I turned. In the sunlight, he looked like a bull – thick neck, thin graceless legs. I wasn't sure about the tail. His partner started to sidle to my flank. There were a couple ways to play it. I decided to be myself. "You talkin' to me, Pancho?" I took my shades out of my jacket pocket and put them on.

They both stopped advancing. They wore cheap sunglasses, plaid shirts and denim pants.

"My name is not Pancho."

"Oh, pardon me," I said. "You reminded me of a cut-rate pimp I knew in Mexicali by that name."

"I am called Geraldo. What are you doing here?" said The-One-Who-Was-Not Pancho. "Who were you talking to?"

"Having lunch, by myself. Ask those ladies." I pointed to the four who were at the table nearest to us. Carlota was just giving them four drafts. A couple of them waved and nodded thanks to me.

"Maybe you should stop coming around, OK, hombre?" said the other one.

"I like this place."

"It's bad for your health," said Geraldo.

"Maybe I'll see a doctor."

"You'll need one if you keep coming around here."

"I've known a lot of tough guys," I said to Geraldo. "Some of 'em have been bigger than you ... at least, when I met them. Some of them needed doctors later. I enjoyed lunch. *Pero ahora voy.*" But now I go. "Maybe we'll chat again next time." I turned and took a couple steps toward my car, then I looked back. They'd stayed put. "You sure you didn't work in Mexicali?"

I winked. He growled at me.

Chapter Twenty-Nine
Desire under the Ash Trees

I took my time getting into the Caddy, trying to look large, dangerous, and crazy, like you do when you back away from a grizzly. Amanda was lying on the seat, head over towards me, hair spread out across the leather cushion, burning brown eyes looking up at me. "Stay down a few minutes, *guapa*," I said, and fired up the big V-8.

"I was hoping you would shoot them," she said. "They're bullies."

"I don't carry a gun anymore."

"You're tough without a gun, Francisco," she purred.

"It's good you were down out of sight. In the bar you gave me the brush off, and I don't think they're sure who I was with outside."

"Why does that matter?"

"I think they want to know who was with Felipe when he was stabbed." Amanda frowned and was quiet after I said that.

When I had gone two blocks and saw no one was tailing us from El Camino, I turned east, and told her, "All right. You can sit up."

She looked around. "Where are you going, Francisco? I need to go back to work."

"You'll be late. We need to talk. There is much to tell, *guapa*." I drove to Max's house.

As we rode along, Amanda asked me, "Are you married, Francisco?"

"No. I loved another woman once...like I love you, but she married someone else. Now she's dead."

"I'm sorry for you." Should I tell her, I wondered, about my daughter?

I pulled up in front of *Casa Rabinowitz*, a one-story

Craftsman style bungalow a few minutes' drive from the Tower Theater. The house had a low-pitched, gabled roof, and a porch out front where a couple wood pillars atop square fieldstone columns supported the roof. The windows were wider than they were high.

I went around and opened the car door for Amanda. She turned her knees toward me, together, like the Land O'Lakes butter squaw, and stood up on the curb with a natural grace. "I am engaged, to Sebastian Diaz," she informed me.

"Bring the wine," I said. The black dog of depression was humping my leg. I'd just found Amanda, after eleven years. If I did my job, and helped Max save Diaz from the electric cure, I'd lose her to him. "So, you love Sebastian?"

"No. Sebastian is a good boy, but I don't love him."

We went inside. It was stuffy. I tossed my hat and my jacket over a kitchen chair, and picked up a pair of sturdy tumblers. We went out back and sat in the hammock, which was in the shade. I needed to know what Amanda was doing in Fresno. I needed to ask her about Sebastian and find out if she could clear him. I needed to ask Amanda about Felipe, too, and see if she knew who'd killed him.

Ah, but it had been so long. And we had a bottle of wine to finish. And there was my madness for Amanda, the urgent passion I felt once again. I'd thought it had ended eleven years ago in a farmer's field in Aragón, destroyed by a bullet from a fascist's gun.

I guess I don't have to tell you what happened before we talked.

Or that it happened in the hammock.

~ ~ ~

Don't get the wrong idea. We didn't scare the wildlife. Max's yard is reasonably secluded, and Amanda kept her dress on. But it was exuberant and loving.

Afterward, we lay side by side in the hammock, swinging in a slow arc like a pendulum.

I explained to Amanda that Max was a lawyer, was defending Sebastian Diaz, and that he'd called me down from San Francisco to help. "You were with Felipe Rios-Ortega the night he died?" I asked.

"Yes." She asked for a smoke, and I got out my Camels.

"Why?"

"Oh, Francisco," she said. "It's not what you think. I could tell you that Felipe was an animal, that he preyed on the girls at the factory, that it meant my job if I refused him. But you know me. I would not be forced by that arrogant vulture."

"What, then?"

"It's complicated." She started to cough out the smoke. Her cheeks were red, but otherwise she was pale.

"Are you all right?" I said.

She nodded that she was, and sat up a bit, gasping. When she began to cough some more, I went inside for some ice water. There was blood on the grass when I returned. I handed her the glass, and climbed back into the hammock. After she drank, I asked her, "Who stabbed Felipe?"

"I don't know. I could not see. I think I heard a key open the door. Someone came in the room. I thought I heard the door close again. The next thing I knew, Felipe had collapsed on my back, and I was pinned under him."

"Could it have been Sebastian?" I asked.

"I don't think so. He didn't like Felipe, but Sebastian is a peaceful, gentle man, a scholar. He wanted to deal with Felipe another way. Besides, he didn't have a key. It sounded like he had to kick the door to come in. Can you help him?"

I sighed inside. "That's why I'm here." I looked up in the ash trees. An ash tree, if it was true, if it was lucky, could be a baseball bat some day. Or maybe a couple dozen bats. If I were good at my job, I could save Sebastian. Right then, I'd rather have been an ash tree. "All right, you may have heard someone come in. Who would want Rios-Ortega dead? Who knew where to find him?"

"Most of the workers at the factory knew Felipe took the girls to the Hotel Californian. But I don't know who knew he'd be there that night, or what room he'd be in."

"You know anything else I could use to help Sebastian?"

"Maybe it was a woman," Amanda said.

"Why do you say that?"

"I may have smelled perfume, either before Felipe was stabbed, or before Sebastian saved me."

There was a smell in the room, Sebastian had told me. *It was not tobacco.* "Would you recognize that perfume if you smelled it again?"

"I don't know. It smelled...expensive. I have not smelled many good perfumes. Francisco, even if I smelled it again, I could never be certain. I had other things on my mind."

"Still, it's a clue." Some Foppiano remained in the bottle. "Let's have some more wine," I said.

"If I drink too much and go back to work, my cigars will not be very straight." She laughed.

"We'll just finish this." I poured the last of the Foppiano into our glasses. There we were lying next to each other in an unstable hammock holding this common, deep-colored, bold and rustic wine. It reminded me of sitting with Amanda and drinking Alejandro's rough country wine in Spain. So Mr. Jones is gonna get a crooked cigar. Do I look like I care?

Amanda said, "You see, I was using Felipe. Or I was going to use him. I told Sebastian I needed to go with Felipe, but not why. I told him I would not let things go too far. He insisted on coming along to the hotel to be sure I'd be safe."

"It appears things did go too far. What do you mean, you were using Felipe?"

"Manuel Ramos. I needed Felipe to take me to his house," she said.

"The Ramos place? Why?"

"Well, the Ramoses, they never come to the factory. I have been here three months and I have not seen them. Only Felipe Rios-Ortega came to work. Felipe though would take the girls out of the factory for a night of play. Sometimes he would take two – to share with Manuel, I think, from what they say. I wanted Felipe to take me to Manuel."

"I saw them yesterday," I said.

"You did? You saw Manuel Ramos?"

"I believe so."

"Tell me about him."

I described the young man I'd seen in the doorway, the one with no right arm visible. "We were not introduced, but they called him Manuel. I saw the father, too. Carlos Ramos."

"A big heavy man?"

I nodded. "He tried to run me down with his horse."

Amanda was quiet now and sipped at her wine. I saw the darkness in her visage again. It hadn't been there at lunch at El Camino, nor in the car, especially not here in the hammock.

"What?" I said, in reaction to her dimming mood.

"I said nothing, Francisco."

"What are you thinking, *guapa*?"

"Can I depend on you?" she said.

"Why are you in Fresno?"

"If I tell you, you must help me."

Now I said nothing.

Amanda rolled out of the hammock and walked to

the French doors at the back of the house. Opening one, she held her glass up to me and in one long drink, drained the rest of her wine. She put down the empty vessel, and standing in the doorframe she pulled her dress over her head. Next she stepped out of her underpants, and beckoned to me. Then she pivoted and walked into the house, her round butt cheeks tight and high, shifting as she disappeared into the dark room. The last thing to fade, like the Cheshire cat's smile, was the long, high crack between them. I followed her inside.

I found her on Max's bed. He had an overhead fan in the room and I switched it on, then stripped. I ran my fingers along the side of her head and traced the faint scar from the bullet. Amanda pressed her body against me lengthwise, and kissed me. I could grow accustomed to the heat if I always had a beautiful dame's flesh pressed to mine.

"There is not much more to tell," she said. "Besides, I cannot talk and kiss you."

"Then kiss me," I said. Amanda kissed me and more.

"You are for justice, Francisco?" I felt her breast, and our hearts were going like mad.

I said "Yes, oh, yes, I am for justice." And how she kissed me under the ceiling fan.

~ ~ ~

"Why are you in Fresno?" I asked. "Who are Carlos and Manuel Ramos?"

Moments ago she was warm and loving. Now Amanda gave a chilling sneer. "I am here for blood, vengeance, and retribution. I am here for justice. If you ask me who the Ramoses are, you must have guessed. I have never seen them but I believe they are Carlos and Manuel Lopez. I followed the Lopezes to California. It must be them."

"Tell me how this happened," I said.

"I recovered from my head wound, but could not go

back to the farm. Carlos Lopez and Manuel thought I was dead. If I went home and lived in the open, they would come and kill me. Instead I went into the hills with Santana and some others."

"You were guerillas?"

"At first, yes, but not for long. After Franco declared his government, the war was over. We were no longer guerrillas, we were 'bandits.' I was picked up one time in Alcaniz by the Guardia Civil." The memory must have disturbed her. "Hold me." I put one arm under her and around her back, the other hand on her hip, and I held her tight.

Amanda told me she'd been sentenced to seven years "penance," a customary term for those who fought against the fascist rebels. She escaped in 1945. She went back to her home village in Aragón. Amanda learned that while she'd been doing penance, "bandits" had hurled a stick of dynamite into Carlos Lopez's home. Don Carlos was unharmed, but one of his sons, Manuel's brother, had been killed.

"So as soon as he could put his affairs in order, he packed his family and left Spain," she said. "You see, Lopez and those like him had won the war, but still they were not secure. People remembered their crimes. I believe he wanted his surviving children, Manuel and his sister, to be safe."

Amanda had missed them by several months and the trail was cold. She spent some time in Madrid, searching for her mother, but found no traces, no records. Then by chance, she ran across Igon, the Basque, in a bar along Ballesta. The Lopezes had left the country from La Coruña in Galicia, he said. "He told me they went to California."

~ ~ ~

Amanda soon closed her eyes. The Foppiano Petite Sirah had done its duty, but now it was gone. I went out to the kitchen. Max had a moka pot, a stovetop espresso maker, and I found his coffee and put some on. I heard Amanda in the bedroom coughing again. When the water had boiled, I took a tray, the pot, and a couple cups back to bed and we sat up, shoulder to shoulder.

The coffee was strong and bitter. So was the truth. There were drops of bright red blood on the sheets under Amanda's chin. She was a lunger, like her father had been. "How long have you had the cough?" I asked.

"It is nothing," she said.

I showed her the blood. "It may be tuberculosis. You know Alejandro had it?"

"Papa? No. He had a cough, but–"

"He knew it was TB. He told me, Amanda."

"I've only been coughing a few weeks," she said. "It's nothing; it's so dry here. My throat is always dry."

"Look at how thin you are," I said.

"I don't eat much. I haven't been hungry. The California food..."

"Your cheeks are red."

"It must be the wine." She gave a weak smile. I realized she'd lost her Mediterranean complexion; the bright red lips and the color in her cheeks emphasized the paleness.

"Are you tired?" I put my wrist on her forehead. She felt warm.

"I cannot have tuberculosis. Not now. Not when I've found the Lopezes. Not now that you and I are together again." Then she started to sob and put her arms around me.

I held her. "Have you seen a doctor?"

She shook her head no, and squeezed out a few words between the sobs, "No, I don't have money for a doctor." And then she started to cough some more. I held her to me and felt the coughs racking her slender body, felt a rattle inside her. "I don't want to die."

"And I don't want to lose you again." She would be all right, I thought. Look at Hammett. He'd been a lunger since World War I; he was still alive – at least, I thought he was. I hadn't read anything by him for a while. "Don't worry, *guapa*."

When the crying subsided I asked, "Does Sebastian know of your plans?"

"No, he know nothing about the Lopezes."

"Why are you two engaged?" I began. "You say you don't love him–"

"I was going to marry him because our son needs a father, Francisco."

"You have a son?

"We have a son together, you and I. A fine beautiful boy. His name is Leon."

~ ~ ~

Leon, I admitted as I drove her back to work, was a swell name. "Does he look like me?" I said.

"A little," she said. "He has dark hair, dark eyes, a face like an angel."

"Sounds as if he looks like you." Nobody ever mistook me for an angel. "He must be very handsome."

She blushed and looked down at her lap. Leon was ten and a half years old. As I drove I recalled us together in April 1938, and worked the math in my head. Yes, "our boy" would be ten and a half. "He stays with Sebastian's parents while I work. In September, he will go to school," she said with pride.

"Amanda, you can't kill two prominent citizens and expect to lead a normal life here. You think you're going to pack his lunch every day and send the boy off to fifth grade at the Fresno schools?" She looked out the window, unconcerned. "The police will be looking for you. If they didn't have Sebastian wrapped up, they'd be looking for you now. Don't you see? You're the missing woman in the Rios-Ortega murder case?"

"Then after I kill Manuel and Don Carlos, you and Leon and I will go away together. Where do you live, San Francisco? Leon can go to school in San Francisco."

"No matter who they are, Amanda, to kill them would be murder."

"It's not murder; it is justice. I'm glad I found you again, Francisco. You are for justice."

"Justice will be if I get Sebastian out of jail, you know."

"You told me once that in your country you have the rule of law," she said. "The law will see Sebastian is innocent. I will help you. We can work together, and when Sebastian is free, you can help me."

"I can't help you kill the Lopezes."

"You must. What if I die? Then Lopez will get away with his crimes."

"You'll live a long time. I'll take care of you, *guapa*. I'll take you to a doctor."

She waved her hand at that idea. "I don't have the time. I cannot let this go."

We rode in silence for a while. The wheels in my brain were turning. I wasn't the law in this burg. I didn't have to stop her. I was just a pacifist private dick who said yes when I had a naked woman in my arms. I couldn't help Amanda, but I didn't have to help Don Carlos Ramos-or-Lopez either. Still, something didn't sit quite right, and it wasn't the cheeseburger from El Camino.

"Amanda," I said, as we arrived downtown, "you said when the guerrillas bombed Carlos Lopez's house, his son was killed. What about his wife?"

"His wife? Lopez was a widower. His wife, Manuel's mother, had died in 1935, before he abducted my mother."

"I wonder ... did he marry again? I saw a woman out there at the house yesterday. She spoke Spanish as you do, not Mexican. She seemed to have authority in the house, as if she were the wife."

"I don't know," she said. "I have not heard that he took a new wife. Perhaps he had a sister?"

I drove on out west, past the airport and down Hughes to the cigar factory. "Do you have a photo of your mother?" I asked.

"A photo? No."

"How old would she be now?"

"46," she said.

"What did she look like?"

"She was beautiful when she was young. I thought she was the most beautiful woman in our village."

I pulled in to the lot at Rosas y Coronas. I kissed Amanda, leaned across and opened her door. "I'll pick you up at 4:30, and drive you home so I can meet Leon. Until then, be careful. Stay with the other workers. And watch out for those two big thugs," I said. "If they suspect you, you could be in danger."

Chapter Thirty
Hair like the Gypsies

Back at Max's office, Flo told me I'd just missed a dame who'd come in. "I think she was the one who'd called on the phone earlier – a Mexican. She waited about 20 minutes."

The public defender's digs was a suite of modest rooms, separated by doors and walls of frosted glass on top, dark wood on the bottom. The clerical staff sat outside the walls at desks behind a thigh-high rail.

"What was her business?" I asked, as I opened the swinging gate in the rail.

"She wouldn't say. She wanted to speak to you. She had Mr. Rabinowitz's card with your name written on the back."

That sounded like the card I'd handed the mysterious women at the Ramos place. "She leave her name or number?"

"No, Mr. Swiver, nothing. It's probably about that Mexican boy Mr. Rabinowitz is defending."

"Yes, I imagine so. Well, if she calls again, put her through at once." I asked Flo for some java and went into Max's office. I closed the door, took off my hat and suit coat, and pointed a floor-standing fan at my chair and sat down to think. There were tall windows across one wall, looking out on the street, and I gazed out at the American scene. In about 10 minutes Flo brought me some joe. Ah, the friendly stimulation of Maxwell House.

I had taken care of Cici's two girls – Meaghan O'Callaghan and my daughter, Brigid – for a year now. It had been a change, and it was no picnic, but I thought it was good for me to have them. I still drank, but I hadn't been slipping into darkness like I'd done so often in the years when I was feeling sorry for myself, missing Cicilia, and in the years when images of Amanda being shot played on the silver screen in my head. Sure, I could get used to having a boy, too. I remembered how I used to play catch in the yard with my dad. I'd show Leon how to throw a curve ball. I'd teach him to cut the grass.

The coffee wasn't as strong as I like it, and I think I drifted off. At any rate soon it was after 4:00, and I had a mild headache. I hadn't done much thinking, nor had the phone rung. I called John Bullfinch, the house detective over at the Californian. He said he would drop by the office the next morning. At 4:15, I said goodnight to Flo and left to pick up Amanda.

I had parked on the west side of the street and my car was now in the shade. When I crossed over to it, two men stepped out of the shadows and started towards me – plaid shirts, jeans, short dark hair, cheaters. One of them was not named Pancho.

I wasn't in the mood for a confrontation so I hustled into the Caddy and fired her up before they reached me. The two men turned on their heels, and jogged for their car. Well if they wanted to tail me to Rosas y Coronas, that was fine. They wouldn't learn anything from tailing me there – that was where they'd come from.

A son. Yes, that was fine, too.

Amanda stepped away from the doorway of the building where she'd been standing when I pulled into the cigar factory lot. She moved across the dry dust and gravel with an elegant languor. It was practical in this heat; it was just her natural grace. I glanced in the rearview mirror looking to see if the two goons had followed from downtown. "Come on, *guapa*," I thought, "move it." She climbed in, and I swung the Cadillac around before she'd pulled her door shut. "*Hola, guapa*," I greeted her. We shot out of the gate, nearly trading paint with my two playmates in their Chevy pickup as they pulled in. "Pardon the dust. Which way's home?"

She told me to turn left. An American gal might have criticized my driving, but Amanda leaned in for a kiss. It may have been the first day Amanda had ridden in a motorcar, so maybe she thought it was normal when the front end started to oscillate on the springs and the gravel spewed in back.

"I made some funny cigars this afternoon – bumpy, crooked," she said. She grinned, to show how she enjoyed the joke of it all. "At Walnut Avenue, turn right." That put us on a course south. I looked in the mirror and saw the blue pickup turn south too. When we reached Jensen, Amanda told me to go left. Unlike her afternoon cigar output, all the roads in this part of town were straight, flat, and met at right angles. I couldn't lose the Mexicans in this neighborhood if I tried.

"So when Max and I left Spain in '38, when you recovered, you found you were pregnant..." I began.

"Yes. I had the baby in the hills. There was a midwife. It was not so bad, to have a baby."

"It must have been rough – on the run, with an infant."

"Everyone helped. And Leon was a good boy. Brave, like his father." Her eyes were large and deep brown in her thin face, and when she looked at me, they were filled with love. Love meant everything to me just then.

"What happened when you were arrested?"

"Santana took Leon to a family in Alcaniz. That was the worst part, being away from our son. That is why I escaped." *Our* son, I thought.

We drove on, and I noticed a nasty odor in the air. I began to roll my window up until I realized it was still about 99 degrees outside, too damn hot to close up the car. "That is the meat packing plant," said Amanda. "It is not very fragrant."

Amanda directed me to a bungalow court, where I

pulled to a vacant spot at the curb. The one-story rectangular shacks came almost up to the sidewalk, separated from the pavement only by a couple feet of dirt and weeds. The bungalows had been painted gray, back whenever they'd been built. They were small for families and looked uncomfortable, like boxes you'd bring a cat home in, but not a box big enough for a cat to really stretch out in. Some residents sat outside on folding chairs or stools. The windows went right up under the eaves, and couldn't provide much light or air. One window had been replaced with plywood. The thick tarpaper shingles on the sloping roofs baked in the sun. The Chevy pickup slowed and cruised on by while we sat in the car. Well, there was nothing I could have done to lose them in this part of town.

"This isn't the best neighborhood for you and the boy," I said.

"Too many Moors," Amanda said. I saw some colored youth walking by a gas station a block up Elm, and realized what she meant. Franco's colonial Moroccan troops were the only dark-skinned people many Spaniards had seen, and they'd been known for their brutality, sowing terror among the Spanish people.

At the near end of the courtyard was an iron fence painted black, connecting the two opposing bungalows. Amanda opened the gate and we went in.

There was a little yard between the first four dwellings, and a boy in black shorts, bare feet, and a white t-shirt was playing alone with a wooden sword, whirling and thrusting.

"Look," said Amanda. "He's playing pirates." The kid could stand there in a dry field and burnt-out grass and make believe he was on the deck of a heaving ship.

"Leon," she called, "come here." She bent at the knees and put her arms out.

The boy turned. "Mama! You're home." He came

running, sword up in his right hand.

"Leon," she said, and hugged him close. Then she stood up, holding his sword hand in her left and faced me. "Leon Swiver Zingaro, this is your father."

I wanted to like the kid. It should have been easy. But I froze. A ten-year old didn't need much of a costume to play pirate. Just a wooden sword would do. A wooden sword and a black eye patch. It was over his right eye.

"My father?" he said and looked up at Amanda. He had the high, lonesome tenor voice of an angel, or at least as sweet as Bill Monroe's. It gave me a chill as I stood there in the sun, feeling the perspiration on my back.

"*Si*," she said to him. "This is Francisco Swiver. I have told you about him." She tousled his glossy, full, dark hair. "Isn't he handsome, Francisco? He has hair like the gypsies."

Those words hit me in the gut. Indeed he did have hair like the gypsies, hair like Maximilian Rabinowitz, and he had an eye patch to boot. I felt my world rocking, as if I were on the deck of that pirate ship. "My son?" I said, and glared into Amanda's face. "**My** son?" I was walking the plank.

"Yes. Say hello to your father, Leon." He was a good boy, ready to do as his mama said. He was putting out his hand to me when I started to back away. I turned. My head spun.

I must have said "no," but I tried to swallow the word. "Amanda–" I started. I struggled inside. Love made me want to do anything for Amanda. And I liked kids – I could love my son. But there was the one question that had stayed in my mind for eleven years since that restless last night at the farmhouse – who was Leon's father? Max? Or me?

"Amanda, this is a lot to grasp." I took the boy's hand in mine, and patted the back of his head, but I looked at her. "I mean, Monday, I thought you were dead. Today I find the woman I've loved, the woman I've never forgotten is still alive."

She smiled at me. "I know, Francisco. After all these years we are reunited!"

"Then this afternoon, you spring the news on me that I'm a father, and now I see the boy–" The sun beat down on us. Beads of sweat soaked my hat brim, and trickled down my nose and cheeks. I took off my hat and wiped my shirtsleeve across my face. Leon put his sword in the air. He spun around on a bare foot in the dirt, still playing. His face came around. I saw the eyepatch. I saw Max.

"And now Leon will have a father," Amanda said.

"A father ... or *his* father?" She said nothing, just looked at me. Maybe the distinction in English was lost on her. "*Un padre o de su padre?*" Did I say that, or just think it? I felt ten pairs of dark eyes on me from around the courtyard, from behind dark windows with tattered screens. I did manage to say, "He looks like Max."

"That's just the eye patch," she said. She pulled it off his head.

I backed off some more and stumbled toward the gate. I turned half-way at the waist and held up my hand and arm towards them. My legs were weak, my muscles cramping and if I didn't keep going, I thought I'd fall down. "No," I said, "Not now. Amanda, I need to think. I need time." I walked out through the gate.

"Francisco! What about your son? Francisco, wait," she called after me.

Leon looked at her. "That was the one you liked, Mama?" I heard him say. Amanda squatted and hugged the boy. He put up his wooden sword and dragged it across the iron bars – clack. Clack, clack, clack, clack.

Chapter Thirty-One
Cream of California

I sat in the car for a few moments, riding curling waves of nausea, feeling a throb in my temples, and hearing a roar in my ears. When I looked up, there was Amanda with a hand on the iron fence. Yes, I could do anything for Amanda. And there was Leon at her side, looking out at me from between the bars. My boy, or another man's boy?

I had to get away. I started up the Caddy, and put the automatic tranny in drive. I wished there was a clutch to ride and manual gears to grind. As I pulled away from the curb, I took one more good look back. Leon stood at his mother's side and smiled at me. He waved the wooden sword over his head, and seemed to mouth "Papa."

I started to drive and when I came to route 99, I turned north. I stopped at a place called Doc's Liquor, where I bought a pint bottle of "Cream of California" brandy. I was hurt, but I was ashamed of myself too, for running, and wanted something nasty.

A few slugs of the stuff down my gullet while I drove took the edge off the pain, and I found myself heading into the Van Ness extension, out to the Ramos place. I would calm down with a nice boring stakeout, and who knew, maybe I'd learn something about the workings of the household. I couldn't help but think of Leon, and how much he looked like Max Rabinowitz, but I didn't want to picture Amanda entwined with my friend so I just drove and drank.

I drove past the Ramos house, hung a U-turn, and settled in under a couple palm trees just northwest of the place with a clear view across the street. The air was still; there was no rustle above me in the fronds.

The wall around the property hid some of the front yard, but I could see the top of the Chevy pickup that had shadowed me earlier parked inside the gate. The ground rose back toward the house and barn, and presented a clear view of the riding track. Someone was riding a horse out behind the house. Hooves thudded in the hot stillness of the afternoon. I took my army surplus field glasses out of the glove compartment and looked. It appeared to be Veronica Rios-Ortega. Her black hair was tied behind her, and swung with the motion of the black mare she was riding. With the glasses I saw strong thighs squeezing the top sides of the saddle. I liked the way she rode. I slid down in my seat and nipped at the Cream of California, and watched her firm ass hovering just above the leather. You can get lost watching a fine fanny in tight pants, and I sat about 45 minutes, relieving my pain, watching Veronica ride.

Around 6 p.m., she rode out of sight behind the house and didn't come back. The gate opened and the pickup came out and turned away from me, toward downtown. I thought of following to see what the boys were up to. I had enough brandy in me now to wade into a fight. But they were just hired hands, and I was after *Señor* Big, so I stayed put. Give 'em at least another hour or two, I told myself. Wait until dark.

"Are there not twelve hours in the day?" I thought. *If a man walks in the day, he does not stumble, because he sees the light of this world. But if he walks in the night, he stumbles, because the light is not in him."* I'd get 'em when they stumbled. I screwed the cap on the brandy. I drink a lot but I know my measure. When I start quoting scripture, I've reached it.

At about 6:30, my straw hat was low on my eyes, my white shirt soaked and sticking to the seat, and I was thinking about the eyepatch. It was just a coincidence from a boy's pirate costume. And the hair like the gypsies? Well, I have dark hair too.

Just then the passenger door opened. Veronica Rios-Ortega climbed in, pulled the door shut and squirmed down low, below the level of the windshield where she wouldn't be seen from outside the car. "Drive," she ordered.

She smelled of horse. She carried a small handbag of stiff, thick, tooled leather. Beads of perspiration hung on her forehead. She wore a white blouse with an open collar, and her chest glistened below the neck. It was a seven-quart shirt, and Vernonica was a two-gallon woman underneath. I turned the key and drove.

We rode south in silence for while. When we'd gone a couple blocks, she sat up in the seat and put her shoulders back. Then she said, "What were you doing outside my gate?"

"Getting drunk." I passed her the bottle. It was down about half a pint.

She looked at it like I'd mucked it out of her stable. "Don't you have a glass?"

"Sorry."

She gave a half-shrug, pulled her shirttail out of her khaki pants, and wiped the neck of the bottle. Then she tipped it up to her lips. A look of surprise came across her face and then she held the bottle up to read the label. "This is brandy?" she asked.

"Yes. Good stuff. Dollar a pint."

She took another swig. "You were robbed," she said. She capped it and handed it back to me.

"Keep it, I have to drive." We headed into the center of Fresno and I decided to go out east toward Max's cabin.

"We told you yesterday to leave. Why did you come back?"

"Veronica Rios-Ortega," I said. I rolled the "r's" across my tongue, and it was a tasty name. "You are the daughter of Don Carlos?"

"Yes."

"Don Carlos Lopez," I mused aloud.

"Yes – *no!* Don Carlos Ramos. Who is Lopez?" She unscrewed the cap of the brandy.

"A man I saw in Aragón. He had a son, Manuel Lopez. You have a brother Manuel, don't you?"

"That means nothing. He is ill. I asked you, why did you come back?" She took another drink.

"I wanted answers. I didn't get them. I'll keep coming back."

We rode a mile or so without talking, and Veronica unbuttoned a button on her blouse and flapped the material up and down. "It is hot. Where are you driving?"

"I'm going up into the hills. It will be cooler. You'll like it there. How long have you been in America?"

"Three years," she said. "But I do not drive. I have not been to the hills."

"Felipe drove?"

"Yes, of course, but he didn't take me anywhere."

"You will like these hills," I said. "They are beautiful on a summer's evening. Beautiful like it is in Aragón."

"When were you in Aragón?" she asked.

"1938. I was a soldier."

"1938? I was 17 then."

The same age as Amanda, I thought. Maybe they went to school together. You might think I was crazy, driving into the Sierras with a head full of booze, but it was uphill, and the concentration it required to drive well helped sober me up. "Your brother, he was shot in the arm, wasn't he? In the war..."

"The shoulder. The doctor in the town, he was a red. Manuel did not get the proper care. Now the shoulder still pains him. There is a fragment of the bullet in his bone. He tries to kill the pain, but–" She broke off, drank, and then, "You were a red, weren't you?"

I said nothing.

"I can tell." She looked straight ahead out the windshield. "You stink like a red."

"Begging your pardon, Veronica Lopez, but that's you. You stink like a lathered-up mare in a closed stall."

She slapped me. For telling her she stunk? "Ramos!" she snarled. Or maybe for calling her Lopez. I grinned at her. She went for me with her nails, but I grabbed her wrist with one hand.

"This is a dangerous way to play," I said. "We're not in Fresno anymore. The road winds."

She relaxed and I let go of her wrist. She opened her handbag and took out a small bottle of perfume, and dabbed it behind her ears and under her shirt. "I want you to leave our family alone," she said.

"Who killed Felipe Rios-Ortega?"

"The lector. Who do you think, you fool?"

"He wasn't even in the room," I said. I thought she might dispute that, but she just took a drink. I pulled off at a small market on the right side of the highway. I didn't know if there was anything fresh in Max's icebox, and this might be the last chance to get food along the road to the park. "Let me get something for dinner. I'll be right back."

Chapter Thirty-Two
Advanced Interrogation Techniques

When we got to Max's cabin I built a fire in the fireplace. Then I pumped enough water to fill two tubs, and warmed it over the flames. I told Veronica Rios-Ortega to get out of her horse-sweat rags and take a bath.

I gave her some privacy for her bath in the kitchen, and went into the backyard. I'd bought some lamb sausages and a loaf of rustic bread at the market, and while she washed I fired up the grill for the sausages. I nearly burnt the damn things peeking in at that statuesque body she was soaping up. She looked like Aphrodite rising out of a pair of wash tubs. Amanda had a good figure, slender and angular. Veronica was all curves, all ripe fruit. I like both kinds. Oh, hell, I like *all* kinds, starting with the kind I'm with.

I just managed to save the sausages. I had put on a pan of onions, garlic, and smoked peppers to soften and I served the sausages on a bed of the veggies along with the bread. There was still plenty of wine in the cabin to choose from, even though Max and I had tried to make a dent in it the previous night. Most were Californians, but I found one Spanish bottle, a '33 Vega Sicilia from an area along the Duero River, not that far west of Aragón. I hoped it would make my guest feel at home. Roses on the nose, chocolatey and nutty with cedar and mint on the palate – the Vega Sicilia lived up to its reputation.

I held one of the Pendleton blankets behind Veronica's naked back. Standing behind her shoulder with my chin in her hair, smelling the perfume that she'd reapplied after washing I wrapped her in the blanket Indian style. We dined inside by the fire. The sausages had good smoky flavor and we both ate and drank well.

The firelight danced on her face, bathing it in a bronze glow. Her damp black hair shined, and her lips were moist and deep red without lipstick. They invited kissing.

"Why did you get in my car?" I asked.

"Why were you watching our house?"

"I want to find out about Don Carlos and Manuel. I want to find out who is in the house. For instance, who was the woman who ordered your father to step off?"

"She does not matter. She is his woman, from Aragón."

"His wife?"

"No, his current mistress," she said. "My mother is dead." Veronica held out her glass, and I refilled it. "I have a question for you. Who was the woman with my husband when he was stabbed?"

"Who says he was with a dame?" I took a drink of my wine.

"What else would he be doing naked in a hotel bed only a few kilometers from his home?"

The Pendleton blanket drooped; the firelight threw dancing shadows across her chest, tantalizing me with hints of the *tetas* below, *pechos* that could have been Felipe's to play with for just a 20-minute drive. "The house dick found no woman in the room. The police found no woman."

"You know who she was, don't you?"

I thought of Amanda and how easily she'd allowed herself to be in that position. She'd maneuvered Sebastian and Felipe to get into that position. I shook it out of my head. "Sebastian Diaz knows who she was," I answered, "and he's not talking to the police."

"Of course not. He's guilty, don't you see? It was a girl from the factory, wasn't it? All day she rolls tobacco on her thighs. Then at night she takes my husband and rolls his *polla* there." She talked earthy, I thought, for a rich girl.

"What do you want, Veronica?"

"I want to know who the woman with my husband was. I want to see Sebastian Diaz convicted and hanged." Her eyes blazed in the firelight. There seemed to be a mark, a flaw in the dark iris of the left eye, a little dagger of yellow. "What do you want, detective?"

"I want justice for Sebastian," I said. "I want to know who chilled your husband. Where were you that night, Veronica Lopez?"

She put her fork in a big piece of her sausage, and raised it to her mouth. "I was at home. I was always at home." She put the tip in her mouth and hesitated. "Veronica *Rios-Ortega.*" Then she drew her lips back and showed straight white teeth, and bit through the sausage. The blanket slid off her white shoulders. "What do you want, detective?"

~ ~ ~

Neither of us seemed to be able to gain an advantage; we pushed our plates and glasses aside and moved on to some advanced interrogation techniques. I looked for an opening, and Veronica Rios-Ortega squeezed me between her legs like she squeezed the saddle on her mare. Her legs were long and solid with muscle, and the firelight showed hard bands of flesh when she flexed her thighs, and a fine down of dark hairs. A lesser man might have broken, but I held firm. She rode me hard, and soon we were both in a lather.

Veronica got up and brought her purse over, then she laid down on her back next to me by the fire. She took out her perfume and sprinkled two or three drops down below her belly, then spread the blanket across herself.

"We should spend the night here," I announced.

"I will be missed," she said.

"By whom?"

"There are servants."

"You can command their silence." Then I began again, "Sometimes, when a husband is unfaithful, if something happens to him, suspicion falls upon the wife."

"Bah."

"Where were you the night Felipe died?"

"I told you, I was at home," she said.

"Did anyone see you?"

"There are servants." This dame didn't miss a beat. "Sebastian Diaz killed my husband."

"He wasn't even in the room," I said.

"They say he was soaked in Felipe's blood. There was a trail of blood from the room, down the fire escape to where the police found the lector. Besides, he was a red. He must die."

She produced a flat silver case with delicate filigree work from her purse and opened it, offering me a cigarette.

"Thanks," I said. "I thought perhaps you rolled your own."

"You are comparing me to the whores at the factory?" she blazed.

"Sorry, I remember it was common in Spain to roll your own. Picadura, no?" I reached across the hearth and held a small piece of kindling to the fire until it caught, then I lit both our smokes.

"We are not in Spain. If we were, Diaz would have been executed by now."

"We have justice here," I said. "This isn't the Generalissimo's Spain."

"More's the pity," she said. "My husband was going to buy a cigar-rolling machine. He would have let 20 workers go, he told me. The machine would pay for itself in six months in reduced costs and increased productivity. But Sebastian Diaz was trying to organize the workers. The girl with my husband, she was one of the workers, wasn't she? That's where Felipe found his women, at the factory."

"Did he threaten to fire them unless they came across?"

"That is too crude, even for Felipe."

~ ~ ~

We slept in the cabin, and on Wednesday morning drove back to town. "Ask Don Carlos or his woman to come and see me today," I said.

"Why should I?" Veronica said.

"I will not leave your family alone until I get some answers."

She was quiet for awhile as the Cadillac sped down the mountain curves. Then she said. "All right. I will do this for you because you made me feel like a woman last night."

"And again this morning," I pointed out.

"And again this morning." A wee smile broke out at the corners of her red lips, and light flashed in her dark, dagger-specked eyes. "But I want to know who the woman was who was with Felipe at the hotel."

"My client is Sebastian Diaz, and he's not saying. Look, I'm not against you Veronica, but I wasn't there. Anything I tell you would be speculation."

When we got to the Ramos place, she showed me a wooden door in the north side of the estate wall. "I will unlock that door tonight after my ride." She pointed to a window in the northwest corner of the house, second floor. "That is my room, see? I will put a candle in the window." And as quickly as she'd climbed in the car last night, she was gone.

Chapter Thirty-Three
Primo

I didn't cover the sixty some miles between the cabin and Fresno in 49 minutes like Max did in his Ferrari, but I'd made it back into Fresno and dropped off Veronica in about an hour and a quarter. I stopped to buy sinkers and java and it was only a little after 9:00 a.m. when I arrived at the public defender's office. Flo was at her desk behind the rail that partitioned the outer office, just taking the cover off her Remington.

"Good morning, Florence. Any word from Mr. Rabinowitz?" I asked her, swinging open the wooden gate and crossing Flo's territory.

"Not yet, sir."

I went into Max's room, closed the frosted-glass door, put my feet up on his desk, and ate my donuts. The cinnamon was fresh and warm, but the powdered sugar was a bit stale.

I'd done some thinking during the drive, and I knew I was wrong about Amanda and Leon. I had no reason to mistrust her, and I'd had no claims on her eleven years ago anyhow. I'd been crazy to get upset and storm off. I loved Amanda. It didn't matter if Leon was my son or Max's; he was Amanda's son. I could love him too. I was taking care of Meaghan, wasn't I? And she was O'Callahan's daughter. If your woman has a child, you treat him like your own. And Amanda was my woman now. She was at work this morning, so I decided to meet her at quitting time, make it up to her, and make a new start with Leon.

At 9:20, Flo knocked and popped her head in to tell me John Bullfinch had arrived. "OK, I said. "Ask him to come in."

He was an inch or so shorter than me, but heftier, maybe 210, and he was carrying the weight around a soft middle. He wore a rumpled, lightweight powder blue suit, and had a bulbous nose with broken veins. I stood up to shake his hand and powdered sugar fell off my lap all over Max's desk.

I thanked him for coming by. He shrugged, as if it didn't make much difference to him. He said he'd take some java, so I buzzed Flo and asked her for a couple more cups.

"Mr. Bullfinch, Max Rabinowitz the public defender has asked me to find evidence to clear Sebastian Diaz."

"I don't know why you're wasting your time. It's pretty clear the Mexican done it."

"I don't believe he was in the room at the time of the murder," I said. Flo brought the coffee, and went back out.

"Look, Diaz was the boy friend," said Bullfinch. "He had to let the boss take his girl for a roll in the hay or they might both lose their jobs. Maybe Diaz was out in the hall to stay close. He hears the girl scream. When he runs in and sees them together, his hot Latin blood boils over. He pulls the knife and stabs Rios-Ortega then."

"Who is this girl?"

"I don't know. She got away. See, Diaz still had time to get his girl out before I got upstairs from the lobby. You have anything to sweeten this?" He jabbed a fat index finger at his coffee. I took a look at his honker and figured he didn't mean sugar.

I found a bottle of cognac in Max's lower desk drawer, and poured some in Bullfinch's cup. He took off his hat and pulled a big yellow hankie out of his jacket pocket and wiped his head with it, then he blew his nose. "What a burg," he said. "It's not even 9:30. Must be 90 degrees already. When I retire, I'm moving north. Where were we? Oh, yeah. I'll tell it another way. Diaz could have been pimping for the chippies from the factory. Maybe the victim went too far. Maybe he was roughing the girl up, or giving it to her, you know, in the back door. She don't like that so she screams. The pimp runs in, tries to break 'em up to protect the merchandise. But Rios-Ortega won't stop, so Diaz stabs him."

"Here's what I think," I said. "Diaz was in the stairwell. He heard the scream – that's the scream the other guests on the eighth floor reported. He run to the room and found Felipe Rios-Ortega with a knife in his back. He helped the girl get out of the room – that's how he got the victim's blood all over himself and on the window sill and fire escape."

"I don't like it," said Bullfinch. "Where'd the killer go? If someone else did it, wouldn't the kid or one of the guests have seen him come out?"

"Could anyone still have been in the room?" I asked.

"Again, Diaz would have seen him."

"Could have been hiding in the john. Or in the closet. Maybe the killer was still there when you came in." I leaned in over the desk.

"I been a dick for 28 years," he said. "Don't you think I'd know if someone was in the room? Don'tcha think I looked around?" But I could tell from the look in his eyes this was the first time the thought had occurred to him.

"I'm not blaming you. You're a good dick, John. You saw the blood; you saw the trail, and you went after your man. But did you hear anything? Smell anything?"

"Naw, there was nobody hiding in the room." His coffee cup was empty and he looked at it with wistful eyes. I went around the desk with the cognac bottle.

"Now, John, what happened after you caught up with Diaz?"

Bullfinch looked reluctant to talk, but he liked Max's cognac. I poured. "I called the police," he said.

"They came to the hotel, and took Diaz into custody,

right?

"Right."

"Did you take the cops up to the room?" I asked.

"Oh, yeah." He sighed, as if I was boring him.

"And what did you find?"

"I didn't find nothing," he said.

"Nothing? The body was still there, right?"

"Of course. It wasn't going nowhere with a knife like that through the back."

"How about the crowd that heard the scream?" I said.

"Oh, I see what you mean. They had come into the room while I was chasing down the fire escape. I guess everybody likes to have a look. The cops had to clear them out to investigate."

That fit in with the scenario that was forming in my head. The killer was in the room when Bullfinch passed through. Then he came out of hiding when the hotel guests came in for a look-see, and walked out with the crowd when the Fresno police cleared the room.

"Tell me about Felipe Rios-Ortega," I said. "Was he a regular guest?"

"Yeah, sure. He'd been coming once or twice a week, maybe about a year. Always took a top floor room."

"You talk to him?"

"Me? No," said Bullfinch.

"So he'd been coming in a year or so, let's say he's been there 60 times, is that about right?"

"Yeah, I guess. Maybe 75. He was a horny bastard." He leered and drank his cognac.

"Seventy-five nights and never talked to the house dick?"

"Well, we did talk a couple times. I knew what he was up to, see. So one time he told me he was married, and if I ever see his wife come in, to call his room and warn him fast."

"How would you know if his wife came in? Did you

know her by sight?"

He looked down in his cup. "I seen her once. She was the kind of dame you'd remember. She's built like a brick shithouse."

Bullfinch drank a little more cognac, sighed and slumped down a little in his chair. "The first time they came to the Californian was for a chamber of commerce shindig. I saw the whole family that time. Well I guess Felipe liked the place. We got air conditioning, you know? So he started bringing his girls there. That's when he stopped and talked to me in the lobby. 'Remember my wife?' he says. 'Sure,' I says, 'who wouldn't?'"

"Did you watch his back out of the kindness of your heart?"

"Naw. He slipped me a fin."

"One time?" I said.

"Most times. If he came in and I was in the lobby, he gimme a five. 'Remember,' he'd say, 'don't let my wife come up.' It got to be our little joke."

Sometimes I was amazed at what a guy would tell. It was as if people were just waiting for somebody to confide in. I have a good face for it. It's a blessing. "John," I said; I poured him another tot, then walked back behind the desk, and put the bottle away. "John, have you had any contact with the family since the murder?"

"Contact? What do you mean?"

"You know, did any of the Ramos family come around and see you?"

"No." He could have left it at that. He could have said nothing. He could have lied. But he went on. Was he bragging? "No, but the Ramos mouthpiece came by the hotel. Funny. He kept talking about avocados. I thought he was goofy. I was going to throw him out. But finally he explained he was a lawyer, and he'd read my statement, and he appreciated my work to catch the killer. He gimme me a c-note. He wanted me to know the Ramos family was grateful for all I'd done. He said as long as I don't change my story, there'd be another c-note coming, maybe more if Diaz was convicted."

The squawkbox on Max's desk buzzed. "Yeah, Flo?"

"Someone to see you, Mr. Swiver. It's that Mexican lady who was here yesterday. She brought a dog. Could you hurry?" I didn't like intercoms. It wasn't very clear. It sounded like Flo'd said something about a dog. But whatever she'd said, it sounded urgent to her.

"Be right there, Flo." I thanked Bullfinch for coming in, and asked him if he'd be at the Californian later.

"Yeah," he said. "I got to get out of this heat." He wiped his face with the yellow hankie again. I steered him by the elbow to the door, and told him maybe I'd drop by.

We stepped into the outer office where Carlos Ramos, looking uncomfortable with a tight collar cutting into the fat of his neck, sat next to the woman, the one I'd seen at the Ramos house. There was a stocky golden-haired dog at their feet, and they were holding hands like any middle-aged couple who'd come to town for some ice cream.

The dog was big enough to start at middle-guard for UCLA, and when we came out of Max's office, it jumped over the rail with a clatter of claws on the wooden floor. "Jesus Christ!" yelled Bullfinch, and stepped back into me. Flo scrambled out of her chair, spilled her coffee, and scooted away in the other direction. The leash had been draped around Don Carlos' pudgy wrist, and he seemed unconcerned about who the dog ate. The animal stood on his hind legs, put his forepaws on Bullfinch's shoulders and his strong-looking jaws and big muzzle up to the man's face.

The woman next to Don Carlos stood and gave a command, "*Abajo!*" and the dog obeyed, just like Don Carlos had obeyed her Monday. "*Sentarse,*" she said and came through the gate to soothe the dog's hackles. The dog put all four feet down, and the dame took up the leash and said to me, "He's still a puppy." She wore a black *mantilla* over her hair, no comb, and a modest grey dress trimmed in black lace. It didn't advertise her body, but still one could see she had a mature, well-turned figure. Her dark eyebrows were arched, her cheekbones prominent, accentuated with a faint dab of rouge, and her face tapered to a V at the chin. She looked to be in her mid-forties.

Bullfinch relaxed a little, stepped around my guests, and walked to the office door. He put his hat on, gave a bit of a sniff with his red nose, and squared his shoulders. "See you around, Swiver," he said, and was gone. I invited my new guests in.

They took seats together on a leather davenport, and I made sure Max's desk was between the puppy and me. The dog laid his head on the floor and watched me with a relaxed, contented expression.

"That's a very impressive dog, *señora*..." I let it hang to see if she might fill in a name.

She didn't. "He is a *mastin pesado*." She smiled.

A Spanish mastiff, I thought, of the heavy variety. "A good-tempered breed," I said, "if he's well-trained."

"You can count on that," she said.

Then Don Carlos spoke, in Spanish. "Now, *señor*, my daughter asked us to come and see you. I would do anything for her, so here I am. But why? Why are we here? What do you want from my family?"

I understood him well, but answered in English, "Don Carlos, *señora*, the public defender has asked me to help him find evidence to clear Sebastian Diaz."

"Clear him? He's guilty! Diaz killed my son-in-law. He is a red," he said.

"I am surprised, *señor*, that you interpret this as a political matter. Your son-in-law was naked in a hotel room. Perhaps it was an affair of the heart," I suggested.

"Don Felipe was married to my daughter. He is an innocent victim. Diaz is the killer," said Don Carlos. "We are eager for justice. Why is there so much talk?"

"Why do you think Diaz is guilty?" I asked. "Had the two men quarreled? Were they enemies?"

"Sebastian Diaz was a red. All reds are my enemies," said Don Carlos.

"Please understand," said the woman, "our family has suffered much in Spain, because of communists."

I gave her an even look. "Your family?" I said. "The Lopezes?"

"The Ramoses," she replied, just as evenly.

"Who are the Lopezes?" Don Carlos shouted. I heard a rumbling noise like a cable car going by, but we weren't in San Francisco. Then I realized, the puppy had growled.

"Forgive me Don Carlos. I knew of a Carlos Lopez in Aragón some years ago. You remind me of him, and I misspoke. I stand corrected, *Señor* Ramos. *Señora*, are you a member of the Ramos family?"

"She is," said Don Carlos.

"I'm sorry, I do not know the *señora's* name," I said, and turned my palms up.

"*Doña* Paz," he said. "*Doña* Paz helps me manage the family, the house." His mind seemed to drift a bit. "My son ... *herido en la guerra*. By the reds. And my wife was killed by the reds – bandits."

"Communists–" I began.

"Socialists, anarchists, bandits–" he broke in.

I interrupted, too. "Republicans?"

"We did not come to quibble about words," said Paz, "nor politics. What questions do you have for us?"

"*Doña* Paz," I said, "do you have a daughter?" Paz already exhibited good posture, but at that she sat up an inch taller and tucked her chin back. She blinked.

"What are you asking?" Her eyes seemed to entreat, to look into me, wondering what I knew.

"What kind of question is that?" boomed Don Carlos. "What can that possibly have to do with Diaz and my son-in-law's murder?"

"I just wondered," I said, "if you had any other family. Perhaps someone you left behind." I paused and looked at them. *Doña* Paz had recovered her composure, and put her poker face back on.

"This is none of your business," said Don Carlos. "Many Spaniards lost family members in the war."

"I apologize for the question," I said. "Don Carlos, do you know any reason why your son-in-law would be naked in a hotel room?"

Doña Paz spoke up, "Don Felipe found the climate in the valley oppressive. The Hotel Californian is one of the few places he could go that was air-conditioned. He was cooling off. He stayed in town one or two nights a week in the summer."

She was good. Firm. Lying through her teeth, but, unless I was prepared to call her on it ... "Did Felipe Rios-Ortega have any enemies?" I said.

"No," said Paz, "none."

"Reds," said Carlos.

"Was the marriage between Felipe and Veronica a happy one?" I asked.

"Yes," they both said at once.

"Could Felipe have been seeing any other women?" I asked.

"No. My daughter provided everything a husband could want," said Don Carlos.

"Ah, but Felipe was a man, no?" I said, and winked at him.

"He was a good Catholic husband," said Paz, as if asserting it made it so.

"Did Veronica have a lover? Someone at the factory, perhaps?"

"She was the perfect wife, obedient to her husband

in all things," said Paz.

"Careful, *señor*," said Don Carlos, "she is my daughter. In Spain I would be within my rights to kill you for insulting her honor."

"The Carlos Lopez I knew of in Spain might have tried to pop me for that," I said. "You know, I even saw Carlos Lopez kill a man once."

"I do not know this man Lopez, but, damn, I wish he had killed you." His hand was closed in a pudgy fist he and he pounded it once on the arm of the davenport. The puppy began his low, deep warning growl again.

"It is the first time he's been downtown," said Paz. "He is excitable." Don Carlos, I wondered, or the mastiff.

"Speaking of that," I said, "Don Carlos, I understand you don't come to the factory very often. Now that Felipe Rios-Ortega has passed, who will take responsibility for day-to-day operations at Rosas y Coronas?" He was angry, so I pressed him about what might be a sore subject. "Your son, Manuel?"

"My son is not well," he said, "I've told you that."

"Yes," I comiserated. "I saw Manuel Lopez shot in the shoulder. He has never recovered from that?"

He stood up. There was the heat, the tight collar. His face and head were turning red. "My son is Manuel *Ramos*. Leave my son out of this."

Paz spoke, "After a suitable period of mourning, Don Carlos will begin overseeing operations."

"Does that include purchasing the new rolling machine?" I said.

"Yes," he said, "Damn you again. And when I do, it will be my pleasure to sack about twenty of those reds who work for me now. Come, Paz. We are through here. *Venir*, Primo." He took the dog's leash from her and pulled on it to lead him out. Let him pull the dog around. He wasn't leading me anywhere.

I rose and walked around the desk to Paz, who was

still getting to her feet.

"Primo?" I said.

"For Primo de Rivera," she said. She gave me a nod. "Good day, *señor*." We were close now, and I stood between her and the office door. She looked hard into my eyes again.

I lowered my voice. "You can trust me," I said to her.

"You should leave our family alone," she said. "You must see we cannot be of any help in your inquiries." She brushed past me, leaving only her scent behind her in the room.

I watched their backs as they passed through the outer office. Then I went to the window. Max's office was on the second floor in the front. In a few minutes, I saw the couple walk out of the municipal building. At the street, one of the two thugs from the cigar factory stepped out of a big Chrysler Town & Country wagon. He opened the passenger doors for the couple, then took Primo around to the back and let him climb in. The Mexican went up front to drive, and the big car pulled away like a sailing ship gliding out of a smooth bay.

Chapter Thirty-Four
Welcome to the Hotel Californian

I drove to Max's house, took a shower, and dressed in clean clothes. I made a sandwich for lunch, and opened a bottle of Musigny that seemed to be calling my name from Max's cellar. I only drank one glass of wine, then made a moka pot of coffee, which I finished while the aroma still filled the kitchen.

Then I went back downtown to the Hotel Californian on Van Ness. I found a parking space on Kern Street and walked to the grand entrance. It was a short walk, but any amount of time in the afternoon sun in Fresno set me to perspiring.

The Californian was a red brick building with vertical white-painted stone trim on the corners of the two wings, and horizontal white stone trim setting off the second, third, and eighth floors. I noted the fire escapes on the wings leading down from the eighth floor to the second-floor roof. The high-ceilinged lobby was hung with crystal. Burgundy runners crossed the marble floor from the entrance to the front desk. I felt comfortable. It took me a moment to realize it was the air conditioning.

John Bullfinch was sitting in a well-stuffed chair with his back to a column, smoking a cigar and holding up the *Fresno Bee*. To his right front, he could watch the registration desk, to his left front, the elevator lobby. He looked like he was doing his job, but I could have sworn I heard a snore coming from his side of the post. There was an old geezer sunk into a sofa across from the registration desk, leaning his flippers on a cane. He could have been a fixture in the lobby like the tall lamps with the yellowing shades, the potted ferns, or the clock that had stopped at 11:20. I nodded to him, but he didn't move. He wore thick glasses and I couldn't tell if his eyes were open. Perhaps the snore had come from him.

"Hey," said Bullfinch when I stepped in front of him. "I'm glad you come by. I had something to tell you. You know, when I was walking out of your office, I caught a whiff of something familiar, and then when I got back here it struck me. It's not very common, whatever it is, and I realized, I did smell something that night – the night of the murder. I think it was the same scent."

"What kind of scent?"

"Well, perfume, maybe," he said.

"What did it smell like?"

"I don't know. It was hard to place. Maybe something you smell in the woods?"

"That could be anything, John. Cedar ... rotting leaves..."

"Nah. Not leaves, something grassy, maybe. Or maybe you're in the woods and you smell an animal. Musk? A cat? Balsam. I don't know, Swiver. But somebody there in your office had the same scent – same kind of thing I smelled upstairs that night."

"OK, thanks." That was something to think about. Could the mysterious Paz have been in the room?

Bullfinch took me up to the scene of the crime. On the way, I asked, "Who was the elevator operator that night? Did he see anything?"

"Hell, no," said Bullfinch. "Remember, Diaz took the stairs up."

"Diaz wasn't the killer."

"So you say," he said. He sighed, as if he were tired of me. "The operator was the night man, Melik. He comes on at 4:30. You can see him later. Ask him yourself."

"I will. Melik?"

"Armenian kid."

The room was spacious, with two windows. One opened onto the fire escape. To the right of the room entrance was another door. It was the bathroom – black and white tiles, chromium fixtures.

"I imagine you've been renting out the room," I said.

"As a matter of fact, no, I don't think anyone's been in here. First of all it was a bitch to clean up. A lot of blood between the bed and the window." He pointed to the window that opened on the fire escape. "I would have just said the hell with it and put in new carpet, but you know how management is. Always lookin' to save a buck. Anyhow, they cleaned it. That took a while. And this isn't our busy season. The hotel ain't been full, so they haven't needed this room."

Along the side wall was a big armoire. I opened the door. It was empty except for some wire coat hangers at odd angles. I closed the armoire, then pulled the door open again and stuck my head in. It stunk.

"John," I said, "put your head in there, smell this."

He came over and stuck his head in, then pulled it out quick. "P-u. Smells like a barnyard."

"Be more specific," I said.

He took another whiff, pulled his head out and gave me a quizzical look. "Stable?" he said.

I sniffed again. I shrugged. "I'm a city boy, myself," I told him. But I recognized it – horse.

~ ~ ~

It was 2:30 when I finished inspecting the murder room. I called the office. Flo said things were quiet. She still hadn't heard from Max. I decided to wait at the hotel until Melik came in. I wouldn't be able to drive Amanda home from work, but I could meet her and Leon soon after.

I went to the hotel bar, The Ash Room, and ordered red wine. It was an afternoon well spent. The bartender liked California wines and showed me some of his older bottles. There was one marked "Brandlin Ranch" in grease pencil. Brandlin had a mataro vineyard planted in the 19th century, and I bought the bottle on a hunch. I was lucky – it was one of the best old vine mataros I'd ever tasted.

After a couple hours I went back to the lobby to see if Melik had come in. Bullfinch was in his soft chair, behind the *Fresno Bee* again. I pulled the paper down and he jumped and let the cigar fall out of his mouth. "Geez, Swiver. You startled me." He scrambled to his feet and picked up the stogie before it could do any damage.

"Melik on duty?"

"Sure. That's him over there." He pointed to a dark-haired boy sitting on a stool in an open car.

"Thanks." I walked over to the elevator lobby. "Melik?" I said to the kid. He had a low hairline and a thick growth of short dark hair. He wore a tunic in the hotel's signature burgundy with white trim and a double row of brass buttons.

"Going up?" he said, and stood up off the stool putting his hand on the control lever.

"No, let's talk." I leaned against the doorframe. "I understand you were on duty here the night of the murder up on eight."

"The Mexican guy? Yeah," said Melik. "Say, what is this? You're not a Fresno dick."

"No, private. And the dead guy was Spanish, not Mex, but never mind that. Who did you take upstairs that night?"

"Mr. Rios-Ortega and his girl. She was one cute little border bunny." He winked.

"What time was that?" I asked.

"I don't know. I ain't got a watch. Maybe around midnight. 11:30 to midnight, somewhere in there," he said.

"Who else?" I asked.

"Hell, I don't remember everyone."

I took a fin out of my pocket, creased it lengthwise

and tucked it in the front of his tunic. "How about after midnight? Anybody then?"

"I don't know," he said. "It slowed down after 11:00. What night was that anyhow?"

"A week ago Tuesday," I said. "Eight days ago."

"I don't think I took anyone up to eight after midnight." A light on the panel lit up a number seven and a bell dinged.

"I got a call," said Melik. I'd been standing in the entrance to the car, back to the open door, and now I stepped in. Melik closed the doors and dialed the lever clockwise. The elevator ascended.

"What if I brought in some pictures? Would you remember anybody then?"

"Hey, I like pictures of dead presidents as much as any working man. But you'd be wasting your money. And I don't need to see no other pictures. I might remember a guy with a hook, or a broad with a wooden leg, but other than that..." He moved the lever up to 12 o'clock and the car bumped to a stop. "I knew Rios-Ortega 'cause he came in once or twice a week, always stayed on eight. Generally though, I don't pay that much attention to the guests." He put his left hand out on the handle and yanked the sliding doors open. We were on seven, and an old gent shuffled in taking six-inch steps. It was the fellow with the coke-bottle glasses I'd seen in the lobby earlier leaning on his cane. He looked even older up close

"Evening Mr. Dugan," said the Armenian boy.

"Good evening, Melik," said the old man. "Lobby, please."

"Next stop, lobby," said Melik, closing the door. He pressed the lever counterclockwise, and we dropped.

"Melik," I said, "were you the only one on duty that night?"

"Usually there are two of us until 11 p.m." he said. "A couple of the cars can be set for self-service if people need them. I was the only boy on from 11 to 2 that night." I looked at the old guy, Dugan. He stood in the corner of the car, stiff and unmoving. He could have been tuning in to our conversation. I couldn't read anything in his eyes with his big thick lenses, but maybe he saw me looking at him, because he spread his lips in a dry smile.

I decided it didn't matter if he listened in. "So the killer could have used self-service?" I said.

"Coulda walked up eight flights," said Melik. "Like I say, it was slow. I don't recall any of the other cars moving. They don't most nights. After two when the late boy goes home, they might use self-service, or the house peeper might take 'em up, if he likes their looks." He winked again.

We came to rest with a gentle bounce. Melik aligned the car with the floor and opened the door. Dugan shuffled out on his cane. "Anyhow," Melik said, "the coppers kept me here that night and asked me the same stuff. I told them, I didn't take anybody else up to eight after Rios-Ortega and his girl."

I decided not to waste any more time. If I left now, I might get to the Diaz place around the same time as Amanda.

"OK, kid," I said. "If you remember anything, give me a call." I wrote Max's office number on the back of my business card and handed it to him.

I nodded at Bullfinch and headed for the Kern Street doors. "Oh, Mr. Detective." I turned. It was old man Dugan, inscrutable behind the thick lenses.

I pointed at my chest. "Me?"

"Yes," he said. "Come here a moment." He was on the sofa, swallowed up by red and green cushions in a Southwestern Indian, *faux* Navajo design. I walked over.

"Young man," he began, "I couldn't help overhearing your conversation with friend Melik. You were asking him about the night of the murder, I take it?"

206

"Yes."

"I might be able to help you. I was sitting down here that night until just about one a.m." Blue veins ridged across along the backs of his hands, which rested on his cane handle. The veins wiggled like snakes when he moved a hand and gestured with a dry index finger. "Sometimes I can't sleep," he went on, "and I prefer the airy openness of the lobby to the claustrophobic room they give me."

I didn't hold much hope for anything this aged geezer could tell me. He was probably lonely. You meet a lot of old cats like that who just want to talk. "Mr. Dugan, I'm running a little late..."

"I understand, Mr. Sleuth. I'll come to the point," he said. "About 12:45 there was a bit of a commotion over by the Kern Street entrance."

"Do tell," I said. "Early edition of Wednesday's *Bee* arrive?"

He chuckled. "No, a bit more unusual. A woman rode a horse right in through the front doors and up the lobby steps."

I pulled on an ear. "Sorry, Mr. Dugan. Sounded as if you said a woman rode a horse into the lobby." He had my attention now.

Dugan nodded. "The doorman was beside himself," he went on. The old man's manner of telling a story was slower than a glacier marching to the sea.. "The woman swung down off her horse and handed him the reins. The doorman struggled to lead the horse back outside. It was a brown mare, a spirited animal."

"You saw from here it was a mare?"

"I'd say so. I don't wear these thick lenses because I can't see; I wear them so I can."

"Of course," I cleared my throat. "I didn't mean..."

"Sure you did, but never mind." He paused and leaned back on the couch. I moved a step closer. "Sit down please," he said. He patted the seat next to him. "Do you know how old I am?"

"How old? No, I don't." I sat.

"I'm 84," he said.

"Congratulations."

He took a hand off his cane and waved as if 84 were no big deal. Then he started again, "Do you know how long it's been since I've had a spontaneous erection?"

"I beg your pardon?" I said, and eased away from him.

"Spontaneous erection. Young men get them all the time. You know what I'm talking about. You're downtown shopping, or you get on a bus. You see a pretty girl, a well-turned ankle, a cantilevered bosom. The periscope goes up."

"Yeah, I get it."

"Well, if you live another 40 or 45 years you won't." I thought I could make out a wistful twinkle in his eyes now, despite the thick lenses.

"Mr. Dugan, I really can't stay too long. The point of this was?"

"The woman who dismounted. She was magnificent. Mediterranean, I think. She shook out her dark hair behind her as she strode along the carpet. Her blouse had several buttons open, but it was still tight against her full breasts. She stank a bit. That's right. She stank of horse, but it was a ripe animal smell, a smell you could wallow in. Her khaki britches were tight across her swaying ass and very snug between her legs. Her hips moved from side to side as she crossed the lobby."

"You paint quite a picture, Mr. Dugan." I felt a stirring in my own loins.

"Yes, well, the periscope went up."

I said nothing to that.

"Just like that, I was harder than I'd been in years. She was such a magnificent creature, the mere sight of her..." He sighed. "I decided to take it upstairs and show Mrs. Dugan."

"Er ... yes. That was wise."

"Yes," said Dugan. "I stood up carefully. As you've no doubt noticed, my trousers are voluminous – baggy pants, the fashion of the old man. At any rate, she crossed to the elevator, and I was right behind her."

"Not too close, I hope," I said.

"Close enough. Though if she noticed anything, I imagine she thought I'd bumped her with my cane. She was looking straight ahead, seeming intent on some purpose. As I say, she stank a bit, and perhaps she noticed it in the elevator. She opened her handbag and applied a bit of perfume."

"You're on seven, right Mr. Dugan?"

"That's correct," he said. "I exited there. So did our horsey friend."

"Did she?"

"Yes. She may have had business on seven. Or she may have walked up to eight. I don't know. I didn't dally in the hallway."

"How many stairways are there?" I said.

"Two. There's one in each wing. At any rate, Mr. Detective, that might explain why friend Melik could not recall taking anyone up to eight. He probably didn't."

And the two stairways might explain how Diaz could be telling me the truth about hiding in one, yet he didn't see the killer, who must have used the other. "Thank you, Mr. Dugan. You've been quite helpful."

"My pleasure," he said. "It's a fine memory."

"The house dick didn't tell me about the incident with the horse in the lobby."

Dugan chuckled and shook his head. "Ah, Mr. Bullfinch."

"Yeah, you'd think the doorman would have called him over to help."

"One of the bellboys helped. They didn't deem it necessary to wake Bullfinch."

"Could you identify this dame if you saw her again?" I asked.

"I'd love to try."

~ ~ ~

It was time to go meet Amanda. There was a florist shop in the arcade off the lobby and I bought 15 red roses. Then I drove around downtown until I found a five and dime. I went in and bought a baseball and a fielder's glove for Leon. I hoped he threw right. I saw a really nice cap pistol that looked like an authentic old double-action Colt revolver, so I bought that, too, and a couple rolls of caps. It was just a toy gun. I played with them when I was a kid, so what the hell? At 4:45, I headed over to the near west side.

Chapter Thirty-Five
A Tough Inning

I parked across the street from the Diaz house, and hopped out with my toys and roses. Then I saw the blue Chevy pickup parked right outside the entrance to the bungalow court and I knew something was wrong. I ran to the gate. Inside, Leon lay in the dust. One of the Mexican goons had a foot on his back, while Amanda struggled with the other one. The guy with Leon was the driver who'd picked up the Ramoses at the municipal building. Amanda was trying to escape the grip of the other tough, the big guy named Geraldo. She was about half his size, and her fists were flying at him but he ignored the blows. I tried the gate – it was locked. I yelled at them. They all paused, and looked my way. Then Geraldo grinned and wrapped one paw around both Amanda's wrists, and gave her a hard blow across the face with the other hand.

I dropped the roses, turned sideways, and loaded the cap gun out of sight of the others. I fired two shots in the air. They were pretty good caps. The shots froze everyone. "Turn her loose, Gordito," I boomed out. Geraldo wasn't grinning anymore. He dropped Amanda's wrists. Leon looked up. When I saw the look in his eyes, I knew I couldn't fail him.

The two *matones* were wearing baseball pants, and high socks. Their shirts read "Smokers," in black script across the top of a diagonal cigar. It was a surreal scene, but I couldn't blink it away. They must have just finished playing ball for Rosas y Coronas, and after the last out, decided to unwind by beating up some women and children. I hoped they'd lost the game. "Step away," I said. I pointed the gun at Geraldo and waved him away from Amanda with the barrel. "Guapa, open the gate!"

Amanda stumbled for her balance and rushed over. "Francisco, thank God." She opened the irongate and turned back for Leon. The driver thug saw her coming and grabbed the boy's shoulders as he was struggling to get up. I fired the cap gun again, but this time it seemed to dawn on them that it didn't have the authoritative boom of a big revolver. Geraldo cut Amanda off before she could get to her son with a push that sent her into the side of one of the houses. She hit it hard and crumpled in the dry dirt. Then they both squared off against me.

I couldn't back down – I gave them my most menacing, confident look. I've been told it's a lot like my crazy man look.

The door to the house on my left opened and a Mexican woman stepped out. She gawked at us open-mouthed and called to Amanda – she called her Pilar, the name Amanda went by at the factory. She must have been Diaz's mom.

"Quick," I told the woman, "back inside. Telephone the police!" She raised a fist to her mouth, but her eyes told me she understood. I yelled, "Hurry!" and she nodded and darted back in. I heard her latch the door. Good, I thought. The two thugs would either have to split up to stop her from calling, or I'd have some law there. If I could just hold them off long enough....

Geraldo picked up a baseball bat I hadn't seen from the dirt by the house. He put it to his shoulder and rushed me. Damn, I thought. Too bad I hadn't bought the kid a bat instead of a cap gun. I dived under Geraldo's swing and rolled into his knees. He missed and toppled over me. Strike one. The driver struggled to pull Leon towards the street. I scrambled to my feet and tackled him in the ribs, separating him from the boy. "Leon, get your mother out of here!" He dashed to Amanda who was using the side of the building to stand up. "Run; I'll hold them," I said to her. I wasn't sure how much a pacifist could do, but I didn't mind taking a beating if I could delay them enough for Amanda and our boy to escape. "Take my car."

Amanda was on her feet now, an arm around Leon. They came towards me. I held out the keys. "I can't drive a car," she said, but grabbed the keys.

"You watched me yesterday. Drive, run – get away from here." I ducked as Geraldo took a vicious swing at me. This goon probably batted cleanup, but he missed again. Strike two. He tried to get me on the back swing, as I struggled to upend him. I felt the bat catch the back of my shoulder. I stumbled. All right, a foul tip. Still strike two. He kicked at my head – he was wearing his baseball cleats. I grabbed his foot with both paws and twisted it. He lost his balance and went down. I scrambled to my feet, and my hat came off. Leon and Amanda reached the gate to the street, and the driver latched on to Leon's shoulders. He pulled the boy away from his mother and back into the courtyard. "Go," I called to her again, "I'll save Leon," but she hesitated, unwilling to leave her son.

Then something crashed into me from behind, glancing off my shoulder, and hitting the back of my head with the solid whack of ash against hide. I went down on my hands and knees. My eyes didn't seem to be working right. Geraldo slammed down on my side and rode me into the dirt. He put a headlock on me and drove his fist into my head, again and again. I tried to turn and get a grip on him, but it was no good. I was all sweaty and my arms were like rubber. Geraldo stood up and kicked me. Colors faded away to shadows. I swung at him, but it was like battling a ghost. Then even the shadows faded out.

~ ~ ~

When I could see again, men in blue pants were spinning around my head. I grabbed one by the leg to stop him from circling. It was one of Fresno's finest. He shook his leg until I let go. I got up to a sitting position, rocked a little there in the dirt and put a hand on the back of my head. Ow! There was quite a bump. But the bump wasn't important. My mind reeled with thoughts of Amanda and Leon. They were gone. Damn! All I'd needed was one more strike.

I still had Geraldo's baseball shoe in my hand, and I tossed it across the yard against the opposite house. I saw my car keys in the dirt by the irongate and I crawled over to retrieve them.

Mrs. Diaz was there, waving her arms, wringing her hands, talking fast. She was telling the police that two men she didn't know took her *nuera* (daughter-in-law) and the *nuera's* son. The Anglo tried to save them but they hit him with a baseball bat. There had been about five cops when I'd first opened my eyes. Now there were only two. Where'd they all go? Did somebody bring donuts?

After a few minutes of sitting on my ass in the dust, I climbed to my feet, told the cops I agreed with what Mrs. Diaz had told them, and salvaged my rose bouquet. I gave it to her. "Put these in some water," I said. I picked up my hat, brushed it off, and went across the street to my Cadillac. Too bad I'd never bothered to note the license plate number of the Chevy pickup the previous times I'd encountered it. I could have put the cops on to it, but now I would have to handle it myself.

Chapter Thirty-Six
The Ramos Knockover

I sped over to Max's place. He still wasn't home, and I couldn't figure it. It was nearly 6 p.m. Even if he hadn't left San Francisco until after lunch, he should have made it to Fresno by now, the way he drove. It was less than 200 miles. What could have happened? Well, I didn't like going up against Ramos and company alone, but Amanda and Leon were at risk, so I had no choice.

I walked past a mirror at Max's and scared myself. I was getting black and blue high on my right cheek and near the right eye. The eye was OK, but my face was swelling to close it. I just rinsed off as best as I could, and put on some bandages. There wasn't time for anything else.

I thought I should make my play after dark. I went into Max's bedroom and borrowed some indigo dungarees that fit me and a t-shirt that was a very dark military green. In the kitchen, I went through the meat drawer of Max's refrigerator. I put the oldest chops he had in a brown paper sack, and I headed out.

There was still light in the western sky, when I drove north to the Van Ness extension. I was anxious about Amanda, but I knew I had to kill an hour or so before dark, so I stopped at the last drug store along the retail district before the residential area. I nursed a cup of joe and poured the rest of the Cream of California brandy in it when the counterman turned away to fix a banana split. It was only a couple swallows of brandy, and it wasn't very good, but on the other hand, it dulled the pain in my shoulder and didn't hurt that coffee any. Who knew what the night might bring?

~ ~ ~

At 8:30, it was dark enough. I left the drug store and drove to the Ramos place. There were no streetlights that far out of town, but there were some spotlights on the outside of the house and in the yard. I rolled past the gate with no headlights on, and saw the blue pickup inside the wall just off the driveway.

I kept going and parked out of sight past the north end of the property. I crept back to the wall on tiptoe. A candle burned in the window on the near end of the second floor of the house. I tried the door in the north wall and found it unlocked. Veronica Rios-Ortega was expecting me.

And Veronica was a dangerous woman. I'd be a fool if I went – a fool, or a man who'd face any risk for his lover and child.

But I wasn't foolish enough to go in on Veronica's terms. I edged along close to the wall until I came to the main gate. The radio in the pickup was playing *Norteño* accordion music. I jumped, put my hands on the top of the wall, and pulled myself up for a quick look. Geraldo and the driver sat in lawn chairs outside the pickup on either side of the driveway. Geraldo had a shotgun across his lap.

I saw Primo the puppy pacing through the front yard. He was quiet on his paws, and if I'd taken Veronica's invitation and entered the compound, Primo could have been on me before I'd gone 30 feet. He wore a *carlanca* to protect his neck from wolves while he was working, or around here, maybe from coyotes. With the traditional spiked collar and his huge slobbering jowls, Primo didn't look like a contender for Mr. Congeniality in the Westminster Kennel Club show.

Pain shot through my right shoulder where the bat had hit me, and I dropped to the ground where I had the chops waiting in their butcher paper. They'd been in the hot car a couple hours now since I'd left Max's, and had that spoiling flesh smell. I hacked them a little with my pocketknife to get the meat juices flowing, then I reached up and put them on top of the wall. I pulled myself up one more time and lobbed the bloody meat into the driver's lap. Then I gave a short, sharp whistle as I let go of the wall, and I saw Primo look my way and trot over before I dropped. I ran north along the outside of the wall.

It sounded as if things were going bad for the Mexicans. One of them started to yell, and Primo was growling and barking. I opened the door in the north wall and slipped into the compound.

It was about 60 yards across the yard to the house, and I covered it on the run. I crouched beside the front steps and caught my breath. So far so good – I doubted anyone had seen me. Then I turned away and went along the house to the back side of the property out of sight of the guards and the dog.

The Ramos place wasn't as big as the Ritz in Madrid, but it was a classy layout for a pile its size. The house was two stories, around an open courtyard in the back. The ground floor rooms opened onto a colonnade. There were dim lights in wall sconces along the columns, and the second tier was a covered balcony. I heard muted voices from deep within the court and focused my attention back in the corner where the voices were coming from.

It looked like the family was dining outside under the balcony. It was now 9 p.m. by my watch, maybe about right for the family meal in the Aragón countryside. Covered lanterns cast a warm glow on the table and the diners. Don Carlos sat at one end of the long wooden table, Doña Paz at the other. Veronica Rios-Ortega sat on the long inside with her back to the house, and Manuel Ramos was opposite her with his back to the courtyard.

The guards were busy with Primo and the family was dining, I had a hunch no one was watching the prisoners.

Keeping out of the light, I entered the arcade on the end and started trying the doors. The walkway was about six feet deep. Solid ebony wood doors set in little gothic arches gave access to the rooms. With the dim lighting and the shadows of the columns, it was duck soup staying out of sight. The first door was locked. I called for Amanda and Leon in a harsh whisper but there was no answer. I glanced out in the courtyard; no one seemed to have heard.

The second room was unlocked. It was a library – empty except for the books. Then a locked room, and I called again. No answer again. The next room was an office or study of sorts. It held a masculine wooden desk with a smooth leather writing surface, a high-back leather chair, and crossed fencing swords on the wall behind the desk. On the sidewall was a bookcase with glass doors. Noticing a bottle of Carlos I Spanish brandy, I bought myself a drink – anesthesia, for the shoulder pain.

I decided to take one of the weapons. Epees, foils, rapiers – I didn't know the difference, but they were fencing swords, with a point to them. As a pacifist, I didn't want to skewer anyone, but rescuing Amanda and Leon was more important than my principles. Maybe it wouldn't come to that. I swished the sword back and forth a couple times until my shoulder made me wince. Maybe it was an epee.

The next room was a music room, with a piano and some dainty chairs. There was a connecting door you could use to walk from that room to a room in the front corner of the house. Much larger, the corner room was perhaps a ballroom or parlor for receiving guests. I looked out the window towards the front gate. There was an overturned lawn chair and an unmoving clump that could have been a body. It was too dark down there for me to tell if it was the body of a big dog or of a man. The pickup truck was gone, the gate was open, and I didn't see Primo prowling about.

I crossed a polished granite floor in a two-story foyer, and passed a double staircase, one leading to each wing of the upstairs. Then I was near the outdoor dining area, where I stopped along the colonnade to listen. The family was quiet at first. When I was able to pick it up, the talk, in Spanish, seemed rather banal – nothing about kidnapping women and children.

"Did you ride this afternoon?" Paz asked.

"Yes," Don Carlos answered. "For about an hour. Did you ride, Veronica?"

"Oh, yes, later than you. I had a good ride. Pass the pork, please." I heard the scraping of silver on china. If they passed their own pork, perhaps there was no kitchen staff.

"Wine, my son?" No answer but he must have moved his glass over for some. I heard the glug, glug, glug of a good pour.

Enough, I thought, and carried on down the hall. There was a lounge, decorated for the women, it appeared. The next door opened unto a billiard room, dominated by a big expanse of green felt, dark wood, and open woven-leather pockets. On the sideboard were cigars, and two bottles of brandy – another Carlos I, and some Osborne with a black bull on the label. I'm the kind of man who never passes a water fountain in a public building without wetting his whistle, so I had another slug of the Carlos I. I felt clear-headed enough. The booze helped me face the danger and the risks; it let me ignore the pain.

At the end of the hall were stairs and I climbed to the second floor, where I found myself outside on the balcony. I tried the doors. There were empty rooms – guest bedrooms, by the look of the furnishings – then a bedroom I took to be Manuel's. It had a sick odor and a hospital odor both. Amanda was not there, but I poked around a little. The top drawer of Manuel's nightstand contained two hypodermic syringes, a length of rubber tubing, and a flat box filled with a dirty white powder. Veronica and Carlos liked to ride. It looked like Manuel had his own horse. From the brownish color of the scag, I was ready to bet the workers at the factory were supplying it – Mexican Mud.

The floor was very solid and I felt safe walking over the dining room without anyone hearing my movements from below. Carrying the epee in front of me, I came to a woman's bedroom in the corner – it looked like Paz slept alone, for what that was worth. I found three bottles of perfume on the dresser – Chypre, Arpege, and My Sin. I'm also the kind of man who never passes a cologne tester in a department store without a quick squirt. I tried the Arpege. It wasn't the same as sniffing wine, but I picked up a little bergamot, and then a flowery scent – some rose, some jasmine. It could have been the scent Paz wore to the office this morning, but I was new at this.

The next room was the master bedroom – masculine and rich. The bed was large; the room was dark – and empty.

I moved down the hall, passed an empty guest bedroom, then entered what may have been the late son-in-law Felipe's chamber. It was stylish and modern, and there was an extension phone. There was a connecting door to a boudoir with a candle in the window – Veronica's. My curiosity kept me there a few minutes. I'd only seen her in her mourning and her riding costumes, but she had quite a collection of fine lace garments, and the whole back of her closet floor was lined with shoes and boots. On her dresser was My Sin by Lanvin. I sprayed it in the air and sniffed behind it. Bingo! Complex, woody, musky. My Sin was a match from last night.

I had been through every room on the first and second floors now, and hadn't found Amanda and Leon. Yet I was sure they were somewhere in the house. The basement? It would be hard to escape from the cellar, and should anyone get into the house, the prisoners' cries might not be heard upstairs. I pulled the door shut and was about to turn and go down the stairs when footsteps approached the corner of the hall from the front of the house. The stairs were too far; I had to duck back into Veronica's bedroom, and I closed the door. The footsteps in the hallway stopped outside the door. I dropped to the floor and moved under the bed just in time, pulling the sword in after me.

The bedroom door opened and Veronica came in. She crossed the room and entered her bathroom, where she opened the taps to draw a bath, then came back out and sat at her dresser. I heard her sniff; the perfume I'd sampled must still be in the air. And with Veronica nearby, I got a whiff of that horse scent again, horse scent with high notes of My Sin. That was a match for the armoire at the Californian.

Veronica stood up and took off her blouse, and draped it over one post of the bed. Plopping herself down above me, she struggled alone to remove her riding boots. Clearly there were no servants around tonight to assist. They must dismiss the help early when they kidnapped people. Veronica slipped out of her riding pants and there was a knock at the door.

"*Quién está ahí?*" she said.

I heard a soft answer from the corridor: "Manolito," her brother. She walked over to the door and I saw her long powerful gams and her strong naked back above her skivvies. Using the door as a modesty panel, she opened it enough to look out. Manuel said, "Are you done with the woman?"

"Yes," Veronica said. "She is the one."

"May I have her?"

"Of course," said Veronica. "You understand, she must die."

"Yes," he said. "That is clear."

"But you may do as you wish with her first. The boy should not leave here alive either, but he is innocent, so..."

"Understood. He won't suffer. *Buenas noches, querida hermana.*" She closed the door, and walked back to the bed, where she slipped out of her underpants, then went into her bathroom.

I waited until I heard some splashing in the tub, then I crawled out from under the bed. Veronica had just passed a death sentence on my love. Perhaps a few moments well spent up here would save time finding Amanda. I stepped into the bathroom, where I found myself behind Veronica's right shoulder. She was in a deep bubble bath, and steam rose gently above the water. When she looked up, she saw a blurry reflection of me in her foggy mirror, and turned her head.

"Detective–"

"Veronica Lopez," I answered and bowed.

"Ramos." There was a flash of anger in her eyes. "I didn't think you were coming."

"I wouldn't miss this for the world."

"Pardon me if I don't get up–" She smiled and flashed white teeth between ruby lips.

"No need," I said. I stepped across to the tub and whipped the epee around from behind my back with a flourish. With great care, I pressed the sharp tip against the flesh of her left breast, buoyant behind the bubbles.

"You don't need that flimsy foil. Show me your big broadsword." She smiled and the golden dagger in her eye gleamed.

"Where is Amanda?" I asked.

"Amanda? Who is Amanda?"

I pressed a little, enough to break the skin. A drop of

bright red welled up around the steel point, until gravity overcame surface tension, and the red dripped into the water. "Remember Zorro, Veronica? A Spanish swordsman in old California. He used to carve a 'Z' into his enemies' flesh. You tell me where Manuel has the woman and the boy, or you'll be wearing my initials on your boobs."

"Are you mad? What are you talking about?" She sat up and squirmed back in the tub, but it was to no avail. She slid forward against the point of the epee.

"Your boys, Geraldo and your father's driver, they followed me and found which woman from the factory I was seeing. You had them pick her up tonight–"

"What happened to you, Frank? Your eye is black. Let me take care of you." She put her hands on the edges of the tub and tried to rise, but I kept the point of the sword planted, and another drop of blood swelled around it.

"You questioned her or you recognized her as the woman who was under Felipe when you killed him."

"No!"

"Don't play with me," I shouted, and I slashed a scratch, just a light scratch, the vertical stroke of an F in her flesh. It was enough.

"Manuel has them in the barn."

Chapter Thirty-Seven
A Hot Time in the Old Barn

Of course, the barn! I pushed Veronica's head down under the water. By the time she'd stopped sputtering and gasping, I had her naked and face down on her bed with a washcloth in her mouth, hog-tied with the drapery cords.

Outside I stayed in the shadows as much as I could, then crossed to the barn and, crouching, looked in.

Manuel had lit an old-fashioned pitch torch and put it in a bracket on a beam in the wall. There was a water wheel set in the center of the barn, a large wooden one, maybe about six feet in diameter, with blades about 15 inches or so across. It was out of use – I saw no source of flowing water in the barn. But the wheel was there, standing on edge and Amanda was tied to it on her back, stretched out like a Vitruvian woman, an arm and a leg on either side of the rim. Manuel stood two or three feet from her, wearing his blue Falangist officer's tunic and his boots. His breeches were off, in the dirt by Leon, who lay crumpled and unmoving in a corner. Leon's hands were tied, and there was a bandana around his mouth as a gag.

In his left arm Manuel held a riding crop. It had rawhide lashes on the end, and he used it to flog Amanda across her bosom and her thighs, slashing the fabric of her dress. He was taking his time, and each blow seemed to crank his sexual desire up a notch. His right sleeve was rolled up, and a soft rubber tube hung around his useless right arm above the elbow. A hypo dangled from his forearm below the tube. The plunger of the hypo was slipping up and blood shot up the dropper's neck, mixing with the contents of the syringe. Flickering light from the torch illuminated the whole scene.

I've seen some sick tableaux in my days as a private dick, but nothing as bad as this. I sprinted for the barn door, and went in at a run. I caught Manuel's left arm on the back swing. Maybe that baseball bat had broken something; I usually hang on like a leech, but the damn junkie was strong enough to wrest his arm loose. He looked surprised, as much as you can tell from pupils too constricted for even the tiniest angels to dance in, but he didn't hesitate. He gave me a back-handed slash across the face with his quirt. I staggered back and heard Amanda call my name. Her head drooped forward, and her voice was weak and raspy.

"Don't worry, *guapa*. I'll get you out of here." Manuel had caught my forehead at the eyebrow, and blood dripped down into my left eye. He swung down again the other way and hacked at my shoulder and upper arm, but I parried that try with the sword. Taking the advantage, I flourished the point near his face, and backed him up a step. The syringe drooped from his arm; I lunged forward and swung at it with the epee, and shattered the glass, breaking it off with the needle still embedded in his flesh.

That was just to worry him, but he was too snowed up to worry much. He whipped the quirt up between my legs. My eyes started to tear up, and my knees felt weak, but I slashed across his quirt hand. An epee has no cutting edge, but it was a good steel weapon, and I put some anger behind it. Manuel dropped his crop and brought his wounded hand up toward his mouth. He shuffled back but I kept after him, and pressed the point of the foil into the cloth of his tunic over his heart and leaned towards him. He straightened, backing up as much as he could and put his hands out, palms facing me. Then his eyes looked over my shoulder and he smiled and seemed to relax. I felt cold metal on my neck.

"Drop the sword, *señor*." It was Paz. Before I could

turn around, there was a precise metallic click. I exhaled, and tossing the sword on the ground in Amanda's direction, I raised my hands. I tried not to lose heart.

"*Gracias*, Paz," said Manuel. He rolled his damaged shoulder and his right arm and hand swung around to cover his crotch, but it hardly mattered. His member had already shrunk out of sight behind his shirttails. I moved my head right and turned my body to glance back at what I was up against. *Doña* Paz had a long double-barreled shotgun, an over-and-under, aimed at my head.

"Paz?" It was a faint, questioning syllable from the water wheel. Amanda was struggling to get a look at the woman.

"I saw you go into the barn when I came out into the courtyard, *señor*," she said to me. "What are you doing here? Talk fast. This gun is heavy for me."

"I'm trying to save Amanda Zingaro," I said.

"He's lying, Paz," said Manuel. "It's just one of my girls from the factory. She's nothing. A Mexican tramp. You know I have to have my girls now and then." He gave a sheepish grin, but I think what I'd said had put a question in the dame's mind.

"Come on," I said to Paz. "Have a closer look at her." She wanted to see, but felt the need to keep her eyes and the shotgun on me. I shuffled a step towards the wheel and kept my hands in sight. "It's all right, *Doña* Paz.

"No," said Manuel. He moved between me and the wheel and snatched up the foil.

"Mama?" said Amanda.

Paz turned her head at this. "What did you say, girl?"

"Mama, it's me. Amanda. You are alive? Here?" Her voice was weak, faint.

"Amanda?" Paz said.

"Let me cut her down, *Doña* Paz," I said. I stepped to Amanda's side; Paz began to lower the weapon, and to tremble. Manuel was watching Paz, and I kicked the sword out of his hand. Then I gave him a kick to the groin that lifted him off his feet.

"This cannot be," she said. "My daughter is dead ... they told me ... ten years..." I took my pocketknife out and keeping watch on Paz out of the corner of my eye, I started to cut the ropes that tied Amanda to the wheel.

"Eleven years, Doña Paz," I said. "I was there. Manuel shot her. But she survived." Red welts were coming up on Amanda's skin where she'd been slashed with the riding crop. She had bright red blood on her chest above the torn neckline of the dress, and she coughed some more up. "Easy, *guapa*, you're safe now."

"Leon?" Amanda whispered.

"He's down, but I don't think they've hurt him. As soon as I cut these ropes I'll go to him," I said.

"What are you doing?" Paz said to me.

"It's your daughter, *Doña* Paz. I have to free her. Come to her. Help her. I mean no harm to either of you." The thought crossed my mind that if she wandered just a few feet closer, I could grab that shotgun.

"Mama, I never imagined you were still alive. What are you doing here?" said Amanda. Her voice was so whispery, I was worried. Maybe the abduction and flogging were too much for an underweight lunger.

I'd cut her left arm and leg free, and crossed between the two women. *Doña* Paz finally lowered the shotgun. "Don Carlos brought me to America."

"You were his prisoner," Amanda said.

"Yes ... at first, but..." said Paz.

"He killed your husband, Mama. Don Carlos killed Papa," said Amanda.

"Carlos and Manuel, they told me you were dead too." Paz sobbed and reached out now, dropping the gun, putting an arm around her daughter.

I went to the boy. Leon seemed dazed but I didn't see any wounds or damage. I stood him on his feet and squatted in front of him holding him by the shoulders. He opened his eyes. When he took me in he said, "Papa?" I hugged him close to my chest with an unconditional love, glad he was alive.

Now I just had to pick that shotgun up before Manuel had any ideas. "It's all right, son. We're going to get your mama out of here, OK?" He nodded, and I took his hand and stood up. Paz had finished freeing Amanda, who slumped against her now on shaky legs, but Manuel was moving on his knees and put his hand on the shotgun before I could get to it. He brought it around to point at me, holding it at waist level with his only good arm, his left, then he waved it towards Paz and Amanda, and back to me again while he struggled to his feet.

"Family reunions make me sick," he said in Spanish. "Yes, Paz. It's your daughter. I thought I'd killed her years ago, but I was wrong. I won't make that mistake again. She's the one who shot me in the shoulder." He swung the gun around to the women. "Ruined my right arm ... eleven years of pain. I was going to give it back to her tonight." Now the shotgun swung back in its arc to me, "Who is this man? One of your red friends, Amanda?"

If I could get my hands on Manuel, Amanda and Leon could get out. I gauged the distance and my chances. They weren't good. While he held the gun on me, he could cut me in two before I reached him. If he swung it back to the women, I might reach him, but if the gun went off then, it would be worse. It was a devil's alternative.

Then with sudden energy, Amanda pushed off her mom's shoulder and picked up the foil. Manuel saw her movement and swung the shotgun around her way. That forced me to play my hand. I went for the gun and knocked it enough that it pointed at the ground as it went off. There was a loud bang; dirt, dust and hay flew up in a cloud. I wrenched the shotgun away from Manuel and ended up on my butt.

Before I could do or say anything more, Amanda had run the point of the epee into Manuel's chest. I don't know if he felt it. Who knows what a junkie can feel? But she kept going and Manuel gave ground until his back was against the barn wall. Pink froth, then red blood flowed out of his mouth. Still she pressed on until she had skewered him to a beam

Part Four

Last
Puffs

Chapter Thirty-Eight
Casa Rabinowitz

When we arrived at Max's house I was running on empty. I hoped Max would be back from San Francisco, but there was still no sign of him.

At the Ramos place, I'd invited Paz to come along with us. She looked wide-eyed at Manuel, still pinned to the wall, eyes open but not seeing, blood running down his tunic from his chest and dripping out of the corner of his mouth.

"Yes," she said, "I will come with my daughter."

She asked about her dog. I figured Primo was big enough to take care of himself, but I wanted to be on good terms with Mama Paz, so after I placed Amanda across the back seat, and the rest of us got in the Cadillac, I swung left into the drive and put my high beams on. There were two overturned lawn chairs. The shape on the lawn was the driver, his flesh ripped at the throat. Geraldo must have fled alone in the pickup. He'd left the gate open.

"I think Primo's fine, but he must be out here, along the road somewhere," I told Paz.

"He'll go home when he's hungry," she said. Or he'll eat the neighbors' pets, I thought. I reversed onto Van Ness, and headed south.

By the time we arrived at Max's, Leon had fallen asleep. I carried Amanda in to Max's bed, fixed Leon up on the living room couch, and showed Paz the spare bedroom. I asked her if she could help me clean up my face and treat my cuts. She seemed to know what she was doing as a nurse. As soon as she was done tending my wounds, I staggered outside and rolled into the hammock. I was asleep before it stopped swinging.

The neighborhood was quiet when I woke up around 6:30, quiet with peaceful sounds – the call of a mourning dove, a fluttering of bird wings, the newspaper boy's bicycle tires whirred softly on the pavement, and a thin paper plopped on Max's porch. It was the coolest part of the day, and the fresh air felt good, but I was aching. I struggled to get the t-shirt over my head and decided my clavicle was definitely broken. I went into the kitchen, took two aspirin, and put on coffee.

I looked in on Amanda. She was sleeping, but her breathing wasn't easy; it sounded like sandpaper drawn across a hardwood floor. There was blood on the sheets. It could have been from her wounds, but my guess is she was spitting it up during the night.

Leon was still asleep. Paz came out of her bedroom while I was having my first cup of joe. I ground some more beans and put on the Moka pot for her.

"Whose house is this?" she asked. "Yours?"

"*Casa Rabinowitz,*" I said. It just comes out. "This is the house of my friend, Max Rabinowitz. He is the public defender. He has the case of Sebastian Diaz."

She looked me up and down. "What are you going to do with us?"

That was a good question. "I need to take your daughter away from here. Maybe to San Francisco, where I live. She's not safe in Fresno. Either the law or the Lopezes are going to be after her. Leon goes with her."

"Do you love her?"

That was an easy one. "Yes. With all my heart. Maybe I should marry Amanda."

She ran her hands through her hair, and put her shoulders back. "To marry does not matter. I have lived with Carlos Lopez 12 years. We did not marry." The espresso was ready. I poured most of it for Paz, and a shot into my cup to warm it up.

"As I understand it, Carlos *was* married," I said.

234

"Yes. But his wife is dead. I also was married."

"You're a widow. Alejandro Zingaro is dead. I saw Carlos Lopez shoot him." She put up her hands, palms out, and turned her face away from me. "Murder him." I told her the story of how Max and I were in Aragón, and came to meet her husband and daughter, how we lived with them for six weeks, and how I came to love Amanda.

"She's ill, you know," I said. "I think she has tuberculosis."

"*Madre di dios!*" She crossed herself.

"Alejandro was dying from TB. But Lopez chilled him first." We finished our coffee. Paz looked at me and asked me how I felt. I told her I was better, and thanked her again for the first aid last night. "Doña Paz," I said, "is there anything you can tell me about the murder of Felipe Rios-Ortega? Anything you couldn't say the yesterday in the office?"

She thought. "No, nothing I can think of."

"Why do you look puzzled?"

She gave a little shrug. "I don't understand why you still doubt it was the lector. Clearly–"

"This is not Spain; you do not decide who is guilty with no evidence," I said. Then I told her I'd better go to Amanda. "She should be waking up. Let me see how she is." I went into Max's bedroom.

~ ~ ~

I sat on the side of the bed, holding Amanda's hand. She smiled and said she was feeling better already, but when I let go of the hand it dropped. I knew she'd put on no make up since I brought her here, but her lips were very red, and her cheeks had color, compared to the paleness of her arms. Her eyes were open but heavy lidded. Her brow was hot, feverish. What a lovely way to burn.

"You should have let me kill Carlos," she said.

"How could you have killed Don Carlos, *guapa?* You

couldn't even stand. I should have stopped you from killing Manuel."

"To kill Manuel was nothing, *fachero.*" She smiled, but she knew it was an old line now, and it died on her red lips. "Where is Mama?"

"You want me to get her?" I said.

"No. Francisco, Mama was sleeping with the enemy. For twelve years!"

I was taken aback at the passion with which she spoke these words. Was it the fever? "People change in wartime, guapa. Paz was trapped, powerless. She had nothing, no one. She was a prisoner. It was the only way to live on."

She seemed to drift off while I spoke, but never far. I heard the whirring of a car starter cranking; from the other direction, someone began to hammer on wood. The neighborhood was coming alive. I sat and held Amanda's hand.

Suddenly, "Don Carlos is evil," she said. "He's a fascist."

I couldn't argue with that. I didn't like him either. "It's not that I want you to like Don Carlos, *guapa.* Yes, he's evil," I said. "But he gave your mother food, shelter. Maybe he gave her more. She was a woman. No matter how bad Carlos was, she needed someone. What if you were alone, confined, and trying to survive? Wouldn't you accept him as a man?"

"Never!" She sat up halfway. "I would kill him before I let him touch me." But that was too much for her. She coughed hard, coughed up a glob of blood onto the sheet. She fell back against the pillow. There was a faint crackling noise. I put my ear down to her chest. It was Amanda's breathing. "Carlos killed Papa," she murmured.

"They told Paz you and your father were dead. Carlos took away your mother's past. She had nothing and no one to return to. She had to adjust. It's been eleven years."

"Too soon, too soon!" Her head lolled from side to side.

I dabbed her lips with a cool wet cloth. "You should let your mother back into your life. She needs you now, like you need her. Doesn't Leon need a grandmother?"

"Who is there?" said Amanda. "I hear something." Her brown eyes were wide, alarmed.

I heard nothing. "You're safe here. It's Max's house."

"Someone's out there."

"I'll go look." I went out the bedroom door and walked right into Max Rabinowitz. Amanda must have heard the Ferrari engine. "Max. You're back. I expected you yesterday."

"Yeah. Things didn't go well," he said. His clothes were wrinkled; he was unshaven and his hair was wild. "We have trouble on the Spring case. I was trying to give somebody the slip and I decided it would be safer to drive down here during the night." He looked around. Paz was in the kitchen. Leon was still asleep in the living room. Then he took a good look at me. "What's going on here, Frank?"

I was covered with bandages around the eye and forehead. You forget what you look like until someone sees you. "The Lopezes made a play to kill Amanda last night. She's safe now, in the bedroom." I hooked a gesture back over my shoulder at the door.

"In there? Amanda?" he asked, and brushed by me. When he saw Amanda, he fell to his knees by the side of the bed, took her hand and whispered her name.

She made him right away and breathed, "Maximiliano, Max."

"What's happened to you, my love?" But "Max" was all she had the strength for and in a few moments drifted off into a feverish sleep.

I was quiet a while as he stroked her hand and forehead, then: "C'mon, Max. She's had a tough time. Let's let her rest." Steering Max out into the kitchen, I introduced Paz as the woman I'd encountered at the Ramos place and explained she was Amanda's mother.

"We thought it was amazing to find Amanda here after eleven years, but now you too," he said. "What are the odds of that? I'll be damned."

We sat in the kitchen and I asked him what had kept him in San Francisco.

"Trouble, man. Don't worry, your girls are safe." He looked up around the kitchen. "You didn't drink all my Cardenal Mendoza did you?"

"What do you mean my girls are safe?" I said. "What's going on?"

"Let's nibble one and I'll tell you about it." Max fetched his brandy and poured three snifters while horrible thoughts about Brigid, Meaghan, and even Bimla swirled through my mind.

"See, I got a call Monday from Cuifen–" he began.

"Cuifen? She's dead, Max."

"No, she isn't. That dead girl in the Lotus House, she wasn't Cuifen."

"Who was she?" I said.

He shrugged. "I don't know. Just some tall Chinese whore."

That was a shocker. I shook my head to drive the thought away, and pursued what was important to me, "What about my Brigid and Meaghan?"

"They're with Cuifen. So is Bimla. I had to get them out of your place. I did it Tuesday night – took them over to Chinatown after dark in your Pontiac. They're all at Cuifen's. She lives with Jade Mama now."

"In a whore house?" I said.

"No, they're done with that," Max said. "Don't worry, I fixed Cuifen up with some money so she wouldn't have to turn tricks and set her up in a flat."

"When?"

"Last year."

"So you knew all along that Cuifen was alive?"

Max nodded.

"Why didn't you tell me?" I said. "I connected the murder of Fang to the murder of her sister Cuifen."

"I know, and I played along, to help you. Look, the killer *was* the chauffeur, Zhao, but he screwed up. He knew his victim worked there and was tall. But he chilled the wrong girl. All look same, you know?"

"All look same? But Zhao's a Chinaman."

"All look same to him, too." Max said. "Anyhow Jade Mama was suspicious when Zhao came in and asked for Cuifen. She sent another girl to entertain him. Cuifen was special, and Jade Mama always protected her."

"Why didn't you tell me? I thought I'd done some good detective work in the case."

"I wasn't working for you, Frank. My client is Joan Spring. I thought it might be better for Joan if you believed that had been Cuifen. Certainly it worked out for Cuifen, because she wasn't in the country legally."

"Oh, God. You lied to me, Max," I said. "I thought you were my friend." I finished my drink and took the bottle from Max. Paz sat quietly. She didn't know the Chinatown angle on this case.

"I am your friend. Cuifen called me and said Bimla and the girls were in danger. I drove to San Francisco and took them to Cuifen's. They'll be safe there. That's what friends do."

"Why did you go? Why didn't you tell me?"

"Honestly, Frank, I thought I should handle it. I knew about Cuifen; you didn't. When she told me about the danger, I knew what was going on. I knew what to do to protect the girls. If I'd sent you into it, there would have been some explaining to do first, and even then, when you got home, you would have been at risk from something you don't know anything about."

"Are you crazy Max? Brigid and Meaghan are my responsibility." I guess I was raising my voice. Anyhow, Leon woke up, and now he'd shuffled, sleepy-eyed, into the kitchen.

Max pointed at Leon and smiled, "And who's this young fellow?"

"That's Leon Zingaro, Amanda's son."

He looked crestfallen. "Her son? Well, a fine looking boy. So she's married now? I thought she was engaged to the lector. Now I'm confused."

"Amanda's not married, Max. The boy is Leon Swiver Zingaro."

Max puzzled at the name. I could see him trying to work it out, understanding the familiar names, remembering the rules for Spanish surnames. "I still don't get it."

"He's my son," I said.

"Yours?" He looked astonished.

"Well, that's what Amanda says."

"Yours?" he said again, his voice rising, astonishment turning to anger.

I nodded.

"Frank, that's low. You knew I was in love with Amanda."

"Yeah, well, I could see that. But I loved her too, you know. I never said anything to you. And then, we both thought she was dead. We saw her shot. So then I thought why bring it up? Max doesn't need to know about Amanda and me."

"I still love her," said Max. He drank his brandy and took the bottle back.

"I still love her, too," I said. I put a friendly arm on his shoulder but he pushed it away, hard.

"Frank, listen to me. I'm not mad at you for not

telling me you loved her. But you knew I loved her and you were screwing her anyhow." Max stood up, knocking his chair down, and headed for his bedroom.

I followed. "What are you doing?"

"I'm getting her out of here. Looks like you've taken over my house. Well, I'm taking my girl." He bent over the bed, and was sliding his arms under her.

"Max, no. She's too weak. She has TB." He straightened up and turned to me. "Like her father. Remember? Alejandro was dying of it."

"Yes, but the fascists got him first," he said. "I'll take her to the hospital. TB doesn't have to be a death sentence."

"I wouldn't take her to a local hospital now."

"Why not?"

"A lot's happened," I said. "Listen, Manuel is dead. Manuel Ramos. He used to be Manuel Lopez. Amanda killed him last night. The cops might be looking for her."

"What?"

"This is no time to do anything rash," I argued. "I think maybe if we keep her here, no one knows where she is—"

"She's not staying here," he said. "Not with you. I thought I could trust you. I was loyal. But you were shtupping the woman I loved."

""Only once," I said. "But *you* were in bed with Amanda for six weeks. When I first saw the boy, I thought he was yours."

"No!" he shouted, as loud as I've ever heard him. "No. I never even saw her those six weeks—"

"C'mon. Don't you think blind men do it?" He pasted me with a right cross. It was a solid punch, and I lost my footing. That was a dumb crack, and I guess I had it coming. I went down on the hardwood floor, and struggled getting up. I was losing count of how many beatings I'd taken the last 18 hours. By the time I got to my feet, Max had Amanda in his arms and was going out the bedroom door. I laid a hand on him and he shook me off. He started across the living room, and I reached him again. He stopped, turned, raised a leg and gave me a hard, downward kick to the kneecap. I went down again.

"You remember what I told you when we were in the barrel in Aragón?" he said. "About how I owed you? About my loyalty?"

I held my knee. I held my tongue, too.

"Forget it. It's over." I heard the screen door slam before I regained my feet.

"What is happening?" said Paz. "I don't understand this."

"Your daughter keeps getting snatched," I said. She finished her brandy, and took the bottle to pour another.

Leon saw Max take Amanda out the front door. "Mama, mama!" He got between me and the door and went out first. At the bottom of the porch he stopped in his tracks and fell back onto the steps. Max, wild-eyed, had whipped the Ferrari around, turfing his lawn close to the front step and Leon's knees and took off down the driveway with Amanda.

Chapter Thirty-Nine
King's Canyon

Max had told me the girls, Brigid and Meaghan, were with Cuifen. I had no idea where that was. Hell, I hadn't even known Cuifen was still alive twenty minutes ago. Max knew I wouldn't abandon them. What did that mean? It meant Max wanted me to follow.

But we both knew I couldn't catch him in his Ferrari. And I doubted Max would take Amanda to the Fresno hospital. Amanda was at risk in Fresno from the law, and possibly from Carlos Lopez. She was hot. And something had gone wrong in San Francisco that caused Max to wait until dark to return to Fresno. Maybe Max was hot, too. Therefore, he must have been headed to his cabin.

So I put on a clean shirt and set off at a steady but sane pace with Leon riding beside me. We left Paz at Max's. At first Leon and I talked. Even though he'd been tossed around, he had a good grasp of what had happened. He knew his mom had killed Manuel. I hoped his memories of Manuel and his perversions and my words with Max weren't as vivid. At least he seemed to know the good guys from the bad guys. I told him Max was one of the good guys.

"Then why did he take Mama?" Leon asked.

"Even the good guys make mistakes sometimes, Leo," I said. When we'd exhausted that topic, I told him a little about the car. "This is a two-door, which we call a coupe."

"Coupe," he said.

"It has a V-8 engine, very reliable, and something that was new back in '41 when it was made, a Hydramatic transmission."

"Hydramatic," he said, and smiled. "That's funny."

As we climbed into the Sierra foothills, I launched into the geography and fauna of California, complete with visual aids. Leon grew quiet and looked out the window.

I had no trouble spotting the turnoff to Max's, and I kept the Caddy moving uphill along the narrow dirt track until the big pine, cedar, and fir trees opened up to the sky and we saw the clearing in front of the cabin. The Ferrari was there. I blocked Max's car in, turning across the driveway between a pair of hundred-year-old trees.

I got out of the car and advanced a few steps toward the center of the yard. "Max," I called. Leon got out of the car, and walked over to me. "Max, this is Amanda's son. You can't take her away from her boy."

The glass crashed out of one of the windowpanes next to the door and the barrel of a rifle poked out, Max's old Springfield from the war. Somehow I'd had a feeling I was going to see it again. "He's your boy, Frank," he called out, in a desperate voice. "You take him. I want Amanda."

"Stay behind me, Leon," I said. He sidestepped behind my leg. "Amanda's sick," I called out. "How are you going to take care of her? You have no electric, no phone. You don't have much food left in there. What are you going to do, lock her in when you go shopping?"

"She nursed me for six weeks. The Zingaros had no electric, no phone. I'm going to care for her."

"She's got TB," I shouted.

"The mountain air will be good for her."

"I'm bringing the boy in, Max. Put down the rifle."

He fired a round in the dirt in front of my feet, and I heard the bolt-action as he slid the next bullet into place.

Leon came out from behind my leg and before I could stop him, he ran for the front door. He clambered onto the porch and the rife turned towards him, but then the barrel tilted up. Leon opened the door and ran in. A few seconds later, Max shuffled out, shoulders slumped, rifle dragging. He threw the gun down into the yard. "C'mon in. Oh, God, I've screwed up. I'm afraid she's dying. I've screwed everything up so bad."

I ran in – without bothering to stop and pick up the rifle.

~ ~ ~

It didn't take a thermometer to know Amanda was burning up. Her breathing was rough and uneven. "Where's the nearest doctor?" I said.

"I think there's one in Hume Lake. That's only about 20 miles back."

"Let's take her there."

And so we put Amanda across the back seat of my car again, with her head in Leon's lap. Max got in front with me. "Why are you bringing the rifle?" I said.

"We might need it. This isn't the only thing I screwed up. I'll tell you about it."

We found a doctor named Ridenour in Hume Lake. He was from San Diego, and semi-retired. He had a small clinic in back of the house where he could treat accident victims and even deliver babies. He didn't seem to care for Max or me, but he was all heart when it came to taking care of Amanda. He told us to wait outside and worked on her the better part of an hour.

We sat on a bench under the eaves at the clinic, a modern brick building. The sun was high in the sky now, and it was a beautiful summer day in the mountains. Max took out his notebook and wrote an address and phone number, and the name "Cuifen" across the page. He tore it out and handed it to me. "They're all at this address in Chinatown, and they're safe." He didn't smile.

I filled Max in on what had gone down in Fresno the last few days while he'd been away, told him how I'd interviewed Sebastian Diaz in the cooler, and was sure he was innocent. I told him about lunch with Amanda and what had happened to her since we left her lying in the

245

field in Aragón. I didn't mention my romantic interlude with Amanda but I did tell him about staking out the Ramos place and bringing Veronica up to his cabin. He looked like he was taking it in but gazed off into the middle distance, as if something else were on his mind. I looked at his fingers, which kept moving. The rifle was in the car about 30 feet away, and I think he wanted his hands on it.

I put him in the picture about the interviews with John Bullfinch and with Don Carlos and Paz. Then there was the snatch of Amanda by the Mexican thugs, and the rescue at the Ramos place with the death of Manuel and the mother and daughter reunion.

"What do you make of it all?" he asked. "Why'd they take her?"

"Seems to me Veronica Rios-Ortega killed her husband. Oh, yeah, I may have a witness who can put her at the Hotel Californian the night of the murder. She would have killed Amanda too, but Sebastian showed up before she could. She heard him at the door and decided to hide, probably in the armoire. Veronica rides her horses hard, and in this heat, there's a stench. It was lingering in the armoire even yesterday. Afterwards she needed to find out who the girl in the room had been. She put her dad's goons on the job, following me. I led them to Amanda." That was about it.

Then I asked Max what happened with Joan Spring. Max leaned forward with his elbows on his knees and hung his head down. He was trying to find the words.

But just then Doc Ridenour came outside, wiping his paws on a white towel. "We'd need to x-ray her lungs to be sure," the Doc said, "but I looked at a sample of the sputum under my microscope and started a culture, and pulmonary tuberculosis is what I'm treating her for. I gave her antibiotics. There's a drug, isoniazid, supposed to be pretty effective. I gave her a shot of that. This is a flare-up and a bad one, but she's young and I don't think she's in immediate danger. Course I'd have to see the lungs to be sure."

Max thanked him. "Anything she needs, Doc. I'll put her in a sanitarium if we have to."

"I don't know," said Ridenour. "There's something else wrong here. She's all marked up. Looks like somebody horsewhipped her or something. Who are you two?"

Max pulled out his wallet and showed his ID. "I'm an officer of the court in Fresno County," he said. That helped. "This woman was victim of a crime. She was abducted and beaten last night."

"By perverts," I said, for good measure.

Ridenour leaned back and looked me up and down. "Yes," he considered. "I guess you would know perverts if you saw them. I think I'll call the state police and see if they have anything to say in the matter."

Max said that was fine, and gave Doc Ridenour $50 and wrote our names down so he could check us out. Ridenour said that $50 would cover his time and medicine today, and he'd prepare a bill if there was any balance due. "She has to take it easy and rest for a couple months, and she has to keep taking the antibiotics," the doc said. "Otherwise the disease could take her at any time. You understand me?"

"Can I drive her to a hospital in San Francisco?" I said.

"You leave the woman rest here tonight. If there's no warrant out for you boys, and if she's stronger in the morning, I guess she could go with you. She can rest in Frisco as well as here."

~ ~ ~

Hume Lake had a hotel, a post office, a gas station, and several lake shore cottages. We had lunch at a café, one with a little blue sign by the door noting they had a public phone.

I ordered Leon a cheeseburger. They were building some sort of bible camp around the lake, and apparently it was a dry town. We all had Coca-Cola.

"Cheeseburger and Coke," said Leon when the food came. "This is a good lunch for American Independence Day." That was the first I realized today was the Fourth of July.

"Hey," I told Max. "We'll dip our bills to celebrate back at the cabin."

"I can't," he said.

"Why not?" I asked.

"I'm a lousy American," Max said.

"What the hell?" I looked at him.

"Not in front of the boy, Frank. I'll tell you later."

Having that mystery hanging over my head took some of the joy out of an otherwise red, white, and blue cheeseburger and a firecracker side of fries. I picked up a *Fresno Bee*. It was yesterday's, but I opened the sports section and while we ate I showed Leon how to read a box score. He was a bright kid. "What's RBI?" he asked. I explained that, and by the time we were done eating I was showing him the formula for calculating an earned run average. It reminded me of how I'd learned math when I was a boy.

~ ~ ~

After lunch, I drove us all back to the cabin so Max could get his car. I was eager to hear what was going on with Joan Spring and why Max was a lousy American, but we headed to Fresno in separate vehicles, so that had to wait. Max offered to drive Leon in his sports car, but all of a sudden I was feeling very protective. "There'll be other times for that, Max," I said. "I'll take him."

Leon and I left first. We were careening downhill, with the Caddy leaning and squealing tires, and had just passed the cutoff for Hume Lake, when there was the toot of an air horn and then a red blur shot by on the left disregarding the double yellow line. Max waved over his shoulder. I was glad the boy rode with me.

We arrived back in Fresno around four. There had been a parade, but it was all over before the heat of the afternoon, though folks were still out relaxing, eating on the streets, and finding spots to view the evening's fireworks. We drove out to Max's house. I stopped at a red light near the Tower Theater, and heard the air horn again. Max pulled up alongside me. My window was down so I smiled and said, "What's up?"

"Just heading home," he said. "I went by the office to check messages, and pick up some files." The light turned green and he chirped his tires and pulled away ahead of me.

Max's bungalow was nearby. When we turned onto East Pine, I saw the Ferrari already in the driveway. It appeared Max was still in the driver's seat. I pulled in behind him. The front door opened and Paz came out, with an anxious look on her face.

"I thought I heard a shot," she said to me.

"Firecrackers," I guessed. "It's the fourth of July…" but then I started to worry. I stepped towards Max. "Hey, man. You need to get your timing checked or something?" I looked in on him and my guts turned to water. Max's head was back at an ugly angle, and a red stain was spreading on the black leather seat.

I rushed over to him from the driver's side. He was still alive, and the blood wasn't pulsing like arterial blood. I put my arms under his shoulders and started to lift him out, but I didn't like the way his head flopped so I let him back down. "Call for an ambulance, Paz. Call the police." She hurried back into the house. I had carried Max the better part of two days across Aragón, and now I couldn't lift him 30 feet to his front door.

Chapter Forty
A Deal with the Devil

The gate at the Ramos place was closed the next morning. At 7:30, I swung into the driveway and rammed it with the front end of the Caddy at about 20 miles per hour. I'd seen them do that in movies, but didn't know if it would work. But twenty mph and 4000 pounds of Detroit iron did the trick. The gate ripped out of its anchor points. I spun my tires up the gravel drive, then cut the wheel and pulled the handbrake as I neared the front steps. I was out of the car and up the steps before I realized I didn't have a battering ram for the front door.

But Paz was with me, and she had the key. "You should calm down," she said.

"You're not talking to your daughter," I said. "Amanda wants him dead. I only want justice." I may have denied it, but I'd been hot under the collar since Max had been shot. We'd had the police the rest of the evening until well after midnight. Then Paz talked me into a few hours rest.

"Carlito," Paz called in the foyer. There were heavy footsteps on the stairs, accompanied by the clicking of a dog's toenails on hardwood, and Don Carlos, dressed in black, appeared on the right side staircase, with Primo, on his leash. He looked like he wanted to embrace Paz, but he saw me and held off.

"The *Civiles* were here all day yesterday," he said to me.

"You'll get no sympathy from me. I told them they ought to come back and see you today about Max," I said.

"I do not know this 'Max,'" said Carlos.

"Rabinowitz. He was defending Sebastian Diaz. Now he's been shot. What did you tell the police?" I said.

"What could I tell them?" he shrugged. "My only son was dead in the barn, pinned to a beam with my epee. My chauffeur was dead on the lawn, his throat ripped out. The gates were open."

"So, ... what did you tell the police?" I repeated.

"I told them that I had been upstairs in bed, that I had taken sleeping powders. I told them to figure it out. I knew nothing. I told them I expected justice for Manuel. Did you kill my son?"

That was pretty good. "No. But I am here to talk to you about justice," I said. "Paz, can you take your dog?"

"Of course you say no–" said Carlos.

"It's true, Carlito. I saw it," said Paz.

Carlos held the leash tightly, then looked at her. "I am glad you're back, Paz. I was worried." He held out the wrist strap of the leash. The mastiff went to the woman with a soft yelp of happiness. "Come," Don Carlos Lopez said to me. He stepped past me and walked into the north wing. I followed him to his office.

He opened the door and poured two brandies – Carlos I. "The heat in Fresno is terrible, señor. This brandy, it evaporates. The 'angel's share,' we called it in Spain. All I know is, the level is down considerably since I was in my office last."

"It's difficult to get trustworthy servants in Fresno, Señor Lopez." He smiled at that, stepped behind his desk and sat in his high back, tufted leather chair with nail heads. Along one wall of the study was a matching leather couch, and I sat on that. The windows behind Lopez opened to the west, and it was dark, almost cool at this early hour. One epee hung alone on the wall over my head. There was a door in the opposite wall. If I remembered correctly, that connected to the library.

"You look like you've had a rough time since I saw you last, Mr. Swiver. Maybe the climate here doesn't agree with you. Why don't you go back to San Francisco?"

I rubbed my busted clavicle and turned my black eye into the light so he could get a good look. "Nothing would please me more." We spoke to each other in Spanish. "I just have some unfinished business with you, then I'll go."

"What do you want, Mr. Swiver?"

"I want the killing to stop now."

He looked puzzled, but said. "What do you offer?"

"Your life, Don Carlos," I said.

"Is it yours to offer?"

"The girl I took out of here last night – the other night – she is the daughter of Alejandro Zingaro. Manuel knew that; I don't know if you knew, but it doesn't matter now. She wants vengeance for her father. Blood vengeance. You killed Zingaro in cold blood eleven years ago. You don't deserve protection, but I can protect you from his daughter."

"Alejandro Zingaro," he reflected. "I recall the man. It was war–"

"It was murder, and you know it," I said. "You took his wife."

He gave a slight shrug. "There were many murders, on both sides. My wife..."

"Let's talk about justice for this one murder, Señor Lopez."

"And there was another murder last night," he said, voice rising. "My son. Don't you think I want justice for that murder?"

"That was self-defense. I saw it. I would have saved Manuel's life," I said. "You can believe that or not. But the fact is, I would have prevented it if I could. Your son was sick. How many poor girls did he torture in that barn? Amanda Zingaro was special to him, but she wasn't the first. You knew what he was doing. You let him take women from the factory for his pleasure, you and your son-in-law Felipe enabled it. Manuel couldn't control himself and you didn't control him. So much for your fascist discipline." Carlos finished his brandy in silence, got up and poured himself another. He returned behind the desk with the bottle and pushed it over to my end. I took the stopper in my teeth and splashed some more in my glass.

"I'm also interested in justice for Sebastian Diaz," I told him.

"Yes, he killed my son-in-law."

"No, it wasn't Diaz. I know who killed Felipe Rios-Ortega. Do you want her to hang for it?"

Lopez switched to English. "Pardon, Senor Swiver. Your Spanish is good. Your accent is American, but you are fluent. However, you said, '*ella*.' That is feminine. Normally, I would not deign to correct you on such a point, but we must be precise."

I answered in English. "I was being precise, Lopez. I *know* who killed Felipe."

We drank our brandy. "On the night of the murder," I continued, "your daughter Veronica went to the Hotel Californian–" There was a glass fronted bookcase along the far wall. I saw something in it and walked over for a closer look.

"Ridiculous! How could she? It must be 15 kilometers into the city, to the hotel. My chauffeur did not take her. She cannot drive an automobile herself." I opened the bookcase and took out a tooled walnut box. I flipped the lid up. There was one large knife or small sword inside, a fine handmade Spanish *espada*. There were places in the box for two. I closed the lid and sat back down with the box in my lap.

"Your driver can no longer testify, Señor Lopez, but I have witnesses. I have a man who saw her ride her horse into the lobby of the hotel. And I have the woman who was underneath your son-in-law when he was killed. She will testify that she saw Veronica."

He put a fist on his desk but kept his voice controlled. "My daughter, Veronica – lucky for you she's still in bed. She said yesterday if she sees you again she will kill you. Apparently she spent a very uncomfortable night Wednesday."

"Girls are spoiled these days," I said. "Reminds me of the story of the Princess and the Pea. Well, she'll be a lot less comfortable in Tehachapi, even if they don't send her to the gas chamber."

He finished his second brandy. "And what do you want me to do?"

I told Lopez he was going to have to answer to murder charges, and since it wasn't practical to bring him to justice for killing Zingaro, I wanted him to take the fall for killing Rios-Ortega. "Plus," I said, "Diaz is innocent. The police will let him go if they have someone else."

"That is absurd," he said. "Why would I kill my son-in-law?"

"Family honor. He was cheating on your daughter. Perhaps under normal circumstances your son would have avenged his sister. But your son was weak, ill. You stepped in and did what the family had to do. You used your *espada,* the one missing from this matched set." I turned the box to face him and opened the lid. "It's the one found in Felipe's back."

I told him he and his men were to make no more attempts on the lives of Amanda Zingaro or Max Rabinowitz. In exchange for his confession, and his word to lay off my friends, I would not use my evidence to prosecute the real killer. I had brought a written statement for him, a confession.

"What if I do not sign? What if I do not confess?"

"Then you lose your daughter. I'll bet we can get the death penalty. You've already lost your son. And I'll turn Amanda Zingaro loose." I paused and took out a cigarette to give him time to reflect. "Your daughter couldn't sleep the other night because despite Primo, despite your Mexican guards, someone got into your house. It could happen again. I wonder how Amanda would kill you, Don Carlos? A shot in the back? Maybe she wants to kill you slowly–"

"All right. I will do it. For Veronica." He took out a fountain pen and scratched his name across the signature line at the bottom. "What of Paz?"

"I leave her with you," I said. "She's a good woman, and resourceful. Perhaps she will support you in your trials. But make no mistake, she will not support you if any harm comes to her only child, Amanda Zingaro."

"No. I will do as you ask," he said, and handed me the signed paper. "There is one thing. I do not know this Max Rabinowitz."

"He is the man you had shot yesterday in his driveway. My friend. The public defender."

Lopez looked blank. "I had no one shot. And I don't know the man."

"He's lying in the hospital right now, Lopez. But you didn't finish him. If he had died, I wouldn't have come in here talking."

Chapter Forty-One
Revolving Doors

Well, I guess I'd about worn out my welcome in Fresno. The cops compared notes and realized the guy they'd found sitting in the dirt at the Diaz place after a fight was the same guy they talked to at Max's when he was shot, and they began to keep an eye on me. An unmarked car sat out on Pine for a few days and tailed me to the city limits when I visited Amanda in Hume Lake. It was time to go.

Paz was back with Carlos Lopez, and Amanda was safe in Hume Lake. She rested in the clinic there the next two weeks. The mountain air (and the doc's drugs) did her a world of good.

Max was in Fresno's Community Regional Medical Center. He was lucky on that score. They had some first-rate trauma doctors. The bullet had been fired from his right side, the one with the eye patch. Although it was at close range – someone walked up to the passenger side of his car, I'm guessing – Max probably never saw the shooter. The slug entered high in his chest, below the neck and went into the big part of the right clavicle at its medial end, the sternoclavicular joint, or in other words where the collarbone's connected to the breast bone. These two bones cracked, but stopped the bullet before it damaged any organs. The impact of the shot snapped Max's head back at a bad angle. He may have hit his head or neck on the hard nearby edge of the convertible's body shell when he was thrown back. That may have caused his paralysis. The docs thought some nerves were pinched or traumatized. They thought the paralysis would be temporary. For now though, he was on a ventilator and couldn't speak, so I still had not found out from him what we were up against in San Francisco.

The day after I'd visited Lopez, I set out early and drove to San Francisco with Leon.

I found Cuifen's apartment, the upper rear of a three-story brick building on the edge of Chinatown. The New China Trading Company occupied the commercial space on the ground floor. It wasn't clear to me looking in the window what they traded.

There were two Chinese lads in the back of New China Trading, watching the entrance to the residences. They weren't as big as the Mexicans, Gordito and the late driver, but they looked menacing enough to me. I asked them to call Bimla down. She vouched for me; she was even happy to see me, and I felt bad, thinking about throwing her over for Amanda. She didn't deserve it. But what could I do? I was in love again.

I saw the girls. They were fine under Bimla's care, and it didn't matter to them they were in Chinatown, in fact I think they liked having Cuifen and Jade Mama around to dote on them. Security was good what with the thugs in the lobby, and Meaghan and Brigid were enjoying their summer. So I told them it was still too dangerous to go home, and that I'd pick them up in a couple weeks.

"We could go with you," said Brigid.

"To Fresno?" said Meaghan. "I'd rather hide out in Chinatown."

It was easy to let Meaghan have her way. The hard part was telling Bimla to play dumb and stay put when I returned. I promised to explain later.

Leon and I headed back to Fresno. "Your daughters are cute," he said. "How am I related to them?"

"The dark-haired one is your half sister."

"So the young one is ... available?" he asked.

He was sounding more and more like my kid.

~ ~ ~

After two weeks, as much for my convenience as

anything else, I brought Amanda down from Hume Lake to Max's place in town. I didn't know who'd shot Max, and I wasn't sure if we were safe at his house, but it was time to take her out of Doc Ridenour's clinic, and I felt I could protect Amanda better in Fresno than up in a rustic cabin with no phone. What if she had another TB flare-up?

I arranged an ambulance ride up to San Francisco for Max. On July 19, Carlos Lopez went in and confessed to the Fresno police that he'd bumped off Felipe Rios-Ortega. July 20, Amanda, Leon, and I drove to the jail to pick up Sebastian Diaz and take him home. We were sitting in the car in the shade opposite the hoosegow, and who should we see climb out of a taxi but Paz.

"I do not know what to think of that woman, Francisco," said Amanda, "but I don't think I like her."

"She is your mother, *guapa*," I said.

" Did she mourn my father? While he lay dying in our yard, she was lying in his killer's bed. How can I call her mother? I call her *puta*." She had her hand on the car door handle.

I reached across and grabbed her wrist. "It was civil war. There was a breakdown of society. Your mother had to do certain things that she wouldn't have done in peacetime. She was trying to stay alive. Remember, Don Carlos abducted her." Even in the shade it was getting hot and stuffy in the car.

"Manuel abducted me," said Amanda. "Did I give in? No, I thought of my father, lying dead, and I fought. I thought of my love for you and I protected my virtue, with a sword."

"And now the killing must stop, *guapa*." I held her with fierce eyes. "I mean it. Let heaven judge Paz."

"She is not even a republican anymore. She is a fascist, like the pig Carlos Lopez." Amanda broke eye contact, pulled out of my grip and opened the door.

"*Madre!*" she yelled, stepping out onto the sidewalk.

Paz turned, put a hand up to shade her eyes from the sun eyes and stepped toward Amanda. "Amanda, child," she said. "You are well again? I am so happy to see you—"

"Child! I wish I were not your child. You have no guilt," said Amanda, "no shame." She advanced on her mother. Leon and I were out of the car on the sidewalk behind Amanda.

Paz stopped where she stood, on the edge of the shade. "What have I done to deserve this? For what should I be guilty or ashamed? I have not murdered anyone." She wrung her hands.

"Mama, please," said Leon to Amanda. "Let's wait for Señor Diaz to come out. We'll sit in the car. It's bad for you to rage like this."

At that moment Carlos Lopez walked out through the main door into the sunshine, alongside a short man with a briefcase. Lopez stopped and took sunglasses out of his pocket and put them on. Paz had her back to him. Amanda saw him and pointed over Paz's shoulder, "Look, there he is! There is the murderer."

I put my hands on her shoulders. Leon wrapped his arms around his mother's waist. Paz turned around. "Carlito," she said, then to us, "Pardon me, I must go to him. He is out on bail. Amanda, I am truly happy to see you. A month ago, I didn't even know you were alive." Amanda squirmed and twisted, but Leon held tight. She came up off her feet, but she was so light that Leon held her and staggered back into me.

I braced him. "Go, now, Paz," I said. "We will take care of Amanda." Paz turned and walked to Lopez.

"No! He killed my father," Amanda shouted. "Don't go to his bed. He killed your husband." She began to cry.

I turned her back toward the car. "Come on, Amanda. Come and sit. Let them get out of here. Enough blood."

"Oh, Francisco," she said. "It's not what you think. It's my father. I loved him so much. He was a man."

Don Carlos stood in the Fresno sunshine, uncowed and unbeaten, a free man, at least for the time being. And with money and lawyers, maybe he'd stay that way. Who cared about Felipe Rios-Ortega now? Don Carlos pulled himself to his full height and gave a slight bow in our direction, as if to say, "I have done as you requested." He came up with a devious grin across his face. I pointed at him and then dragged my index finger across my throat. Paz hailed another hack and they walked to it, Carlos holding up his trousers. They'd taken his belt.

Sebastian Diaz was next to come through the revolving doors of justice. Don Carlos was out on bond; Diaz was now a free man, all charges dropped. I shook his hand, and he embraced me. "Thank you, thank you, señor, for all you have done, not only for me but also for Pilar."

"Chico, you may as well know, my name is not Pilar Avila," Amanda said.

"You two have some catching up to do," I said. "Come on." Leon and I sat up front and they got in the back. I drove them to the bungalow courts on Elm, the Diaz home. Amanda had not been there since the abduction. I told her to go in and say her goodbyes to Señora Diaz and Sebastian, but encouraged her to be quick. "I won't breathe easy until I get you out of town. Who knows what else Carlos Lopez told the police?"

They went in and I stood outside and smoked a Camel. It was probably warmer indoors. After a little bit Leon came out with his ball and glove, and we played catch.

Chapter Forty-Two
Cyrgryzs

Back in San Francisco I picked up the girls in Chinatown, while Amanda waited in the car. I said an awkward farewell to Bimla, who seemed to take it in stride. That only made me feel more awkward. Amanda and Leon moved in with Brigid, Meaghan and me.

At first, Max still had a ventilator in and couldn't talk, so I wasn't able to question him about the shooting. Some days I dropped Amanda at his hospital room to keep him company. Maybe I was mastering my jealousy. I felt confident in my love for Amanda and hers for me. On the other hand, Max *was* paralyzed.

I didn't know what was going on with Joan Spring and the trouble Max had alluded to with her case. So one of those times when Amanda sat with Max at San Francisco General, I went to see Joan Spring at County Jail #1 on Washington Street. Most of the prisoners were men; there were fewer than two dozen women locked up. One or two were murderesses. Others were narcotics users, thieves, pickpockets, and parole violators. I met Joan Spring in a private visiting room, cooler, but otherwise not much different from the green room where I'd talked to Sebastian Diaz in the clink in Fresno.

It had been more than six months since I'd seen her. Her hair was cut shorter, but was still straight, black and shining. She wore a light blue denim shirt, not silks, a denim skirt and canvas shoes with soft soles. She had no lipstick on, but her lips were a rich black cherry, her skin a soft pure vanilla. Her eyebrows and eyelashes were not made up, but her eyes were still violet and when they locked on me, I couldn't look away. Without her makeup, and in the cold harsh light of the prison, I judged her age to be about 35. Then I remembered she was a monkey in the Chinese zodiac, so she'd been born in 1908. She was 41, four years older than me. Even without makeup and in the cold harsh light of the jail, she looked younger than that. She sat. I stood across a table from her.

"Hello, Joan. You're looking well."

"Hello, detective. Thank you. I am as well as can be expected."

"I suppose you're wondering why I'm here," I said.

She looked as if nothing could interest her less. "No, I wonder why I'm here," she said.

"My friend, attorney Maximilian Rabinowitz was here to see you at the beginning of this month." I started to walk around the table, and I glanced down the front of the blue denim shirt. Did they not issue undergarments to women in San Francisco jails?

"Earlier this month? Yes, I guess it was – July. What has he been doing since then? Where is he?"

"He's been shot," I said.

"Oh dear," she said. "Where?"

"Fresno. What did you two talk about when he was here?" I was surprised at the effect her eyes had on me, after all this time.

"My defense, of course."

"Anything new on that?" I said.

"No, not really," she answered.

"Anything you can tell me that might help me understand why Max was shot?"

She seemed to roll it over in her mind. "No, nothing. I can't imagine. Did he have any enemies?" She licked her full lips. There was that tug again on the line from the violet eyes.

"Joan," I said, "does the name Cyrgryzs mean anything to you?"

"Cyrgryzs?" The violet eyes blinked. I broke away from their pull and walked across the room. "No. It is not a Chinese name." she said.

"Think. Cornelius was supposed to see Cyrgryzs the night he died."

"How do you know?" Joan said.

I didn't answer that. I couldn't say I walked in, found Connie dead, and looked in his appointment book.

"You're probably going to walk out of here, you know," I began, instead. "Your husband was shot while you were on ice. That reduces the credibility of the attempted murder charge against you. Besides, you're not talking, and the only evidence against you is circumstantial. No one was there when you bopped Fang. The government could try to get your driver, Zhao, to testify, but you can't compel him to incriminate himself, and he probably wouldn't give evidence against you."

"They might offer him life in prison instead of the death penalty to say I was behind Cuifen's murder."

"They might," I said. "Would that turn him?"

She drew the corners of her mouth up into a mirthless smile. "Many Chinese of Zhao's age consider loyalty a great virtue."

"And when you walk out, you get all of Connie's money."

"I hope I can walk out soon," she said.

"I'm just asking you to help me," I said. "He's my friend, your lawyer... Who shot Max?"

"I'm sure I don't know."

"I'll bet you know Cyrgryzs."

"How badly was Mr. Rabinowitz hurt?" she said. "Is he still alive?"

I didn't answer. I felt her eyes probing me.

"Well, ask Mr. Rabinowitz about Cyrgryzs," she said.

And then I remembered where I'd heard that name. It was the morning after I'd met Joan Spring. Max had been smiling and said to me, "I just saved Louie Cyrgryzs from the electric chair." And I had made some wisecrack.

I slapped my forehead. "Of course! Thanks, Joan. You want to tell me anything else?"

"I've said enough."

"See you on the outside, kitten." I winked.

Chapter Forty-Three
The Honey Trap

Amanda Zingaro's presence seemed to do Max a world of good. Although he wore a stiff neck brace, the bed was cranked up, and Max was upright. More important his breathing apparatus was out and he was talking again. His voice was weak, but it was clear and audible. I pulled a chair up close to the bed, next to Amanda.

Max occupied a private room. Even so, it was nothing fancy. The walls were a regulation hospital green. He had a jug of water on his nightstand, a radio, a brown metal tray table positioned on an arm over his bed, and a window with a view to the west. The sun was beginning to shine in from the top corner of the window when I arrived. "Feeling better?" I asked.

He nodded. "Still hurts to talk," he said.

"Max had some soup today. Chicken," said Amanda.

"Not like Ma used to make it." He smiled a little, but it belied the weakness in his voice.

"That's OK," I said. "Drink it. It'll help you get your strength back."

"Yes, mother," he said.

"Max, I'm sorry it hurts, but it's time to talk," I said. "I need to know what's going on with Joan Spring, and why you returned to Fresno after dark."

He shrugged with his eyebrows. "Maybe not, Frank. We're not in Fresno anymore. Maybe it no longer matters."

"Who shot you?" I said.

"Blind side. I couldn't see him."

"It was Cyrgryzs," I said.

It was quiet. Max closed his eye, and I thought maybe I was losing him. Amanda reached out and took his right

267

hand, and rubbed her fingers on it from the wrist across the knuckles. His eye fluttered.

"You don't know that," said Max.

"Cyrgryzs chilled Connie Spring," I said. I took out the small lined notebook I'd picked up from the house the night I'd found the body. "Spring had an appointment book. It's like the one you were using in Fresno, you know." Max's eye widened as I held it out. Then I opened it to the last entries.

"*Friday, June 28,*" I read, "*Frank Swiver – 7:00 p.m., home. Cyrgryzs – 7:30.* Only thing is, Cyrgryzs must have showed up early. Maybe about 6:50."

Max closed his eye again, and looked tired.

"Tell me about Cyrgryzs."

He turned toward Amanda. "Take a walk, honey. It's better you don't know about this."

Amanda rose, kissed Max on the forehead, and said to me, "I'll go to the cafeteria for a smoke, OK Francisco?" I nodded, and she picked up Max's sack of Bull Durham off the night table.

When she walked out I said to Max, "All right – Cyrgryzs. Let's have it."

"Physicist from Stanford. Accused of passing secrets to the Red Chinese. I defended him. Government didn't have a case."

"What's his connection with the Springs?" I said.

Max squeezed his eye shut as if in pain, and lowered his chin a fraction toward his chest. Then he slid down an inch in bed, let his head sink back against the pillow, and opened his eye again. "The secrets were passing through the Lotus House. Cyrgryzs to Princess Cuifen, Cuifen to her sister, Comrade Joan."

"Joan Spring's a spy?"

Max tried to nod but really couldn't with the neck brace. "Maoist agent," he said.

"Who knew?"

"I'm tired Frank. Can't talk now."

"We need to get it over with, Max," I insisted. "Who knew?"

"I did," said Max. "It's no coincidence I let myself be drawn into the Spring case with you. Joan Spring knew my politics. When Cyrgryzs was picked up by the feds, Joan came to me, hired me to defend him. She was paying the bills all along."

"Is that when you started going to the Lotus House?"

"Yes. Cyrgryzs talked about the place, talked about Cuifen. Joan Spring comped me. Anyhow, when you told me you were working for Joan, I invited myself into the case to keep an eye on things. I drove you out to Spring's place in St. Francis Wood. And I stayed close to you, trying to shield Comrade Joan."

"She was in deep," I said.

"Too deep," Max agreed. "She didn't think the suicide angle would hold up. She wanted a private dick. If I had known, I would have told her to just let it go. Her bad luck she got you."

"Was it luck?"

"Well, Overby and Snoots don't think you're the brightest guy. They didn't want any trouble with Cornelius Spring and thought you'd be safe. They just don't understand how relentless you are, how you'll work a case to death. That's what makes you so good."

It was best to take that as a compliment. I lit one of my Pall Malls and offered Max one. He shook his head. "I could see you were attracted to Joan," he said. "I suggested she ... uh ... get to know you a little better. I thought she might be able to use her feminine wiles to throw you off the scent. You have your weaknesses, Frank."

"Max, I thought you were my best friend. I saved your life. How could you screw with me like that?"

" You got no beef. You did the screwing. I'm the one's

been shot." He was silent for a moment. "Anyhow, I didn't know it then, but you have Amanda, so we're even."

Were we even? The man I'd trusted all these years, the man I'd thought was like a brother to me – now I realized he was a liar. I'd always accepted his communist politics. I'm pretty far left myself. Communist Party USA was one thing. They were an influential force for democratic rights for the working man, for integration, the same rights I supported even though I'd never joined the party. But Max was not only a card-carrying commie, now he was working for a Red Chinese agent, a foreign spy. And now, because of Amanda, I could no longer count on Max as a friend.

"What about Cornelius Spring?" I said. "What did he know?"

Max bit his upper lip. "I'm not sure the extent of it all. I think Joan had been the lover of someone high up in the party – someone close to Mao in the '30s. They selected her. Ever hear of a honey trap?"

"Like in Winnie-the-Pooh?"

"I think that's 'honey jar,'" said Max. "Joan was a honey trap in China after the war. She was bait for Cornelius Spring. When he went to Nanking in '46, he got stuck in the trap. Connie was such a greedy bastard, he would have collaborated with the reds just to get the money in his bank, but they wanted to have something on him for insurance. What better way? So Connie got a wife and became the secret U.S. banker to Mao Tse-Tung and the Chinese commies."

"And Mao and the reds gained a running capitalist dog to do their banking, placed an agent in the U.S. in a long-term relationship, and opened a line of communications through the Lotus House," I said.

"That's about the size of it, yeah."

I stood up and walked to the window, and looked out

to the west. I could see the tower of the Mission Dolores Basilica.

"Frank."

It was barely a whisper. I went back to the bed and sat down. "I'm here." I leaned in.

"Gimme some water," he said. I filled his glass and put a straw in it, held it for him while he drank.

"When Comrade Joan went in stir, she gave me power of attorney for the red gold in Connie's bank," he began again. "Cyrgryzs needed money. I wrote him a small check, but I didn't like doing business with him. I was starting to regret my involvement with Joan. But you can't quit these things so easily. I decided to get out of town – get away from Cyrgryzs. I closed down my practice. Went to Fresno."

"Then the next time Cyrgryzs needed dough, he went to Connie Spring," I theorized.

"Right. Maybe Connie didn't come across," Max said. "Or maybe Joan drew a line through Connie's name with a pencil."

"And that was the end for him. What happened with my girls? Cyrgryzs again?"

Max nodded. His voice was getting weaker. "He spotted Bimla downtown, recognized her. She made him too, and bolted. But he followed her to your place. She locked the house up and called Cuifen on the phone. It's a good house. O'Callaghan, being an old gangster, built a fortress. Cyrgryzs couldn't bust in."

I tried to take some of the burden of speech off him. "Cuifen called you, you drove up."

He nodded. "I saw Cyrgryzs lurking across the street in the park, waiting for them to come out."

"Bimla let you in, and after dark you drove the three of them to Chinatown." He nodded again. "Why did you wait until dark the next night to drive back to Fresno?"

"I went to the jail to see Comrade Joan the second

day up here. I wanted her to call off Cyrgryzs. I know I'm up to my neck in this, but your girls shouldn't be. I thought I still had some influence over Joan, and some power with my control of her bank account. But she plays a ruthless game. When I left her, Cyrgryzs spotted me on the street and tailed me. I thought my best chance of losing him would be to travel after dark. And drive fast."

"Where do I find him?" I said.

"Cyrgryzs?" Max said. "I don't know, man. My advice, don't. Don't try. Don't get involved."

"But we are involved, Max."

Max didn't say anything. He was fading on me. I let him fade.

Chapter Forty-Four
Low Tide, July 30

I went back to the jail to see Joan Spring around eleven one morning at the end of July. She looked about the same; beautiful lush black hair, violet eyes, creamy skin, wine-dark lips, blue denim workshirt, unbuttoned to mid-bosom, and it was chilly in the jail. They don't call it the cooler for nothing.

She hadn't had any makeup on the first time I'd seen her. I couldn't imagine what all she used, but I did buy her a bottle of perfume, Shalimar. I don't know if it was what she'd been wearing when we had our rendezvous at the Clift Hotel last December, but it was close.

"For me?" she said.

"I thought it might make you more comfortable," I said.

"Shalimar is my scent. Thank you, detective."

"Frank."

"You never cease to surprise me, Frank," she said.

"Tell me where I can find Cyrgryzs, Joan."

"What did attorney Rabinowitz tell you?"

"He doesn't know anything. But I do." I told her what I knew about Cyrgryzs, the killing spree, and the spy ring.

"An interesting story, detective. Maybe you should write it up for the pulps. Evil Chinese agent, yellow peril ... exciting stuff, umm?" She asked me for a smoke. I gave her a Pall Mall. She steadied my hand while I lit her up and when her fingers touched me again, an electric charge shot up my wrist.

"Tell me where to find Cyrgryzs," I repeated.

"Why should I?" she said.

"I'll tell you what, Joan. You think you're walking out of here soon. You're going to get a pass on the murder and attempted murder charges. Well, I think I have enough on you to send you to the chair on a federal espionage rap. I have proof – Chairman Mao's checking account records at the WellSpring Bank, with your name on them – and witnesses. Even if they don't fry you, you'll never see the light of day. But I'm willing to zip my lip, for old times' sake, kitten – if you give me Cyrgryzs."

"If you used those bank records, what would happen to your friend, Max?"

"He's only power-of-attorney. He doesn't know what he's onto."

"Mr. Rabinowitz is a good cadre. All right, I'll give you Cyrgryzs, for old times' sake, Frank. And in exchange for your promise to forget about espionage. But Rabinowitz knows more than you think, and if you put me on trial, I'll see that Max takes the fall, not me." She blew a cloud of smoke at me. "What is today's date, detective? Prison life is such a dull routine. All the days run together."

I looked at my watch. It wasn't a calendar watch, but what did she know? "It's Tuesday, July 30," I said.

"Well, it may be too stop him then, but I agreed to tell you. Cyrgryzs will be sailing through the Golden Gate soon."

"What?"

"Connie gave him money, but Cyrgryzs killed the poor fool anyhow. We arranged passage on a freighter sailing for Macao July 30 on the tide. I don't have the tide tables, but if you haven't missed him already, I'm sure he'll be sailing before you can do anything about it. Louie Cyrgryzs will soon be an honored guest of the People's Republic of China, and a physics professor at the University of Peking."

I still had hope. There were two high tides each day – and at least a fifty-fifty chance the ship was sailing on the evening tide. I might have six hours, maybe even more. "Button up, kitten," I said, and pointed a finger at her breasts. "You don't want to catch a chest cold."

~ ~ ~

All good so far, but I'd still have to move fast to nab Cyrgryzs. I picked up a morning paper outside the jail and turned to weather. High tide this afternoon was at 3:31. I'm no seaman, but I figured most captains, would weigh anchor in the three hours or so after that. Then I turned to the shipping news. Shipping had dropped off in the years since the war. In San Francisco, the freighter *Mar Branco*, leaving from Pier 35 that evening – evening tide! Yes! – was the only ship sailing today that listed Macao as a port of call. Unless our rogue physicist was leaving from Oakland, the *Mar Branco* had to be my meat. I called the FBI.

"There's a Red Chinese spy sailing tonight on the *Mar Branco*," I told them.

"Who's calling?"

"This is Frank Swiver speaking. I'm a private sleuth."

"One moment." It was more like three or four.

"Mr. Swiver, we have your file here. You fought for the reds in Spain in '37 and '38. Then you told your draft board in 1942 that you were a conscientious objector. Is that correct?"

"That's the other Frank Swiver," I said. "I'm Francis X. Swiver, the right-wing patriot and hawk."

"What's the name of this alleged commie spy?" said the agent.

"Louie Cyrgryzs."

"Spell that for me."

"I can't," I said. "He's the Stanford physicist."

"I remember that case," said the G-man.

"Can you pick him up? He's defecting, trying to get away to China."

"He was found not guilty at his trial. On what grounds could we detain him?"

I tried to give him the short version. I mentioned Joan Spring and the Lotus House, but I kept Max out of it. I realized

I didn't have much – enough to bluff Joan, maybe, but no hard evidence, no proof connecting Cyrgryzs to any of it, except maybe a notation of an appointment in a dead man's notebook.

"If I go to my chief with that, Mr. Swiver, he'd laugh at me."

"Mr. Hoover's not going to laugh about a red Chinese agent," I told him.

"Mr. Hoover's 3,000 miles away, Mr. Swiver. Thanks for calling." The line went dead.

I went back to my office on Post Street, took off my hat and draped my jacket over the chair. I opened a window, and lit up a Pall Mall for myself. I poured a large glass of Sebastiani Casa de Sonoma, an unusual red but a good one. Espionage was a federal crime, but I couldn't interest the FBI. I didn't have any credibility with them. Who could I sell it to?

I went back to my desk, got a dial tone, and called Lieutenant Overby.

"Bureau of Inspectors, Overby speaking."

"Lieutenant, it's good to hear your voice," I began.

~ ~ ~

Overby wasn't too happy to speak to me. "Why didn't you tell me about Spring's notebook when we came by your place at the end of June?" he said. "You didn't even tell us you'd found a homicide victim. That's a crime you know."

"I did call it in," I said.

"Balls," he said. "We got an anonymous call."

"That was me. Closest pay phone was at a service station on Woodside."

"You lied to me and Snoots. And you left town when I told you not to."

"I'm sorry, Lieutenant–"

"That's what I wanted to hear," he said. "All right. We can haul this guy off the ship on suspicion of murder. Give me the details."

Chapter Forty-Five
Mar Branco

In fact Overby's men were able to determine the *Mar Branco* was not leaving port until six. I stopped in to see Max, and learned that the hospital intended to discharge him later that same day. I was surprised. He hadn't walked yet; he'd said he still couldn't move his legs.

It appeared Max would be my houseguest for a while. He had given his house in Fresno to Sebastian and his mother. Casa Rabinowitz, Fresno was now Casa Diaz. It had seemed damned generous of him at the time, but now I realized he was paying for everything – the house, the Ferrari – with Chinese commie money, Mao's gold. He had asked me to find him a new place, in San Francisco, a flat on one level with wide doors in case he needed a wheel chair for a while. But I'd put the real estate search on the back burner while putting the last pieces of the Spring case together. So Amanda and I agreed to bring Max home with us to the big house on Lafayette Park for a time.

But now I had to meet Overby and Snoots at Pier 35. "Can I pick him up tomorrow morning?" I asked the head nurse.

"Why, Frank? Now that I know they're willing to let me go, I don't want to spend another night here," said Max.

"I have an appointment this evening," I said.

"That's OK," said the nurse, snapping on a rubber glove, and smiling. "We're open all night here. If you settle the bill while the office is open, you can come by any time to collect him."

Max had a checkbook out, and was looking over his bill. "Max, is that Joan Spring's account there?"

"Force of habit," he said.

"Why don't you write me a check for my services? How long has it been? Let's see, the Spring case started in December … that's eight months, about 240 days … at $25 a day."

"C'mon. You didn't put all that time into her case," he said.

"She's always on my mind," I said, "and I'm still working on it now. Let's say an even five thousand. We'll give her a discount for being a long-term customer."

"That's crazy," Max protested.

"Not so much as you think. If she's paying me, she's entitled to private-detective-client confidentiality, and that could keep her out of federal prison. So for your client's sake, write the check. Mao won't miss five grand. How many *yuan* did you spend on that Ferrari?"

~ ~ ~

Max wrote the check and I took it to my bank before closing time. I took out $1500 in cash, and deposited the balance. I drove to Cuifen's, where I invited Bimla out for that coffee we didn't have back in December. She ordered a double espresso and asked for evaporated milk. I gave her a grand, and explained I now had a son and a wife to go with the two girls. She understood the grand. Next stop was Old St. Mary's church on California Street, where I put $250 in the poor box.

At 5 p.m. my car was parked, and I was walking along the Embarcadero. There was a bulkhead building at Pier 35, concealing the docks behind. I walked south, smelling the oily sea water, listening to the lapping of the waves on my left and the sounds of the city at night on my right, until I saw *Mar Branco* painted in white letters high above the waterline on the stern of a large ship. I turned around and walked back, and met Overby and Sergeant Snoots, just getting out of their prowl car.

"She's back there," I told the flatties.

"How about our man?" said Snoots. "Is he aboard?"

"I don't know what Cyrgryzs looks like." I said.

Snoots took a newspaper clipping out of his inner jacket pocket and passed it to me. "This is from the trial," he said. The black and white picture showed a man with a receding hairline, dark straight hair, and a goatee.

"Sergeant, take two uniforms and Swiver," said Overby. "Go on board and find our man if he's there."

"Right," said Snoots. "What if he gives us the slip?"

"I'll be out here with Miller to stop anyone who comes off the pier," said Overby.

Snoots and I made our way onto Pier 35 and boarded the *Mar Branco*, a long freighter with one stack in the rear. Snoots posted one uniformed patrolman by the gangplank, and a seaman took us to the bridge. The ship's officers seemed busy, getting everything ready in time to sail with the tide. Captain Airth, a grim-looking Scot, didn't want to waste his time talking to "any fooking peelers." I said he probably didn't want to miss the tide, either, but I told him he might if he didn't cooperate with the fooking peelers now. Airth called the purser, a burly Russian with a thick accent, to the bridge to deal with us.

"We're equipped to carry 12 passengers," said the purser. "There are seven booked for this cruise. Six are already on board."

I showed him the news photo. "This man among them?"

"He don't look familiar. Let's go see them," the Russian said.

Snoots left the other patrolman outside the bridge, and we went to meet the folks who'd boarded – a 40-something school marm on holiday to the Orient, a young Indochinese couple traveling on French passports, an Indian doctor, an international business traveler. Snoots handled them with kid gloves. He seemed out of sorts. "Let's talk," I said to Snoots.

We walked down the corridor away from the purser and lit a couple smokes. "It ain't the old maid," said Snoots.

"Not likely. What about the Indian doctor?"

"No, his skin's too dark. The businessman's too fat, too old."

"You went easy on them," I said.

"Sometimes I'm subtle, Swiver," he said. "I poked the last guy's stomach for padding when I turned him around. It was fat. I wiped the Indian's hand with a little alcohol swab when I looked at his passport. No color came off. They're legit. No sense getting rough."

"All right. Let's try this last fellow."

He was thin, clean shaven, looked young – maybe late twenties. His hair was sandy blond, even his eyebrows. If Louie Cyrgryzs was any good at disguises, he could have done a dye job, and maybe he looked younger without his goatee. We looked in his luggage and slanted around the compartment. "I like this one," I whispered to Snoots when we passed. I tried to think of a way to trick the man into revealing himself, but I didn't know any Chinese, and less physics.

Snoots looked at the man's passport. "Alan Brown, eh? What line of work are you in, Mr. Brown?"

"Sales," the man said.

"What do you sell?" I asked.

"Medical equipment," he said.

"Do you have a sample case?" Brown pointed to a trunk that was standing upright by the foot of the bed. I didn't know what I was looking for, but I opened it. I saw stethoscopes, scalpels, syringes, scales and surgeons' masks. Snoots looked in over my shoulder, and I straightened up and stepped away. I looked in Mr. Brown's suit coat, which was draped over the desk chair. In the inside pocket were two pens. One was a fountain pen, but the other was thicker than a regular pen, and said "SIPD" on it. There was a magnifying window labeled "Roentgen" on the barrel. I held it up to the light to see inside. A lined dial floated under a hairline, and I started to have some glimmer of an idea of what I was holding.

"Snoots–" I began, but Mr. Brown gave me a left hook that caught my neck. "Look out!" I gasped too late, as he kicked Snoots in the nuts. Brown put a foot to his back and the Sergeant toppled into the open trunk.

Brown bolted for the door. I dropped the personal dosimeter I'd been eyeing and managed to grab an ankle as he passed me. I held on. Snootsie turned and sat up, drawing his service revolver, but Brown kicked the gun away with his other foot. He lost his balance and fell, and that pulled him out of my grip.

Brown scrambled to his feet faster than a three-legged cheetah, and shot out into the corridor, pulling the door closed behind him. I opened it to follow, and two gunshots blazed from the companionway. I dropped into a crouch behind the door. It sounded like both bullets hit steel around the bulkhead. Then I heard a thump and a crash and peeked out.

Brown had collided with the Russian purser, who'd been standing just outside the cabin when he'd tried to flee. They'd both gone down and were still tangled up in the tight quarters. I lunged out, grabbed for Brown's gun hand, and slammed his wrist into the raised sill of the door. His pistol clattered to the floor, and I crawled over to retrieve it. By now Snoots was on his feet. He grabbed Brown by the collar and I picked him up by the belt. Together, we tossed him into the compartment. Snoots stepped back in and I closed the door. This time the sergeant wasn't so subtle.

~ ~ ~

It wasn't long before Mr. Brown – we were both sure now he was Cyrgryzs – was lying on the bed with his hands cuffed behind him. Snoots was sitting on the floor next to the bed catching his breath. I helped him to his feet and picked up his hat for him.

"Thanks, Frank." I don't recall him calling me "Frank" before, or since. He held his hat out and put a crease in the crown with the edge of his hand, put it on and snapped the front brim down. "Well, let's get this guy off the boat so they can sail." Snoots grabbed Cyrgryzs by a shoulder and the two of us pulled him to his feet.

Then the purser dragged in a short cabin boy, and told him, "Straighten this mess up." The cabin boy had his head down. He was dressed in something like a People's Liberation Army uniform – soft cap with shaggy black hair underneath, dark olive-green tunic buttoned to the neck, and baggy trousers.

Cyrgryzs started to struggle when he saw him. "It's you!" he said. He bit my arm and made a dive toward the cabin boy, whose eyes flashed when he looked up, but at that, Snoots lost patience.

"I've had enough play for tonight," he said. He pulled his sap off his hip pocket, and tapped Cyrgryzs with it.

Head down, the cabin boy set to work righting furniture and sweeping broken remnants into a dust pan with his whisk broom. When he bent over, his baggy pant legs went up high enough to show a slim vanilla-skinned ankle. I caught a whiff of jasmine and rose, but didn't place it. In another setting, I might have thought it was Shalimar.

Snoots and I each pinioned an arm and steered Cyrgryzs, feet dragging between us, up to the deck, then pushed him down the gangplank.

Lieutenant Overby was waiting. "Good work, Sergeant. Did he give you any trouble?"

"Nothing I couldn't handle, sir," said Snoots.

"Miller," said Overby, "make sure the captain knows the *Mar Branco's* cleared to sail." The police loaded Cyrgryzs into a black maria. Snoots and Overby and I stood by the Lieutenant's car and lit some smokes.

We heard the ship cranking up its anchor chain, and the orders to cast off lines echoed through the night air along the Embarcadero. The *Mar Branco* blew its foghorn twice, and water splashed as the prop spun.

"I guess they're not waiting for that seventh passenger," I said.

"By the way," Overby told me, "while you were on board, some news came over the radio that might interest you." The lieutenant pronounced the first syllable in "radio" like I say "radish."

"The D.A. decided to throw out the case against Mrs. Spring late this afternoon," he continued. "They decided they didn't have enough evidence to convict her. I guess your boy Rabinowitz wins another one, eh?"

"What about resisting arrest? She could have shot Snoots or me. We'd testify," I said.

"She's done eight months, Swiver. They figure time already served." His voice tapered off.

"What are they going to do with her?" I asked.

"Well, the only thing they can do now is release her," said Overby. "In fact, they let her out earlier this evening."

The scent of jasmine and rose – Shalimar. The flash of the eyes – violet. The cabin boy, I thought. Joan Spring had outmaneuvered me.

Chater Forty-Six
My Sin

I wheeled Max in his chair from my Cadillac to the front door of my house. "Joan Spring fed us Louie Crygryzs, but when we picked him up," I said, "she slipped in in disguise and took his place."

"She's quite a chess player," said Max. It was about nine on a quiet night; Max's voice was still weak, but there was little competition that night from urban crickets. "She offered you a poisoned pawn, and when you took him, she made a clean sneak."

"A Queen's Gambit," She showed me her gams and sap that I am, I bit – I thought it, but it was too corny to say. "Maybe Joan drew a line through your name with a pencil, too. Maybe Cuifen calling you up here from Fresno was part of the setup. Maybe Joan had Cyrgryzs outside the cooler, waiting to pick up your trail for you."

"Maybe, maybe, maybe," he smiled. "Maybe comrade Joan Spring outmaneuvered me, too." He shrugged.

"Do you trust Cuifen? She worked for Joan."

"She's all I've got. I'll trust her. In fact, I should move over to her place tomorrow. Then I won't be a burden or a danger to you and Amanda."

After I said goodnight to Snoots and Overby, I'd driven directly to the hospital to pick up Max. I'd brought Amanda home in the afternoon, and left her there with Leon and the girls while I'd been at the pier. She knew I was worried about her safety, and I'd told her to keep the house locked up. So I was uneasy to see a crack of light creeping around the edges of the front door. But then I thought, I'm sure Brigid and Meaghan would tell her we always keep the drawbridge up. Maybe someone heard us drive up, and opened the door so I wouldn't have to get my key out. Very considerate. I put my back to the door and pulled Max over the threshold.

If the open door wasn't a warning, right away the smell of "My Sin," by Lanvin, with a bottom note of horse sure was – the smell in the car when I drove Veronica Rios-Ortega to the cabin. The smell in the room where Felipe Rios-Ortega died. The hair on the back of my neck began to stand up. I pushed Max fast across the foyer and into the living room.

Veronica Rios-Ortega came in behind us; she had a grip on Amanda, and steered her in at knifepoint – the point of that double-edged *espada* I'd seen in Carlos Lopez's study to be specific. Without losing control of Amanda, she turned halfway and slid the pocket doors behind us closed. "Brigid! Leon!" I called.

"Your children? They are locked in the cellar," Veronica said in Spanish. "They are safe for now, but I must kill them all before I leave. The boy I remember from Fresno. He has seen too much already. Sit over there." She gestured towards a chair on the left, catty corner from Amanda. "Leave the cripple."

"If you harm any of the children, you'll die here tonight," I said. I backed slowly to the chair, keeping my eyes on her, trying to think. Behind Veronica, I could see Max, with his one eye intent on the scene.

"Big talk. That is why I kill you, first. Then the children." She was dressed all in black. Her pants appeared to be black leather. "I came to kill this *puta*, so that there are no witnesses to the death of Felipe. I kill you because you know too much. Then I have to kill this cripple; I don't know who he is, but it is his bad luck that he is here." The little flaw in her iris blazed yellow.

"You're insane."

She laughed without mirth, a near-hysterical cackle. Her head twitched to the side an inch or two, then back. She blinked. Then she said, "What does it matter, detective? Once you are dead there is no one left to connect me to the Hotel Californian. Someone may have seen me, but do they know who I am? Where to find me? I doubt it. You are the key."

"Bullfinch, the house dick. He knows you."

"I don't believe he saw me at the hotel the night of the murder. I walked right past him with the crowd when the police cleared the murder room. If he knew I was there, he would have said something then. Enough talk." She tightened her hammerlock on Amanda's arm, and aligned the sharp tip of the *espada* along Amanda's breastbone. My heart raced. I didn't see how I could save her

"You think you can overpower us all and kill us with that sword?" I said.

Veronica released the hammerlock, but the point of the short sword kept Amanda close. She reached over her shoulder and pulled out a cylinder wrapped in a red *muleta*. Unfurling the red cloth, she revealed a shotgun. It looked like the old over-and-under model Paz had brandished in the barn.

Quiet and unseen, Max braced his hands on the wheel chair arms to lift himself. I made a silent supplication to St. Giles, patron of cripples, to raise him up.

"No. I think I kill the *puta* with the *espada* and let you watch her bleed. Then I blast you with one barrel and turn the other on your friend." Again Veronica tossed her hair and head toward Max without glancing back. She put the shotgun to the small of Amanda's back, pushed her away, and turned the shotgun towards me.

Max was on his feet now, but looking unsteady. He hadn't used them for more than three weeks. I watched his progress, fascinated, but careful not to betray his movement with my expression.

"You don't have to do this," I said to Veronica. "I

made a deal with your father that I would not pursue justice against you."

"A deal! You are an even bigger fool than I thought. I prefer to do it my way," Veronica said. "Then I control my own fate." She held the shotgun in her left, at waist level, pointed my way, and the *espada* in her right hand, raising it to strike.

Max was only a step and a half behind Veronica now. He shook a little as if he had balance problems, then slid his foot forward. It was slow progress.

Not a night for slow dancing – when things started to happen, they would happen fast. I had to make a move now if I was going to save Amanda. I dove out of the chair to knock Amanda aside. Good for me. The shotgun boomed and ripped a hole in the cream-colored seatback of the chair where I'd been sitting an instant before.

I don't know if Veronica had been familiar with Newton's third law, but she went to school on the kickback of the shotgun. Trying to control the recoil with one arm disrupted her balance.

I was on top of Amanda now, trying to shield her with my body. "NO! Don't shoot him," she screamed as she had screamed when Carlos Lopez had cut down Alejandro. Lying on her side, she kicked with a heel at Veronica's shin. "Veronica Lopez, I am your enemy; do not hurt this good man." Somehow, she squirmed out from under, and sat up in front of me.

Veronica lunged forward and slashed with the knife at Amanda's breast. Then Max arrived and looped an arm around Veronica's throat and yanked back. The other barrel roared, but the shot flew wildly over the sofa. I scrambled to my feet and lunged for Veronica's sword hand. But Amanda came between us. The point of the deadly blade pierced Amanda's blouse. Her mouth formed an *O* but no sound came out. Pain filled her eyes.

Max wrestled the big woman from behind. Veronica

turned her sword and attention on him. Out of the corner of my eye, I saw her kick at him with her boot.

Frothy blood oozed out of Amanda's chest. Her eyes pleaded with me. I took her in my arms. She tried to speak, but coughed. She coughed blood. "Francisco," she mouthed, "it's hard to breathe." I laid her back on the carpet and grabbed a small pillow off the couch.

Pulling her blouse open, I saw a deep gash two inches in length. "It's not your heart," I said. "Hang on. You can make it." A whistling sound rose from the wound as she tried to inhale. It was a lung. I pressed the cushion against her wound. I pressed hard to stop the flow of blood. Holding the pressure, I maneuvered Amanda across the floor to the phone, and I called for an ambulance. Across the room, Max and Veronica were rolling on the floor in a death struggle. But Amanda was dying in my arms.

I looked in her eyes, and I saw it was the end. She put an arm up and pulled my head down, so my ear was near her mouth. "I love you, Francisco. Take care of Leon."

"I will. I love you, Amanda."

She shuddered, then she whispered her last words.

EPILOGUE

I knelt beside Amanda's body; I held her; I grieved until my devastation reached bottom. When I finally glanced up, Veronica was lying by the door. Max was gone. I rose to my feet and walked over. Veronica had some lacerations, but the twin-edged blade was still in her hand. She'd been throttled and choked to death with human hands. It must have been brutal, maybe like that fascist officer I'd killed, so many years ago and so many miles away

I found a light trail of blood out the door, down the walk, and around to the open garage. My Cadillac was gone. The Ferrari, the color of Max's blood trail, of Amanda's blood on my hands and on my shirt, was still parked in there, and the keys were on the seat. Clearly, Max had been hurt. The Ferrari's presence suggested he was too incapacitated to handle a manual transmission.

I let the kids out of the cellar. They were scared but safe. Leon was inconsolable. Only his grief for his mother could match my grief for Amanda. That gave me someone to be strong for. All I could do was hold him, and tell him his mother's last thoughts had been of him.

I called the cops. It was too late for the ambulance. When Lieutenant Overby heard the address of the call, he came over with Snoots. Even though there were a lot of questions, Overby saw to it that the dicks who answered the call went easy on me. Snoots even put a hand on my back. I was grateful.

I took about ten days off and spent time with the kids, time when I wasn't downtown at the Hall of Justice giving statements. Bimla came over some days and helped me out. For a while, I had the feeling I'd get a radiogram from Joan Spring, perhaps taunting me, perhaps saying, "Wish you were here." But I didn't hear from her. I guess it wasn't her style.

Then I received an envelope with a City postmark, and no return address. Inside was another envelope addressed in a familiar hand. I drove out to Ocean Beach again, and sat by a window at the Cliff House. I bought a bottle of cabernet from Freemark Abbey.

I read:

"Dear Frank,

Well, I imagine I've caused you a bit of trouble. I don't expect to see you for a while. If you've received this, it was re-mailed by Cuifen. Please don't try to find me.

Keep the Ferrari. You'll find the title with my papers in a box in your garage. It's worth more than your '41 Caddy anyhow. I must say, that Cadillac was a comfort with the stab wounds in my side and left leg.

I couldn't stick around you know. Even if Veronica Rios-Ortega hadn't busted up my homecoming, I would have disappeared as soon as I'd regained a little more of my strength. For all I knew, you were going to turn me in for espionage or treason. And why the hell not? I was guilty. I crossed the line. Most of all I betrayed you. Oh, hell. I lost my way somewhere, Frank.

I stopped in Half Moon the first night. Then I spent a few days holed up in Big Sur regaining my strength. I made a farewell appearance in Fresno. Carlos Lopez won't give you any more trouble. I finished him, for Alejandro's sake and for Amanda. Now I'm on the road again, but that's as much of my itinerary as I can share.

I hope we're even.
Your pal,
Max"

I drank half the Freemark Abbey, and I re-read the letter a couple of times. Then I put the cork back in the bottle and slipped it under my armpit and walked out to the beach.

The blood feud was over. Good old Max.

I sat on the beach and drank from the bottle while the wind from the Pacific blew needles of sand into my face. I thought again of Amanda's last words.

What were they? "We'll always have Fresno." No, nothing like that. "Kill Carlos Lopez for me." That was more likely, but no. She pulled my ear close to her mouth and whispered, "I'm sorry, *guapo*. I do not even know who is Leon's father. But I love you so."

Ah, I knew it.

EL FINAL

293

Author's Acknowledgments

I enrolled in a writing class on "Plot" at Stanford U. when I was working on this novel. I owe many thanks to Malena Watrous, the teacher of that class, for nurturing any talent I brought to class, and for her encouragement, which kept me going.

I'm indebted to some fellow students from that class who joined me in an online writers' critique group after the class ended, and have put up for many years with *Last Puffs* and other Frank Swiver adventures, (even though private eye fiction is probably not their cup of tea). Thank you Siri Chateaubriand, Arlene MacLeod, and Jenn Stroud Rossman, (all fine authors too), for your time and invaluable help. —HM

About the Author

Harley Mazuk was born and raised in Cleveland, Ohio. He earned a B.A. in English Literature from Hiram College, and studied at Elphinstone College, Bombay, India. He worked in the music business in New York, then joined the Federal Government, for a 29-year run, first in Information Technology, later as a writer and editor in corporate communications.

Retired now, Mr. Mazuk likes to write pulp fiction, mainly private eye stories, several of which have appeared in *Ellery Queen Mystery Magazine*. His first story, "The Tall Blonde with the Hot Boiler," resulted in his first sale, to *EQMM* (Jan. 2011). He has sold longer fiction (novelettes/novellas) to Dead Guns Press and Dark Passages. His first full length novel, *White with Fish, Red with Murder*, was released Feb. 28, 2017, by Driven Press.

Mr. Mazuk's passions are his family, writing, reading, running, peace, Italian cars, and California wine. He lives with his wife, Anastasia, in Maryland, where they have raised two children.

NewPulpPress.com